"All [...] [...]fia. Singi[...]

He couldn't stop his twitching mouth any longer and gave in to a full-on smile. An unfamiliar feeling.

"Then what does the singer mean when he says he wants to get lost in the rock and roll? Huh?" Her huff made something tight inside his chest loosen.

"He wants to get lost in the beat," he said reasonably, inhaling the vanilla-musk scent of her hair. "Here. Listen again." He started the song over. At the chorus, he sang the correct line.

A quick glance to his right revealed Sofia's frown. Her dark eyebrows met over her nose and that full pink mouth of hers, the one he hadn't been able to stop staring at since they'd met last night, pursed. He forced his gaze back on the road where it belonged.

He had no business thinking Jesse's girl was pretty.

Dear Reader,

The holidays hold unique memories for all of us. Some of them are warm and wonderful as we remember happy gatherings around a Christmas tree laden with gifts or cozy evenings eating homemade treats beside a fire while listening to carols. But for people who don't have homes, or family, the holidays can be riddled with unpleasant memories.

For struggling single mother Sofia Gallardo, the holidays evoke a mix of emotions. Her only Christmas wish is to give her six-year-old son, Javi, a real Christmas, a home and a family to be proud of. For the Cades, the holidays are a time they pretend doesn't exist as it brings back painful memories of a beloved family member they've recently lost.

I'm inspired by Sofia's perseverance and determination to provide a better life for her child, and am moved by the Cades' grief and need to come together as a family again. The magic of Christmas heals wounds and brings a couple and child the love and family they deserve. I welcome you to the first book in my Rocky Mountain Cowboys series and hope you find it as uplifting and inspiring as I did!

Wishing you a holiday season filled with joy, laughter and love.

Happy reading,

Karen Rock

HEARTWARMING

Christmas at Cade Ranch

—

Karen Rock

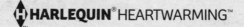

Recycling programs
for this product may
not exist in your area.

ISBN-13: 978-0-373-36861-7

Christmas at Cade Ranch

Copyright © 2017 by Karen Rock

Printed in U.S.A.

Karen Rock is an award-winning young adult and adult contemporary author. She holds a master's degree in English and worked as an ELA instructor before becoming a full-time author. Most recently, her Harlequin Heartwarming novels have won the 2015 National Excellence in Romance Fiction Award and the 2015 Booksellers' Best Award. When she's not writing, Karen loves scouring estate sales, cooking and hiking. She lives in the Adirondack Mountain region with her husband, daughter and Cavalier King Charles spaniels. Visit her at karenrock.com.

Books by Karen Rock

Harlequin Heartwarming

To my husband and daughter,
whose love is the greatest gift
I receive every Christmas and
the whole year through.

CHAPTER ONE

"Is Daddy down there?"

Sofia Gallardo knelt beside her five-year-old son, Javi, on frozen grass and snuggled him close. All around them, poinsettia and pinecone Christmas wreaths bedecked the surrounding gravesites. She pulled in a ragged breath of balsam-scented air and blinked stinging eyes.

How to explain the afterlife to a child? An animated film they'd watched at a public library came to mind. "No, honey. Daddy went 'up.'"

Javi traced the plaque's engraved letters with a fingertip poking through his faded red glove. The white tops of Carbondale, Colorado's nearby Rocky Mountain range breathed chill late-November air down at them. It rustled through the Douglas firs dotting Rosebud Cemetery and jingled bell-shaped ornaments looped around a wintergreen boxwood. "Like in the movie?"

"Just like that."

"With balloons?"

"Maybe."

Brown eyes slanted up at her beneath a drooping toque a size too big for his head. He looked thinner, she assessed, gnawing on her lip. Pale. When was the last time he'd had milk? Fruit? Two days ago?

No. Three.

Four.

"He can't go up without balloons." Javi pulled a creased picture from his backpack and peered at it. "And he wasn't old like Mr. Fredisson."

"Fredricksen," she corrected automatically, then closed her eyes for a moment and gathered her thoughts. How to make sense of something she hadn't yet fully processed? Outside the cemetery's gates, the swish-hiss of a sander slipped past, ahead of this afternoon's predicted storm.

She shivered in her sweater and wished for a winter coat, gloves and a better set for Javi, too, than his mismatched pair.

Wishes.

At least they didn't cost a thing.

"You don't have to be old to go up."

Her ex, Jesse Cade, was dead at only twenty-six, gone from her life before Javi's first birth-day when Jesse relapsed into heroin addiction. Gone from this world two years ago without her knowing until a stranger, Jesse's mother, Joy Cade, tracked her down last week and phoned with the news. Sofia had promised to meet her here during her Portland-bound bus's layover from Albuquerque.

Her stomach knotted. When Joy had pleaded for the chance to meet her grandson, Sofia heard a mother's pain and found it hard to re-fuse. After wrestling with the decision, she'd finally called Joy this morning and accepted the invite.

Not that she'd made peace with the plan.

Sofia avoided people who associated her with her own addiction history. What if Joy divulged Sofia's shameful past to Javi?

She wouldn't be able to bear it.

Javi sprawled forward and pressed his cheek to the stone. His Batman hoodie—a dingy black thing he'd plucked from the shelter's discard pile—rose above his waist. "I don't want to go up. Ever."

"You won't, sweetie. Promise." She brushed back his dark hair and clamped her chattering teeth. Growing up in the inner city and forced at times to live in shelters, Javi had already endured a harsher life than some adults. She'd do everything in her power to keep him safe.

Even from herself.

"But what if they don't have free lunches in—in— Where are we going?"

"Portland." She gathered him close and the familiar fear of not knowing where their next meal would come from curdled inside her. "No more being hungry."

Hopefully her friend's job lead panned out. Finding steady, decent-paying employment wasn't easy for former felons without high school degrees. She'd run out of options in Albuquerque.

But maybe in Portland she had a chance at a position that'd last more than a few months, a career, maybe even a real home for Javi. One she'd decorate for the holidays in every inch of its space to make up for all the Christmases he'd had to do without.

It might be a pie-in-the-sky idea, but when you had nothing, you had nothing to lose by dreaming big.

She had two bus tickets and three hundred and forty-two dollars in her wallet. Since being laid off from her latest job and evicted from another apartment, it was all she had in the world besides her little guy. Her grip tightened on Javi.

She'd made a lot of mistakes. Failing to provide for her son, making him ashamed of who he was or where he came from, would not be part of them.

This had to work.

"Never ever?"

"Never ever," she vowed, fierce.

She would not, could not, break this promise.

Society had judged her a disgrace, as had her father when he'd tossed her out at age sixteen. What her deceased mother thought... she'd never know.

Didn't want to know.

Most important of all, though, was how Javi would judge her someday. If he knew she was a former junkie, he might stop believing in her. Which was one reason she needed to keep Joy's visit short—to prevent any damaging revelations.

Her "respectable mom" persona had been crashing around her ears recently. A former addict "friend" had tracked Sofia down and begged to crash at her apartment. Feeling bad for the woman, Sofia agreed to let her stay, just for a couple of nights. But then their houseguest spiraled into a drug-induced manic state where she'd threatened Javi with a gun and hollered about Sofia being a hypocrite. The woman created such a ruckus that it had caused Sofia's eviction. It also confirmed that the only way to truly erase who she'd once been was to start over in a place where no one knew her.

No more reminders of her old ways.

Javi wriggled away and pulled a toy Batmobile from his pocket. He clicked on the red headlights. "Did Daddy love me?"

She pictured Jesse, the easygoing cowboy she'd met in court-ordered rehab and once believed she might marry. Stupid, foolish girl. "He did."

"How come he left?"

"He was sick." A shiver trailed an icy fingertip down her spine as the afternoon sun finally succumbed to cloud cover. Addiction was a sickness, she justified, so it wasn't a lie.

"Did he get sick and die?"

She started to shake her head, then nodded instead. There were no easy answers when drugs and violence mixed. According to Joy, drug dealers murdered Jesse for unpaid funds.

Javi propped himself on his elbows, and

his sneaker-clad feet, crossed at the ankles, swung. He pointed at the lettering again. "Is Grandma coming?"

"She said so…" Though Joy should have arrived by now.

"Will she like me?"

"How could she not?"

"My teacher doesn't like me."

"That's only because you won't stop eating all of her erasers."

"She told Mrs. Penn she couldn't keep bringing in paper for me anymore. She sounded angry."

Sofia bit her lip. School supplies. Another thing she struggled to provide. "Honey, sometimes grown-ups just have bad days. I know she likes you."

"What's that say?" Javi pointed at the marker, switching subjects with the whiplash speed of a child.

"I've read it to you twice, honey."

"Please," he wheedled, and she sighed. Where was Joy? Their bus departed in twenty minutes. She'd breathe easier once she put this part of the world, this part of herself, in the rearview mirror for good.

"That's a *J*," Sofia began.

Javi traced the first letter at the top of the plaque. "Like me."

"Right." Jesse's siblings' names all began with *J* and he'd wanted to follow the tradition with Javi.

"What's this say?"

"'Jesse Andrew Cade. Beloved son and brother.'"

In the distance, a lone cardinal perched in a skeletal maple, bright as a leftover leaf. A gray-haired woman approached, wearing navy shoes and carrying a matching purse. A sensible-looking gray wool coat fell past her knees. Joy?

Sofia turned away, her heart picking up speed.

"Cade like me!"

She felt her smile falter. "And that says, 'Free spirit. Roam in peace.'"

Free spirit. Yes. That'd been Jesse. The quality that had attracted her and made her believe in a better life, a better her.

"I'm hugging Daddy goodbye." Javi rolled back on his stomach and curved his arms around the plaque. Then he leaped to his feet and slipped a hand in hers. His lone, left-sided dimple, the only trait that resembled Jesse, appeared when he smiled up at her. "How many brothers did Daddy have?"

"Four," someone replied softly behind them.

Sofia whirled and came face-to-face with the gray-haired woman she'd spied. Her pale pink lips lifted slightly in an uncertain smile and a gust blew strands of her neatly clipped bob across her thin face. It was relatively unlined and pretty in an understated way, her age younger than her hair color suggested. Wire-framed lenses magnified the hazel eyes that darted between Javi and Sofia. That color…the light yellow-green surrounded by a ring of brown. She'd seen it only once before…

Her heart beat a fast tap.

"Did you know my daddy?" Javi skidded to a stop in front of the stranger and gaped up at her.

"I'm his mother," came her quiet, tremulous voice. She pulled her purse closer to her body and her wool coat sleeve rode up to reveal an elastic-wrap bandage crisscrossing her left wrist. "And you must be…?"

"Javi!"

Joy swayed and her face paled. Concern shoved caution aside. Sofia swept an arm around the woman's waist and guided her to a bench beneath a cluster of towering pines. "Thank you," Joy murmured once she sat. "Now. Come closer, dear."

She crooked a finger, and Javi clambered up on the bench beside her. His short legs dangled, scuffed sneakers kicking the air.

"Are you my grandma?" His left-sided dimple appeared in a quick smile.

Joy gasped. "Yes."

"You don't look so old."

Despite the tense moment, Sofia held in a short laugh. Joy's warm eyes met hers. "Well. I appreciate that. And how old are you?"

He held up four fingers, and Sofia shook her head. Red stained his cheeks as he peeled up one more digit.

"And do you go to school?"

He nodded. "Yesterday my teacher had a party for me. She brought in cupcakes, and they were free."

"Javi goes to—went—to preschool in Albuquerque," Sofia interjected.

"Education is important."

Javi scrunched his face.

"Yes," Sofia agreed, feeling like a hypocrite. How she wished she'd gotten her diploma. Without it, the label High School

Dropout followed her wherever she went, like an invisible capital *F* sewn to her clothes. At least she would not fail at being a good mother, the one and only thing she was proud of.

"I have to go to a new school and make new friends." Javi nibbled on his thumbnail, then dropped it at Sofia's head shake.

"Are you excited about that?"

"What if they call me Free Lunch like back home?"

Joy blinked. "Excuse me?"

"Oh. It's just something kids say," Sofia said quickly, hating how a few children had picked on Javi for his secondhand clothes and the card he used instead of money in the cafeteria. Someday she'd give him everything that other kids had so no one would ever make fun of him again. "It doesn't mean anything."

"Yes, it does," Javi insisted through hands covering his face. "It means we're poor trash. Least that's what Timmy Rice says."

"That's a mean thing to say," Joy insisted, indignant. "It's better to have no money than no heart."

Javi peeked up through his fingers. "Is that true?"

"I swear."

"A lady at a desk called me a waste of space. Is that true?"

"Absolutely not," declared Joy, her voice firm.

Javi threw his arms around her. "I like you."

Joy smiled, blinking fast. Her trembling hand passed over his hair. "I like you, too, honey. A lot."

He angled his head to peer up at her. "How come?"

"Because you're a Cade, and Cades always stick together."

"Mama says the Cades ride on top of mountains and don't ever fall off. Their hats touch the clouds. Right, Mama?"

Sofia dropped her eyes at Joy's surprised look. Okay. Maybe she'd exaggerated a bit about Jesse's family, but she'd wanted Javi to believe he came from good people...strong men and women...a family he could be proud of, unlike her.

"That's right, Javi." Time to change the subject. "Joy, I'm not sure if you ever mentioned how you found us...?"

Joy produced a cell phone with a familiar rodeo buckle cover. Jesse's phone.

"The police returned this to us a couple

years ago, but I didn't… I couldn't bring myself to look through it. Not until recently. Then I saw this."

She flipped the phone around to show a picture of Sofia in a hospital bed, a newborn Javi in her arms. Jesse grinned as he crouched beside them. The name Cade was scrawled in big letters on the empty baby pen nearby.

"That's me!" Javi exclaimed.

"Yes. Yes, it is."

"Mama said I cried a lot. Is that why Daddy left?"

"Honey!" Sofia exclaimed. Out of the mouths of babes. Javi had been a colicky baby. True, she had worried at one point that taking care of a demanding baby had driven Jesse back to drugs, but she knew that was not the case at all.

"Mama said he got sick."

Joy nodded. "Yes. She has the right of it." She cleared her throat. "Javi, would you find me some holly berries?" She pointed to a patch of bushes beyond the pine bunch. "Celtics believed they were good luck."

"Like basketball?"

"No, honey. Ancient people. They're all gone now."

"Like Atlantis? Mummies?"

"Something like that…"

"Got it!" Javi leaped off the bench and raced away, eager as always to help. He lived to save the day like his beloved superheroes.

"Don't eat them, now!" Joy called.

The bushes were in their line of vision but out of earshot. Sofia admired the woman's deft handling of this tricky moment. She pressed clammy palms on her jeans and perched on the edge of the bench. Her insides felt frozen, her heart beating in a block of ice.

"So Javi doesn't know about Jesse's addiction."

"No," Sofia said swiftly. "I don't want him knowing about any of that."

Joy studied her for a long moment, then nodded. "He won't hear of it from me."

Sofia released a breath. "Thank you."

"I've been searching for you ever since I found this." Joy tucked the phone in her purse. "I figured out who you were by searching his contacts, but your number no longer worked."

"I've moved around a lot."

And Sofia couldn't afford a phone, or this conversation. It brought up too much of her past. She needed to leave. Now.

Joy's eyes glistened as she studied Javi

scuttling across the whitened ground on his hands and knees. The sky spit a few snow flurries. A first volley of more to come, Sofia worried. A low howl rose in her ears.

"I—I—" Sofia was struggling to think of a graceful way to extricate herself when Joy buried her face in her hands and her shoulders shook. Overhead, a pair of cooing mourning doves alighted on a branch. "I'm sorry I upset you."

"No!" Joy lifted a tearstained face and a left-sided dimple appeared. "This is wonderful. It's just hitting me that this is real." She released a shaky breath. "Javi's my first grandchild. Knowing there's a part of my Jesse still here on this earth, well, it's the first thing that's made me feel alive in a long, long time."

Sofia's heart felt like it might explode. "I wish we could stay longer and visit, but our bus leaves soon. May I call you when Javi and I are settled?"

"I'd appreciate that. Will I see you again?" Joy rose.

"I'm not sure," Sofia temporized. She reached for her wallet and came up empty.

Had she left it by the grave? Her eyes flew to the area and landed on Javi's backpack.

Perhaps she'd stowed it in there. The events of this anxious morning blurred. Her panicked thoughts knocked against each other, and her temple throbbed. When was the last time she'd had it?

"Javi, have you seen my wallet?" she asked, hustling to the backpack.

"Uh-uh."

She scrounged through Javi's backpack and her purse. Nothing.

"Our bus tickets were in there. Money. Identification…"

"Let's retrace your steps. If we can't find it, you'll stay at the ranch until everything's sorted," Joy declared in a tone that brooked no argument.

"Wooo-hooo!" Javi shouted. "I want to see Daddy's ranch! Can we, Mama? Can we?"

She stared into two pairs of hopeful eyes. Her throat constricted as though someone slipped a noose around it and tugged. If she didn't find her wallet, they'd be out of options, and this small town didn't look like it had a shelter.

Where would she and Javi sleep during the blizzard?

It's only one night, a voice whispered. *A*

chance for Javi to see what a real family looks like and meet his aunt and uncles.
   Fine.

CHAPTER TWO

"MOVE IT! MOVE IT!" James Cade hollered as he thundered at breakneck speed alongside a stampeding herd of longhorns. His siblings' bloodthirsty howls filled the broad valley. Pelting snow obscured his vision and froze his throat. He yanked up his bandanna to cover his nose and mouth, leaned low over his palomino's neck and galloped flat out to redirect the rampaging group before they plunged off the bluff ahead. His heart drummed. Stinging sweat dripped in his eyes.

"Hee-yah!" pealed his younger brother Jared, his lusty shout ringing above the bellowing cattle's din.

Their trampling hooves slapped the hard, rocky earth in a heart-pounding rhythm. At James's finger point, Jared swerved away in the white murk and chased after a breakout group of cows and heifers, his face animated, eyes intent, back straight. He looked as unruffled as he had when they'd begun searching for the runaways who'd broken from their winter pasture hours ago. Of course, it'd take a lot more than a hundred out-of-control livestock to rattle golden-child Jared's bone-deep confidence.

As for him? Chaos got under James's skin, made it itch. And whenever chaos hit, James's restless thoughts didn't quit until everything on the family ranch he managed was in its proper, predetermined place. The rules he'd instituted after his youngest brother Jesse died and older brother, Jack, left to seek justice were needed to protect his family and their way of life. Otherwise, their carefully pieced-back world risked falling apart again.

"Yip! Yip! Yip!" hooted his sister, Jewel. She barreled at lightning speed along the right side of the cattle atop her large bay. Her dark eyes flashed, and her mouth curled slightly at the edges in a fearless smirk. She'd lost her black Stetson, he noticed, and snowflakes clung to her dark, braided hair. Red filled in the pale skin between her freckles. If she was tired after their grueling day, she wasn't showing it. Not that she ever would.

In fact, since Jesse's death, she'd thrown herself into ranching as if possessed. As though she could somehow make up for the shattering loss.

At James's signal, Jewel nodded then fell back slightly. The maneuver allowed him to begin arcing the cattle her way into an open, snowy space, turning the stampede in on itself so they'd mill instead of run.

More important, it'd stop them from mingling with the Brahman herd owned by their archenemies and neighbors, the Lovelands. Their bitter family feud went back over a hundred years, beginning with a tale of deception, theft and murder, the rivalry still fresh as it played out in water access disputes and missing cattle.

James pursed his lips and whistled long and high, urging on the Border collies. They lunged at the longhorns' ankles, dodging horns, driving the livestock to the right. With the bluff drawing alarmingly close, they needed to make the turn in the next thirty seconds or it'd be too late. Devastating tragedy. Not on his watch.

He squeezed Trigger's heaving sides and rode harder still, James's body steaming and slick beneath his plaid shirt and flannel-lined jean jacket. He ignored the deep ache in his shoulders and the way his teeth ground with each jarring stride. All around him rose the thick, musky scent of animals. Their eyes rolled and they bleated loudly, showing no signs of slowing.

Out of the worsening blizzard, his youngest sibling Justin emerged, a lone, dark figure between the herd and the bluff's edge.

"Get out of there!" James bellowed.

He ripped off his bandanna and waved at his reckless brother. Immediately, the wild swirl of icy wind and blowing snow snatched away his breath. Anger and concern roared in his bloodstream. Cool, unaffected Justin, however, didn't budge. He sat slim and ramrod straight in the saddle and stared down the charging herd as if he dared them to mow him over. The fool. Their departed father taught them better when they'd begun working the family's ten-thousand-acre ranch as kids.

Some said Justin had a death wish. Given his reckless antics since losing his twin, Jesse, James agreed. But he wouldn't let anything happen to his little brother, to any of them, ever again. However, when he got Justin to safety, he'd kill him.

James kicked Trigger with his heels, dragging forth the blowing horse's last bit of steam. At his command, Trigger neighed, then veered directly at the lead cow, obeying without hesitation. Make-or-break time. James flashed his red bandanna at the cattle, flaunting the "fish" to make them more afraid of him than whatever had spooked them.

The livestock balked, then broke to the right. The rest of the herd dashed pell-mell after their leaders, turning back. Confused and confronted by themselves, they slowed, raising the snow, tearing the naked brush, letting out hoarse bawls as they began to mill and spread farther down the white valley, no longer in danger. Out of the corner of his eye, he spotted Justin chasing off any stragglers who approached the bluff. James released a long breath.

Jared flashed by, effortlessly driving the group he'd wrangled back into the now-organized mob. Jewel pulled her mount around in a neat circle, scooped up her trampled hat, then trotted up beside James. After rounding up the last of the strays, the Cades corralled the bawling, red-and-white-spotted herd and guided them back on the long trail home.

Silence reigned as the herd's lowing dropped down to its usual buzz. The Cades settled into their saddles and thoughts. Thick snow poured from the sky and clung to their hat brims, their noses and shoulders. They followed a meandering, beaten trail down the mountain slope.

The pungent scent of spruce filled the air and seeped into James's nose, making his shoulders drop, his rigid spine bend and flex. He felt pummeled, his muscles tender and worn out the way he liked best. This was the right kind of tired, the type that followed a long, honest day's work. It sometimes let him escape his worries about the ranch, his siblings and his grieving mother by falling into oblivious sleep.

The world dimmed further as the sun, buried underneath heavy-bellied clouds, slipped behind Mount Sopris's craggy top. The valley floor billowed away, raw and untamed, growing gray in the dawning dusk. Walls of ice on stone, gleaming with the last of the light, enclosed the valley, stretching away toward the long, low Elk Mountain range.

The place was wild, beautiful and open with something nameless that made the highland spaces different from any other country to James. That made it home. The isolation, the vast, untouched stretches of valley and bluffs, soothed his restless spirit, lowered his guard and gave him peace.

He felt a bone-deep kinship with the land. It configured his DNA. His ancestors had labored, sacrificed and fought to protect it, to claim it as their own. It was his responsibility to maintain that legacy and pass it on to the next generation. No threats would cross its border again, not so long as he drew breath, he vowed, his own personal cowboy's prayer.

The horses nickered as they clomped past barren aspen clumps, tails swishing. "That was fun," Jewel drawled. She swayed in perfect rhythm with her enormous steed. It was the ranch's largest mount, which, of course, made it the only one the petite roughrider would mount.

"Then you don't get out much," Jared said, then flinched to avoid Jewel's trademark shoulder jab.

"Just wait till we get home. We'll see how tough you are," Jewel huffed. She rammed her misshapen hat on her head and pulled the brim low over her braids.

"I'm a lover, not a fighter," Jared protested, riding with the easy grace born of years in the saddle. His perfect white teeth flashed in his lady-killer grin.

The family's Romeo had left a swath of broken hearts across the valley. Jared's ease at meeting women, at achieving anything in life, was downright irritating. Opportunities like college football scholarships and a starting NFL position seemed to fall into the small-town hero's lap.

"That's your excuse? Pathetic." Jewel rolled her eyes and brushed snow from her horse's forelock. "Don't know why girls throw themselves at you."

"Must be desperate," Justin said through a yawn, looking ready to fall asleep despite today's excitement. A thick belt of snow encircled his hat brim.

"Who is it this time?" teased Jewel, wagging a finger. "Mandy? Mindy? Mona?"

"It's Melanie," Jared clarified. He rubbed the back of his neck, then gave a rueful laugh. "Nope. It's Melody."

"See." Jewel snapped her fingers. "They're all starting to blur together. Even for you."

She burst out laughing and Justin joined her. "Seriously, dude. Pick a girl. Any girl."

"They pick me, bro."

A wild howl pealed down the slope and Trigger's ears shot up. It was loud and harsh, then softened to a mourn, lonely and haunting. The hair on the back of James's neck rose. Wolf.

A pack of coyotes barked in answer, a sharp, staccato yelping chorus, the piercing notes biting on the chilly early-evening air. Trigger sidestepped, nickering, and James swiftly brought him under control on the slippery terrain.

"You're so full of yourself," scoffed Jewel once they'd settled their jittery horses. Their hooves clattered against the frigid slope.

"And you're so full of—"

"Knock it off." James's fingers tightened around the leather straps in his left hand. "We've got more important things to worry about than Jared's love life."

Had his mother gotten out of bed this morning? Eaten? Dressed?

"At least I've got one, big bro."

James opened his mouth but the denial dissolved, bitter on his tongue. Jared was right. Since Jesse's murder, he'd worked nonstop to shore up the ranch and didn't have time for anything, or anyone, else. He loved his family. That was enough.

So why did he sometimes wish for a confidante? A hand in his? A person to hold... someone to share a bag of peanuts with at a football game. The pelting snow slackened.

"Let's pick up the pace or Ma's meat loaf

will be cold," he said, needing to deflect, hoping that by saying those words they might be true and she'd had a good day.

"*If* Ma's cooking… Didn't see her up this morning." A line appeared, bisecting Justin's brow.

"Yesterday wasn't one of her good days." Jewel patted her horse's sweat-streaked neck. "She was going through Jesse's phone again. She still thinks those pictures are his son."

James shook his head. "If that was true, Jesse would have told us." Jesse had messed up a lot, but James didn't believe his brother capable of turning his back on his own child. Besides, Jesse loved kids, all living things, in fact… Jesse keeping his child a secret made no sense. There had to be another explanation for the photo.

"I don't like Ma getting her hopes up," Jewel fretted.

"Obsessing is more like it," James worried out loud. "Like when Jesse was alive."

A collective moan rose from his siblings. Their mother's fixation on healing their brother had taken a horrible toll on her physical and emotional health.

James's hands tightened on the reins. He'd convince her to put away the phone and stop torturing herself. With the holidays approaching, this false hope came at an already painful time.

Jared deftly guided his horse away from a depression in the snowy field. "Should we get Ma help?"

"No. She's getting stronger," James insisted. They didn't need outsiders poking through their business. Once they got through Christmas, Ma would improve. He'd make sure of it. "She's been mostly keeping up with routines."

"And that's all that counts, right?" Justin asked out of the side of his mouth. "That she follows your schedules?"

"They keep things running smoothly," James protested. A night wind hummed softly through the gnarled, stunted cedars they passed.

Yes. He was a micromanager. No denying it. But if he'd been more vigilant, he would have spotted the threats to Jesse, like his connections to the Denver-based drug group who'd tracked him to Carbondale, then killed for unpaid debt.

And then there was his own, more direct role in the tragedy—a failure he'd never forget—or forgive. "I'm protecting us. Plus, the schedules help Ma."

He closed his eyes against the sudden vision of Jesse, pale and still in his coffin. They'd all struggled to make it through that day and every day since, especially around the holidays when he'd passed away.

Giving his mother direction, a routine, gave her a purpose, something positive to focus on. Seeing her wander the house, or worse, staying in bed, with that empty look in her eye as if her heart had been scraped right out, broke him in two.

"Meat loaf," Justin said solemnly. "Yeah. That right there is a real lifesaver."

James nudged Trigger and trotted ahead, leaving his siblings behind in the gathering darkness. They meant well, and he wouldn't trade them for anything. But they didn't understand the need to keep a tight rein on the ranch, the family and especially Ma. He didn't give two hoots if they ate meat loaf. They'd lost too many Cades already. With his mother lumbering through life like a zombie, he feared they'd lose her, too, if he wasn't extra careful. Better to worry too much than not enough, he'd learned in the hardest way possible.

He would always be vigilant in preventing negative forces from infiltrating their clan as they had with Jesse.

His brothers and sister quieted and joined him a moment later, fanning out on either side, their solid support palpable. Despite the tweaking, quarreling and outright brawling, especially Jewel and that fierce uppercut of hers, they always had each other's backs.

The terrain grew gentler, rolling. Below, on the level floor of the valley, lay the rambling old ranch house with cabins nestling around and the corrals leading out to the soft, snow-dusted hay fields, misty and gray in twilight. A single light gleamed like a beacon.

Home.

His spirits lifted.

An hour later, showered and ravenous, he tromped up the front porch of his family's main house. Built with rough-hewn cedar, it seemed to spring from the earth, a part of the landscape, its lines as majestic as its surrounding mountains.

Log pillars held up a steep, snow-covered portico and peaked gables broke up the roofline. Numerous windows gleamed in the dark. They must have cost a fortune when they'd been installed. 1882. The year his gold-mining, prospecting ancestor stumbled on a lucky strike that'd made his fortune and allowed him to purchase the property.

He pushed through the screen door and stopped short at the scene before him. No set table. No meat loaf. Where was his mother? She must have had another tough day. His chest squeezed.

Then his eyes alighted on his ma holding hands with a dark-haired young woman.

"James!" Ma exclaimed and stood, as did the stranger. She was slim and tall, her midnight hair a thick tangle around a beautiful face the color of a candle's glow, her obsidian eyes wide. They shifted out from under his direct gaze, her nervous reaction instantly jangling his suspicious nature. A child stopped waving a wooden spoon like it was a sword and stared with large, unblinking eyes, as though sizing up a threat.

"Is it that time already?" His mother's hand fluttered to her cross necklace and she twisted it. "We must have gotten sidetracked. Sofia, this is my second eldest, James. James, this is Sofia Gallardo, mother of Jesse's child,

Javi, my first grandson and your nephew. Isn't it a miracle?"

And just like that, the safe haven he'd labored to create turned itself inside out.

CHAPTER THREE

PULL BACK. STEADY. Steady. Don't come off the vein.

Blood rushed in the half-full syringe, curling red. Sofia held her arm still and slowly pushed the plunger. She wanted to make this last. Anticipation sizzled over her nerves.

Pull it out again. The blood swirled back inside.

Now. Squeeze.

This was what she wanted. Yes. Here it was. The rush. It flooded up her arm and tingled.

Then it hit. It was like a mini explosion of unadulterated pleasure.

Everything turned blissful and beautiful. And she loved everything. It was a pure joy to be alive, to have a body; a heavenly awareness.

The hand of God, cradling her to sleep.

Sleep.

No.

Don't go to sleep.

Don't. Go. To. Sleep.

Sofia lurched upright in bed, and her gasp cracked through the small, dark room. Her heart thrummed, deafening in her ears, almost painful. Was she having a heart attack?

Had she taken a bad hit?

She groped for the syringe and came up empty. Where? Where? Where?

"Mama?"

She shoved her hair from her hot face and peered at the small shape hovering by her bed.

"Javi?"

His eyes looked as big as saucers. "Are you okay?"

"Yes." She hoisted him up and pulled him close. "I just had a bad dream."

Terrifyingly real.

Remembering the good was worse than the bad.

"A monster?"

"A big one," she said, recalling the horrible creature she'd once been—thinking of nothing, no one, but her next fix.

She rested her cheek on Javi's head and strove to calm her breathing. Kids needed their parents to protect them, but in her case, it felt the other way around. She'd gotten sober for Javi, and because of him she stayed on the straight and narrow.

"I can sleep with you till you feel better," he whispered around what sounded like his thumb. A flash of worry popped inside. The old habit reappeared whenever he felt stressed.

"I'd like that, sweetie. Thanks."

Ten minutes later, Sofia stared up into dark and listened to Javi's soft, regular breathing.

Another addiction dream.

She squished her pricking eyes shut. Foolish her for hoping the nightmares would end after she'd left her drug-ridden neighborhood. She'd finally escaped, yet her addiction followed, a zombielike thing lurching toward her up US 285 from Albuquerque to drag her and Javi down.

No.

She had to stay one step ahead and get farther away than Colorado. Another coast. Maybe even a different country.

You cannot fall.

Though you could, whispered another voice. *You know how easy it would be.* An innocent mistake, even. Never meaning harm, exactly…

Prescription pills were more addictive than heroin.

She clamped her hands over her ears, a useless move since the taunting rose from within, the horrible refrain of her lonely life. She blew out a breath, disentangled Javi's limbs from hers and slid out of bed. She needed air.

After slipping on a thick robe and slippers, Sofia eased out of the room. She padded down the staircase, pushed open the screen door and stepped onto the porch.

The black night folded around Cade Ranch like velvet, as cold and soft as a bat's wing. The storm had cleared, and overhead, glinting stars clustered. She inhaled the aroma of the rich, slumbering earth. It seemed to hold the mystery of nature and life, a smell that, in a strange way, soothed her some, gave her a tiny bit of hope. As if she, like the rest of the world, could afford to settle down, too, for a bit.

She leaned on the banister and peered into the night. Her heart lifted at the majestic vista. The Rocky Mountains' shadowed outlines scaled the distant horizon. They surrounded the ranch's valley in a semicircle, stone sentinels guarding against the outside world, shielding and protecting this isolated countryside.

But could they protect her—and Javi—from herself?

It was a constant gnawing fear.

One she bore alone.

But how strong could one person be?

Why didn't you ever tell them about us? she silently asked Jesse, her eyes on the sky, her leaden heart at her feet. *Why didn't you come back for us? Were you ashamed? Incapable? Afraid?*

She wished she and Javi could settle here, but Jesse's tragedy was also her tragedy. His addiction story hers. Shared history. She could never be someone else, someone worthy of being Javi's mother, around a family who'd already lost a drug-abusing son, people who knew who she really was, who she might turn into if she wasn't careful.

At a light cough, she jumped. A dark figure detached itself from the shadows, and she stumbled back, panic scrambling over her skin. A newel post stopped her flight. When she spun around, a firm hand landed on her upper arm and checked her momentum.

"It's me. James."

His rich baritone cut through her flustered

fog. James. One of Jesse's older brothers. The strict, reserved one. He hadn't said much earlier as she and Joy had slapped sandwiches together to feed the rest of the boisterous Cade clan. In fact, he hadn't spoken at all. As he ate, he'd simply watched while his siblings peppered her with questions. They'd seemed to accept her and Javi immediately. James, however, had held back, his shuttered expression hard to read.

It'd made her nervous.

He made her nervous.

Her past experience with controlling men like her father had taught her to be wary of them as triggers for her addiction.

She shivered and crossed her arms. *You're free now*, she reminded herself, firmly. *Javi got you sober. No more worrying.*

Right?

Her recent nightmare, however, told another tale.

And now she stood alone with James in the dead of night. Anxious awareness zipped along her nerve endings.

"What—what are you doing out here?" she gasped, her words full of air and apprehension.

Moon rays illuminated the tall, rangy man.

He had wide shoulders, a slightly crooked nose and incredibly long eyelashes that would have made a handsome man look effeminate. Instead, they made this rugged cowboy a tiny bit beautiful. His full lips twisted. "I live here."

She checked her eye roll. "Right. Well. Night." She turned to leave but his voice stopped her.

"Tell me about Jesse."

"What do you mean?"

"The stuff you left out earlier because Javi was listening. Why didn't Jesse tell us about you?" He leaned against the railing, folded his arms on his chest and peered down at her from his great height. She could make out the pronounced curve of his biceps beneath his white thermal shirtsleeves. He looked strong. A man used to getting what he wanted... And now he wanted her to talk about a time she'd rather forget.

Not happening.

Thinking, talking, reliving her darkest hours was like walking backward on broken glass, each word drawing blood.

She licked dry lips. "I don't know why he kept us a secret."

You threw him out... Told him never to con-

tact you again until he was sure he was completely sober...heartless woman...

"Jesse loved children."

Not Javi...not more than drugs, anyway, and the pain of that thought pierced her side. "Jesse's not here to explain himself. There's nothing more I can tell you."

"Or nothing more that you *want* to tell me."

"Excuse me?" she asked, stung by his answer. It struck too close to the truth.

"I've been called a lot of names in my life." He squinted at her. "Fool isn't one of them."

"What are you suggesting?"

"That you're hiding something." He leaned a hand on the newel post behind her, his proximity hemming her in. She ducked from beneath his arm and spoke over her shoulder, avoiding him, just as she dodged all confrontations. *Physically remove yourself from bad situations*, her rehab counselor had told her, *before you explore other ways to escape.*

She'd hung on to those words all these years. They were some of the rare bits of sobriety advice she'd received, given she'd never attended any NA meetings. Without childcare, she'd struggled to go. Besides, she'd told herself she didn't need extra help when she only had to look at her child to know why she had to stay sober. "I'd better go in."

"Please stay."

"No, really, I—"

"Humor me. You are under my roof..."

She bristled at his tone, recalling it from her youth, the oppressive sound of her father. She'd checked out of her prison-like, motherless childhood the only way she thought she could, starting with prescription pills a school friend promised would take everything away, including a painful sports injury. It'd seemed innocent at first. Fun. Rebellious without causing any real trouble. Who didn't have pills in their bathroom cabinets? And the painkillers had taken away everything...including herself. When her need to stay numb had gotten too expensive, she'd turned to heroin, a cheaper, deadlier fix.

"This is Joy's home," she protested to James, projecting calmness despite the pressure building inside.

"I run the place, and I'm part owner with my brothers and sister."

"Joy invited me. I'm *her* guest."

"And how did that happen?" He lifted one of his thick, slanted eyebrows.

"I lost my wallet. Otherwise we'd be in Oregon."

"You didn't plan on meeting the rest of us? Even for your son's sake?" Suspicion edged his voice.

"No. It's just that I…we didn't have time."

"Right. The tickets to Portland." The way he drew out the city's name made it sound like a fictitious place, a destination she'd fabricated. "Who do you know there?"

"That's none of your business," she murmured through rigid lips. The wind picked up and fluttered strands of hair in her face. She shoved them behind her ears.

"It is, *if* it involves a relation of mine."

"Javi's your nephew," she gasped. So now he didn't believe Javi was Jesse's son? Fury corroded her tongue. She hated feeling backed into a corner. Trapped like she had been during her childhood.

"I only have your word for it." His sober voice descended on her, as heavy as a gavel.

"And his birth certificate."

"And where's that?"

"My wallet."

"The one that's missing…" He cocked his head, studying her.

"I'm leaving."

He held out a hand. "You misunderstand me." Something about the plea in his voice halted her feet. She'd heard it before, in her own head, that same desire for someone to understand her. "I don't know you, where you come from or who your people are. Since Jesse's murder, I don't trust strangers."

Her eyes met his, and she gnawed on her lower lip, thinking fast. She wasn't about to talk about who her people were. Bringing up her father was another trigger, and she wouldn't compound this tense moment by invoking his name. "I'm just passing through," she said, knowing it sounded weak. But it was the best she could do.

He nodded slowly, his dark eyes shiny and a touch sad. The moon sank beneath a scuttle of clouds and the world seemed to collapse in on itself. A black hole.

"I'd like your promise to be on the Portland bus tomorrow. If you delay, Ma will get attached. She looks strong, but she's fragile, especially this time of year."

"Don't worry. I'll be gone tomorrow. I'm definitely not staying for the holidays."

Though how she wished, just once, that she could give Javi a real Christmas.

"Her heart's been broken too many times by…"

"Jesse," she murmured.

When James averted his face, the firm cut of his jaw drew her eye. A day's worth of dark stubble shaded it, giving him a dangerous edge, yet she also sensed a profound loneliness in him that echoed her own. There was nothing worse than feeling alone in crowds of people. He'd held himself back during the boisterous family dinner, his vigilant eyes rarely straying from his mother. He wanted to protect her, and Sofia admired his determination, especially since she was equally resolute in shielding her son.

Wind chimes jangled from a corner of the porch, their silvery notes shivering on the breeze. "Jesse caused Ma a lot of pain. Still does."

"You love your mother a lot."

"She's the greatest person I know."

Sofia ached at his simple, heartfelt declaration. All her life she'd wished for a mother to love and knew she'd have been just as protective and loyal as James. "Jesse's addiction must have been hard on her."

He turned and his dark eyes glimmered in the gloom. "Were you an addict, too?"

"Jesse and I got clean together."

And when he relapsed, you kicked him out. You never gave him the support you should have.

"How long have you been sober?"

"Six years." Did he think her a closet junkie bent on taking advantage of his family?

Her throat tightened at his possible bad opinion, though why it mattered, she hadn't a clue. Nearly everyone she'd ever met assumed the worst, so why would James be different?

Maybe the reason stemmed from her long-held wish for Javi to be a part of Cade Ranch, a world she never got to experience: one full of strong values and family, where he'd be safe and secure—even if she slipped again. Every night, she told him Rocky Mountain cowboys' bedtime stories, describing legendary men to make him proud of his dad.

And now James's suspicious manner made her want to flee. He reminded her of who she was, not who she wanted to become.

"No relapses?" he pressed.

"Nope." She forced a pained smile and spoke through her clenched teeth. "See. Not rotting. I'm not a meth head."

"What about your arms?"

She extended one, and he slid her sleeve

up over her elbow to peer at her track lines, scars that disfigured her, showed the world the ugliness that lurked within.

A shivery tremble began in her lower stomach as his calloused fingers grazed her marks. His gaze lifted and locked with hers. Instead of the disgust she expected, his face fell. A crazy urge to wrap her arms around him and hold *him* up seized her.

"Seen enough?" Her voice broke.

When he didn't answer, she shoved up the other sleeve and extended the scarred underside of her elbow.

"Enough." He lifted his hands, then dropped them, backing away, looking slightly stunned.

"They're not fresh," she insisted, shaking inside.

His chest rose and fell with the force of his sigh. "But you were with Jesse when he relapsed."

"Yes," she answered fast, relieved to get past this awkward moment of physical awareness.

"Were you friends with his dealer?"

A bitter laugh escaped her as she pictured her neighborhood's thugs. "Hardly."

"But you knew them." He looked her dead

in the eye, and she nodded, unable to hold in the truth at the anguish she glimpsed in their depths.

"Did you know Jesse's murderers?"

"Of course not. I was raising a child." And trying, trying, trying to move on with her life. Guilt flashed inside over how she'd had to push Jesse away to do that. If she'd stuck by him, been stronger for him, would he be alive today?

James studied her and the stern planes of his face softened. "Heroin ruined Jesse's life." His voice seemed to vibrate across the short space between them, bending the frigid night air, making her insides jump. "I won't have anyone associated with drugs here at the ranch."

The old, familiar shame of being an addict, a felon, a homeless teenager and single mother dredged through her. It raked over her hopes to become something more.

"My addiction cost me my dreams. Single-parenting added another challenge," she divulged. "But I'm going to make something of myself and have a fresh start." One she delayed every minute spent in Carbondale. She needed to begin again where no one knew the bad in her.

"I hope you do."

"I'll leave once I find my wallet. A couple of the places I wanted to check yesterday evening were closed. I'll visit them first thing tomorrow."

"And I'll accompany you after I've finished my chores."

"What? Why?!"

"To help you get that fresh start." A ghost of a smile appeared on his face, a faint dimple denting his left cheek like an innocent child's memory. "Good night, Sofia," he said, his voice a deep rumble between them. Then he turned, trotted down the stairs and strode toward one of the cabins.

She watched his large frame stalk across the snowy field, unsure whether to call the Cades friends or foe.

Certainly not family, as much as she wished otherwise.

Joy wasn't the only one in danger of getting her heart broken. Sofia could fall for this warmhearted clan—minus haunted, brooding James—as quickly and painfully as she had for Jesse. Hopefully, she'd find her wallet tomorrow and be on her way before any real damage was done.

CHAPTER FOUR

JAMES SLUGGED A hot draw of black coffee the next afternoon and set the thermos in his truck's cup holder. A boot-stomping country-rock tune blared from his sound system and Sofia perched beside him, her arms hugging her knees to her chest.

Sofia sang softly, a low sound he found himself straining to hear. They were lyrics to a familiar song that she nearly had right…

"It's 'beat boys,'" he corrected, mouth curling, unable to stop himself. An annoyed breath of air escaped him. After spending too much time dwelling on the strange effect the feel of Sofia's scars had on him, he'd vowed to interact as little as possible with her today.

"And feet off the seat, please." He angled his head side to side, working the kinks that'd formed in his neck after another sleepless night. Layered brown, tan and beige mesas flashed by his window, rising above the white-banked Colorado river that followed alongside I-70. The hum of his tires, eating up the miles to Carbondale, were a bass note accompaniment to the thumping tune.

Out of the corner of his eye, he glimpsed the swing of Sofia's thick black hair as she dropped her feet to the mat and twisted around to face him. "It's the Beach Boys. You know? Like the group?"

"Might have heard of them," he drawled, biting back a grin. "But the lyrics are 'beat boys.'"

"Uh-uh. Listen again." She restarted the song and then sang "Beach Boys" on the chorus. "See?"

"All I could hear was you. Singing the wrong words." He couldn't stop his upward twitching mouth any longer and gave in to a full-on smile. An unfamiliar feeling.

"Then who does the singer mean when he says that he wants to 'get lost in the rock and roll'? Huh?" Her annoyed huff made something tight inside his chest loosen.

"He wants to get lost in the beat," he said reasonably, inhaling the vanilla-musk scent that rose from her hair. The soft, shining tresses curled close. "Here. Listen again." He started the song over. At the chorus, he sang the correct line.

A quick glance to his right revealed Sofia's frown. Her dark eyebrows met over her nose, and that full pink mouth of hers, the one he hadn't been able to stop staring at since they'd met last night, pursed. He shoved down the unwanted attraction and forced his gaze back on the road where it belonged. He had no business thinking Jesse's girl was pretty.

Focus on your mission: retrieve Sofia's wallet and put her and Javi on the next train to Portland. ASAP.

"Play it again."

When the song finished, she punched off the player and flopped back in her seat, arms folded over her chest. She plunked her heels on the seat again and dropped her chin on top of her knees. "How come no one corrected me before?"

"Maybe they were afraid of you," he teased, then sobered at her horrified expression. Had he struck a nerve? Why?

Without a word, she jerked around to face the window and rolled the glass lower. Crisp, crystal-fresh air flowed inside the cab. It carried a hint of smooth pine and diesel. Red cones appeared as they crested a small hill. A cordoned-off lane indicated upcoming roadwork and he slowed, dialing the radio tuner until he caught a Broncos away game against his favorite team, the Cowboys.

They rode in tense silence for a few minutes.

"Jesse used to do that," he said. "Sing the wrong words."

"Whenever he sang 'Hush Little Baby' to Javi, he'd change all the gifts around." She spoke without turning her head. "He'd always ask, 'Now, what's a baby gonna do with a diamond ring?'"

That caught him with an unexpected warmth. "Sounds like Jesse. What'd he swap them for?"

"I think it was something like, 'Daddy's gonna buy you a quarter horse. And if that quarter horse won't canter, Daddy's gonna buy you an alligator.'"

A short laugh escaped him. "Yep. That's Jesse all right."

"He was good with Javi."

James squinted his eyes and kept his expression stone. "Jesse always loved babies. So, he never gave any reason for leaving you two?"

She bit down on the corner of her thumb for a long moment, then said, "I didn't give him much choice when he relapsed. Didn't want drugs around Javi—"

Her voice broke off, and he shot her a swift look. Her hurt seemed genuine... Had his brother abandoned his child? It went against everything James knew about Jesse. Then again, his brother had kept a lot of secrets, though never one as big as this.

"Why are they playing Jackson?" Sofia exclaimed, dragging him from his thoughts.

Surprised she knew the name of the Cowboys' starting wide receiver, he met her large, intelligent eyes briefly, then forced his gaze forward again. "Not a fan?"

"After last week's backward punt return fumble?" she exclaimed. "We need to pull the plug on him." She jerked her bent thumb out the open window. With her hair blowing wildly around her heart-shaped face, her upward-tilting nose flaring over her rosebud mouth, she knocked the breath right out of him.

"You saw that game?"

Her shoulders, encased in a puffy white ski jacket his sister used to wear, lifted and fell. "The diner I worked in had a radio and the owner was a Cowboys fan. You sound surprised."

Eyes on the road, he chanted in his head. "I guess I'm just used to my family. They're die-hard Broncos fans."

A scoffing noise erupted from the passenger side. "Guess they have to be, living up here and all."

He lifted his hat, then settled it on again, curving the brim in a C. "Yeah, it's practically a requirement."

Her quick bark of laughter warmed his blood. "So how'd you turn traitor?"

"Michael Irvin."

"The Playmaker." She whistled. "Three Super Bowl titles."

"And three All-Pro selections. The man was a legend."

"A Hall of Famer." She lifted her chin slightly. "Caught seven hundred and fifty passes."

"Sixty-five touchdowns."

"He was Jesse's favorite, too." An appalled silence descended. "I'm sorry." Out of the corner of his eye, he noticed her reach out, as if to touch his arm, and stop. His body tensed. The sudden wish for that touch staggered him.

He cleared his throat. "Right. Just me and Jesse. Otherwise it's all about the Broncos.

My brother Jared, you probably know, was their starting wide receiver until he tore his ACL six months ago."

"Which one is Jared again?"

James puzzled over how best to distinguish among his dark-haired siblings and went for the obvious. "The handsome one."

She spread her hands. "That doesn't help. You're all good-looking. Genetic mutants, really."

"Ha," he scoffed. At her continued silence, he glanced at her, taken aback by her serious face. "Everyone says he looks like Orlando Bloom."

She flicked a graceful hand. "Pretty boy, then. I prefer a Jon Snow, personally."

He felt, rather than saw, her eyes land on him and it did something funny to his gut.

A roar sounded through the speakers, and he gripped the wheel. Sofia dropped her feet to the mat and leaned forward. "Come on, come on. Get to the end zone," she chanted. Then they both hollered.

"Touchdown!"

"Wooo-hooo!"

"This puts them in playoff contention."

Despite speaking over each other, he heard every one of her words perfectly, as if they were the keys in some old-fashioned type-writer, pressing into his brain, leaving an indelible mark.

"There's the bank!" she exclaimed once he'd exited the interstate and onto Main Street. They cruised down the quaint downtown thoroughfare filled with a continuous line of two- and three-story brick and stone facades. Ma claimed many were the original structures built back when Carbondale became a depot town, servicing ranchers and prospectors in 1887.

It certainly had a rustic, Western atmosphere. Boot-and-cowboy-hat-clad residents thronged the wide sidewalks. Overhead, Christmas wreaths bursting with greenery, pinecones and bright red ribbons dangled from black streetlights.

As they parked and exited the truck, he inhaled the tangy scent of barbecue wafting from Shorty's, a family restaurant run by an old high school friend. A marquee broadcast a country-western concert taking place later that night, Heath Loveland listed as one of the performers, and the Festival of Lights, Carbondale's holiday season kickoff event set for next week. He hadn't been to it since Jesse's passing.

Sofia's animated face seemed closed now that they'd hit the street. She ducked her head, and her eyes darted left to right, her hands shoved deep into coat pockets. What had happened to his lyric-substituting football enthusiast? Back was the cagey woman who'd raised his suspicions last night. It reminded him not to let down his guard, no matter how easily she disarmed him.

A couple of hours later, after checking various establishments for Sofia's wallet, James fed another coin into the parking meter, then joined her at Timeless Gifts' front window.

"Javi would love this." The wistful note in her voice caught at him, as did the still way that she stood, as if breathing wasn't a given.

A miniature train rattled by. It barreled through a replica Christmas village.

"We had a set like this when we were kids. We were obsessed with it, especially Jesse. Every birthday and holiday, we'd beg for new tracks, buildings, landscape, accessories until it'd taken up most of the living room. We even changed it up with the seasons, and Christmas used to be our favorite time to transform it into a wonderland."

Where was it now?

Probably moldering in the attic with the

rest of the decorations since Jesse's passing. He should toss the items. Just thinking about them was like worrying a cavity, his thoughts running over them this time of year automatically, unconsciously, checking to see if the memories still hurt.

They did.

"It sounds amazing." She dabbed at her red nose with a tissue. "I never had toys like that."

"How come?" He tucked in the loose end of her scarf, his fingers lingering on her throat's silken flesh.

Her expression grew guarded. "It's getting colder," she said, her silent I-don't-want-to-talk-about-it equally clear.

He squashed down his rising curiosity. "Any other place you might have visited yesterday?"

"No. That's it." She shoved her hair off her face and her forehead scrunched as if she had a headache. "I thought we'd find it at the diner. It's the last place I remember using it."

"No one turned it in yesterday or today."

When the driver of a passing pickup honked, he waved, then dropped his hand quick. It was Boyd Loveland and his adopted son, Daryl. They passed by in a beat-up Chevy with the number 812 painted on its doors. Must be entering it in tonight's smashup derby, he mused. The last of the season. If so, Justin would be gunning for them.

"What am I going to do?" Sofia asked quietly, eyes closed, only speaking to herself.

"Let me pay for the tickets." It was the perfect solution, one that'd save his mother from becoming more attached the longer Javi and Sofia stayed.

"No."

"What?" He gaped at her.

"I don't take handouts."

"Then pay me back once you're settled and begin your new job."

"I—I can't. You see, I need my wallet."

Her intensity took him aback. As did her pinched expression. She looked afraid. But of what? Did she have pills in there? Drugs? She'd reassured him of her recovery last night, but this desperation brought back bad memories of Jesse and the frantic lengths he'd go to for his next fix.

"You can get new IDs. I'll give you money beyond the fares. Enough to help you have your fresh start. Nothing is irreplaceable."

Except drugs. He would not allow another abuser near his mother.

"Some things are. Please take me back to the ranch."

"Then let's at least report it to the police," he insisted. What was she hiding? "You can send them your Portland information once you're settled. They'll let you know if it turns up."

Her tan skin turned a sickly yellow, and she backed up a step. "No. No cops." She turned in a small circle, her eyes darting. "Please take me back to the ranch." She ran a shaking hand through her locks. "I need to think."

He nodded, resigned, then led the way to the truck, his doubts rising. Based on her erratic behavior, his gut told him she threatened his ranch's peace. He held open the door and breathed in Sofia's light vanilla scent as she scooted up onto the seat.

She was a damsel in distress, yet he couldn't be her hero. He'd never get close to a wild card like Sofia. So why was he attracted to a woman he couldn't trust? One with a child who might—or might not—be his nephew? Clearly, Jesse had cared about the child enough to sing him lullabies. That fact, however, didn't make Javi his son.

Or a Cade.

To believe in Sofia, James needed solid

proof. Without it, he'd put his mother at risk. His thoughts returned to Sofia and how she'd charmed him earlier.

Was his mother's heart all he needed to worry about?

CHAPTER FIVE

"Doggone it!"

At a clattering bang, Sofia stopped tossing a salad and whirled from her place at the ranch's granite kitchen island. Javi peered up from a coloring book spread across an oval table before a bay window. Over his shoulder loomed Mount Sopris. The setting sun gilded its jagged, snow-covered peak gold.

Joy gaped at an upended kettle and cradled her Ace-wrapped wrist. Steaming brown stew spilled onto the red Native American–style rug covering the pine floor. The mouthwatering smell of bay leaves, cooked carrots and braised beef, already filling the vaulted kitchen, intensified.

"Let me help." Sofia grabbed the pot and dropped it into one of the countertops' built-in stainless-steel sinks. She flipped on the garbage disposal and dumped the ruined dinner down the grinding mechanism. James had mentioned looking forward to beef stew on the drive home earlier. Would he be disappointed? And why did she care?!

Clearly, he was suspicious of her. After she'd refused to visit the police, a trip that would have triggered bad memories and risked revealing her old felony, he'd barely spoken to her.

"I want to help!" Javi scampered over, his face glowing, his compact body practically vibrating with excitement.

Resistance was futile. The kid lived to help.

She ruffled his hair and handed him a couple of paper towels. "Get down with your bad self."

"I'm using my superpowers." Javi sank to the floor, the tip of his pink tongue clamped between his teeth as he concentrated. His long sweeps smeared the stew farther into the small spaces between the wood planks.

"Supper's ruined." Joy sighed when she returned from the laundry room, where she'd dropped off the rug. "I wanted to make tonight special for you." She leaned against one of the natural wood cabinets that matched the floor and the exposed-beam, slanted ceiling. Her apron tie knot unraveled in her hands.

Javi sat back on his heels and waved a dripping towel. "I don't like beef stew anyway. Celery is bleh."

"Hush," Sofia hissed, mortified. They were guests here, at least for one more night, while she figured out her options.

Her wallet couldn't have just disappeared. Someone had to have it. Worse, Javi and Joy seemed to be joined at the hip already, spending every minute forming a bond that was becoming harder and harder to imagine severing when they left.

Was a lasting relationship with the Cades possible? At least from a distance? Joy seemed to be comforted by Javi, and Javi bloomed under his grandmother's doting.

Or would staying in touch keep her chained to her past?

"It is kind of bleh," Joy said, her tone conspiratorial. A sparkle brightened her eyes. "Don't tell anyone I said that."

Javi moved close and dropped his voice. "It's our secret?"

"Exactly."

"I don't like secrets."

Sofia cringed inside.

Please, oh please, don't ever learn about mine.

"Honesty's a good policy to have, young

man. And you can put those paper towels outside in the trash."

"What else can I throw out?" Javi picked up a chipped ceramic saltshaker. "This is old."

"It is. It came all the way from Chicago when your great-great-great-great-grandfather ordered it from the Sears and Roebuck catalog over a hundred years ago."

"What's a catalog?"

"A book with pictures of different things you can buy."

"What kinds of things?"

"Oh, anything back then. You name it. Rifles, chickens, fur coats, even a house. There's one in town I can show you someday if you're still here. They decorate it like it's a Las Vegas casino. Blinking lights everywhere, a singing snowman and Santa on the roof."

When her hopeful eyes met Sofia's, Sofia hurried to the broom closet. She had plenty of reasons to stick around, the most disturbing of which was her sudden interest in James Cade. When he'd smiled at her bungled lyrics, her breath had caught for a second, long enough for interest in the man to take hold.

"Santa doesn't like me." Javi raced out the

back door. A thunderclap of joyous howls rose from the Border collies.

"He thinks Santa doesn't like him?"

"I've tried telling him that Santa loves all kids the same, even if they don't get a visit, but..." Her words stumbled to a halt. It pained her to think of all the holidays they'd had to do without, the times she'd had to explain to Javi why Santa hadn't come that year. Or the next.

"Well, now. That's a sad enough thing."

"We have each other. Plus, Javi's never known anything different."

"Christmas used to be Jesse's favorite holiday."

They smiled faintly at each other. "I remember."

"Guess we haven't done much celebrating here, either, not since..." Sadness weighed down Joy's friendly face, making her seem older and less present somehow. It was like looking at a hologram. Sofia's heart went out to her.

"Anyway," Joy said, straightening, brisk. "Here I am thinking of myself, when you've only just learned about Jesse. I wish you hadn't had to find out this way."

"Yes."

"Where did you and Jesse meet?"

Sofia glanced at the shut door and lowered her voice. Her heart pounded. How she hated dredging up this old stuff, but she couldn't deny another mother details about her son. "At the Alano House."

"Six years ago."

"Yes."

Joy's chest rose and fell with the force of her sigh. "Jesse couldn't stay sober. And Lord, but I couldn't help him, either. He lived to assist others but couldn't take care of himself."

"He was good with Javi."

Joy's face brightened. "He always loved kids. We used to joke that moms had to watch out, or Jesse would steal their children. He'd carry off any old baby he could get his hands on without even checking if it was okay with the parent, when he was sober, of course. When he wasn't…"

Sofia winced, remembering a strung-out Jesse pacing her apartment, hands over his ears as Javi had screamed and shrieked. "Yes."

"How did you two break up? It's hard thinking Jesse left his own child and then didn't even tell us about Javi all these years."

Sofia struggled to keep the hurt off her

face. She wouldn't run down a son to his own mother. "I told him not to contact me unless he was sober. He was probably waiting to get clean."

She ran a mop over the floor, careful not to dampen Joy's rose-pink heels. Given she wore a beaded necklace in the same color, along with a headband in an identical shade, Joy had a color story going on that Sofia didn't want to mess with. Especially now that the kind woman had lost hours' worth of work literally down the drain.

"And it never happened…not long enough for him to be sure of his sobriety, I'm guessing." Joy dabbed at her eyes, not placing blame as Sofia had feared, her acceptance filling Sofia with unexpected warmth.

"How's your wrist?" she asked to break the emotionally fraught moment.

"Getting worse." Joy's elbows jerked as she scrubbed the pot. White, frothy water bubbled over the metal sides. Sofia stowed the mop and grabbed a dish towel, its pattern a mirror image of the rugs scattered around the room. "The steroid shots aren't working on my rheumatoid arthritis. Dr. Billings says I need to stop postponing surgery."

Joy's glasses slipped down her nose, and

Sofia pushed them back up. They exchanged a quick smile. For a moment, Sofia imagined what it'd be like to have a mother like Joy. Or a mother at all, given hers had died in childbirth.

Her father must have blamed her for the loss, she'd often thought during those awful and numerous times when she was consumed with guilt. It explained his constant anger and dismissal. No matter what Sofia did, it was never good enough to make up for his beloved wife.

While she didn't know what it felt like to be a loved daughter, she'd always be the best mother possible to Javi. Everything she'd missed, she gave. Tenfold.

Sofia grabbed the rinsed pot and began drying it. "What's stopping you from getting the procedure?"

Joy shrugged. "I'd be out of commission for four to six weeks, depending on how fast I heal. Who would look after the family?"

Concern for kindhearted Joy rocketed through Sofia. "Your kids?"

"The ranch takes up all their time."

"A relative could step in maybe?"

"My husband and I were both only children. Our parents have passed. But not to

worry, dear. I'll get by. I always have. Unless…"

"Unless…?"

"There's any chance you might be willing
to help out," Joy said, offhandedly, though a
light now filled her eyes, an undeniable wish,
easy to read, that she wanted them to stay.

Sofia froze.

"If you could spare the time," Joy babbled
on in the awkward silence, her glasses slightly
foggy around the edges. "I'd insist on com-
pensating you. You could save up for Portland. Though I don't mean to pressure."

"Thank you, but…"

Here was Sofia's chance to explain why
she couldn't say yes…to confess her secret
fears. Yet she hesitated. She didn't want Joy
to see her as weak. A potentially bad parent.

How she wished Javi could be part of a real
family for the first time in his life. And have
guaranteed meals. A warm house. A bed of
his own to sleep in over the holidays. Even if
the Cades didn't celebrate them any longer,
it'd be a step up from anything she and Javi
ever experienced.

All pros.

But the con? She'd have to live with the
constant drumbeat of her past failings. Plus,

what if the Portland job lead dried up? The position, a receptionist post held by a pregnant doctor's wife, needed to be filled soon. Although they were flexible on the start date, according to Sofia's friend Mary, and were willing to wait for Sofia, as they were happy to help a struggling single mother, she couldn't impose on their patience forever. At the very least, she'd need to call them with an updated arrival date and hope they didn't see her as unreliable and change their minds.

"But I don't…"

The back door flung open and Javi skidded through it, accompanied by a frigid gust. "Guess what I found!"

"What, honey?"

"This!" Javi held up a stocking nearly as big as he was. Red glitter emblazoned the letter *J* across the top.

"Where did you find that?" Joy asked, her voice faint.

"It was by the trash. Can I keep it, Mama? It's so big. Maybe Santa will see it, and he won't forget me this year."

"Oh. Honey."

"Of course Santa won't forget you."

"He doesn't come for kids who don't have houses. Will we have one in Portland?"

Joy placed a hand over her heart.

Sofia thought of the struggle they'd have getting started in that new city, especially if she didn't have their IDs or cash. Javi would go another holiday without.

She took a deep breath and turned over her options. Perhaps, in the short term, she could put aside her insecurities to help a deserving woman and give Javi a real Christmas with family.

"We can stay, but only for a month and maybe an extra week or two, at most," she hedged, looking at Joy.

"Thank you!" She threw her arms around Sofia and tears sprang to her eyes. Javi whooped and raced around their legs.

She returned Joy's hug, breathing in the light floral scent that rose from her neck, overwhelmed at the rush of emotion and the sense of rightness. If only this could be forever.

Shutting down her own pity party with a firm hand, she hustled to the refrigerator and evaluated possible ingredients for a replacement meal.

Tomatoes. Red onion. Cucumber...

Her time on Cade Ranch had a shelf life she needed to remember lest she grow too attached. And that included one very masculine member of the Cade clan as well, she firmly reminded herself.

Bell pepper, garlic, Worcestershire sauce...

Joy joined her at the fridge, swiping damp cheeks.

Sofia cleared her throat. "How does gazpacho sound?"

Joy cocked her head. "I'd like to try it. Not sure about James, though. He doesn't like different."

Of course he didn't. "Well, he'll learn to like it. Do you have jalapeño peppers?"

"They're Justin's favorite snack."

An hour later, Sofia sat across from James at the eat-in kitchen's table. She felt his dark eyes on her and her cheeks grew warm. He shouldn't stare. Was he staring? She glanced up and caught his gaze. Great. Now she was staring.

She poured Javi another glass of milk, then passed the cold glass pitcher to Justin. His resemblance to Jesse unnerved her, despite the beard, mustache, cuts, bruises and scars transecting his face. It raised the specter of Jesse and her past. Why, oh why, had she volunteered to stay at Cade Ranch?

"This is good." Jewel dipped her spoon

in the gazpacho. "I like it. Spicy." The light cast from an old-time wagon wheel fixture gleamed on her French braids and glinted on the arrowhead pendant tied around her throat.

"It's different." James held his spoon aloft, eyeing the dripping red concoction.

"And we know how much you love different," drawled Jared, the good-looking one, James had said. She eyed Jared's sculpted features. His fine-boned nose and high cheekbones. She guessed he looked like Orlando Bloom, though it did nothing for her.

Now, James, on the other hand... Her eyes drifted to the rugged cowboy, met his gaze and dropped again. He was a dramatically attractive man. Lean strength and work-rumpled sexiness. He was getting under her skin in the worst way.

And what was so "different" about gazpacho?!

"Weren't we supposed to have stew tonight?" he asked in his low baritone; his direct way of looking at her, his squint, jumbling her thoughts.

Jared coughed, "Schedule," behind his fist, and Jewel chucked a bread roll at James. He snatched it easily out of the air, split it and began buttering, the nonchalant move comical. At her quick snort of laughter, he smiled at her, lines deepening on either side of his brown eyes with their ridiculous eyelashes. She felt an urge to run her fingers over his thick brush of hair.

"Joy dropped it. Blam!" Javi jumped in his chair. "Can I call you Grandma?"

"Javi. Eat please." Sofia eyed her son's untouched bowl, the dark circles beneath his eyes, the hollows of his cheeks.

"You can call me anything you like, honey." Joy reached out and guided Javi back down into his seat.

James's smile faded. "Was it your wrist again? You've put off your surgery too long and—"

"I'm scheduling it for next week," Joy cut in, a tad breathless.

The Cade siblings slowly put down their spoons and glasses.

"It's about time." Jared reached across the table and patted his mother's hand.

"That's wonderful, Mama!" cried Jewel. "And I'll help with the housework like I promised," she added slowly, dragging the words from her throat. "Maybe I can finally learn how to cook. I could make those Christmas cookies. The ones with the frosting. You haven't made those since…since…"

"Noooooooo," groaned Jared and Justin.

Joy shook her head. "You stay in the saddle where you're needed, honey. Sofia kindly offered to stay on and help us out."

Amid the exclamations of gratitude, Sofia noticed one very silent and very disapproving Cade.

James. His opinion shouldn't matter, but for some insane reason she wanted him to be just the tiniest bit happy that she would be sticking around.

SOFIA AND JAVI…staying another month…

James let out a held breath, rinsed off the last plate and stowed it in the dishwasher, his thoughts in an unpleasant tangle.

Were his suspicions that she'd lost a drug stash and wouldn't leave Carbondale without it correct? She'd refused to report her missing wallet to the police. Why? And if she deceived him regarding that, what else might she be lying about? Jesse being Javi's father? He looked nothing like Jesse, save for the left-sided dimple, which, admittedly, was a Cade trademark.

He wiped his hands on a dish towel, then

carefully hung it on the oven door handle beside its matching counterpart. He straightened it, squared the edges and eyed the conformation until satisfied that all was back in its rightful place.

Confusion.

The enemy of an orderly, safe life.

Everything Sofia represented. His brother had taught him not to trust addicts. The temptation to use was too strong, and someone with years of sobriety could still relapse. Even if Sofia was clean, she might resume old habits, do anything for a fix, including breaking his mother's heart.

Across the room, he spied Sofia coaxing an uninterested Javi to finish a bowl of grapes. All evening, she'd waged an unflagging war to get him to eat fruit and vegetables. Despite his misgivings about her, he admired her determination. Her devotion, too. Yet her opaqueness discomfited him.

Making matters worse, she'd pledged to help on the ranch as his mother recuperated from the surgery. He couldn't refuse the offer, especially since his ma had begun smiling again and seemed, for the first time in a long time, to be a tiny bit happy.

Yet the unsettled feeling of being outmaneuvered churned in his gut. This time of year turned his mother inside out. They got through the holiday season by ignoring Christmas while the rest of the world erupted in celebration of hearth, home and family, something they'd never fully get back.

"How about you eat a grape for each one that I catch in my mouth, little man?" he heard Jared say as he joined the group in their two-story living room.

A floor-to-ceiling stone hearth dominated one end and he pictured it bedecked in Christmas stockings and lit boughs the way it had once been. They used to hang red and green ornaments from the massive set of mounted elk antlers above it. A warm, crackling fire spewed hickory-scented puffs of heat. How long since they'd burned a yule log? He dropped into a high-backed blue armchair and eyed his family. Too long.

"Okay, deal!" Javi laughed. He leaped up on one of the tan couches grouped around a crosscut tree-trunk coffee table. When Sofia didn't correct him, James shook his head at the child. Javi's knees buckled, and he perched on his heels instead.

"You don't know what you're in for," Joy warned, seating herself on Javi's other side.

She plumped a blue-and-tan-checkered pillow and placed it behind her back. "Jared doesn't miss often."

"I bet I can catch more." Jewel leaned over the living room's loft railing, ready as ever to compete with one of her brothers.

"Ladies first, then," Jared said easily, looking characteristically unperturbed when it came to competition. He won so many, he had every reason to back up that confidence.

"Watch and learn." Jewel jogged down the open spiral staircase and grabbed the bowl. "Whoever gets the most out of ten wins."

Javi bounced on the couch, then stilled at James's small, corrective frown. Admiration sparked inside for the child. He was boisterous, like all kids, but he wanted to do right. If only James could be equally sure about Sofia.

Jewel caught the first four, missed the next three, caught another two, and the last bounced off her nose. "I meant to do that." She chuckled and passed the bowl to Jared. "Good luck."

"It's all skill, sis," he said with a wink, then caught ten in rapid succession. No surprise there.

"You su—" Jewel cut off at Joy's swat. "I

mean, you duck," she amended, glaring at Jared. "You really, really duck."

"Quack you very much," Jared rejoined and the brothers guffawed, the family rhythms returning, temporarily loosening the pressure valve that'd been present since Jesse's death.

James had given up hoping things would ever return to the way they'd been. A time when his mother hadn't cried at odd times of the day, Jewel hadn't retreated into her saddle, Jared hadn't spent all his free time away from the ranch, Justin hadn't risked his life with his reckless antics and Jackson had been home…

No. This was their new normal. Though it didn't stop James from missing the old days—especially during the holidays. He wished December would disappear right off his calendar to end another painful year.

Javi climbed on Jared's lap and patted his cheeks. "Can you teach me?"

"Sure."

"After you eat your ten grapes," James said, feeling a growing sense of duty to this child who might be a Cade.

"Ugh. Always the lecturer," Jewel groaned.

"A man honors his word," James insisted.

"As does a woman," Sofia added. They exchanged a quick searching glance and the morning's easy rapport returned to him, followed by her inconsistencies about her wallet.

A car revved outside and backfired. The sound cracked through the air like a gunshot. Javi jumped, spilling the bowl of grapes. He bolted around the back of the couch and started crying.

The family swapped concerned glances as Sofia crouched by the small space. "It's just a car, honey."

"Justin's hunk-a-junk," Jewel said over Sofia's shoulder. "He'll show it to you before he goes to the demolition derby."

"No," Javi sobbed. "Shooting."

"Honey. You're safe," soothed Sofia.

"No," he choked out, hyperventilating, by the sound of it.

It amazed James how quickly Javi had gone from rambunctious to fearful. Spirited to terrified. What had happened in his life to make him react this way? No one should ever feel afraid on Cade Ranch, especially not a child.

He leaned over and spoke firmly, steadily. "Javi. I want you to take a deep breath in through your nose, then push it out through your mouth. Can you do that ten times, bud?"

"Yes."

Sofia gripped the back of the sofa and the

sides of their hands touched. The urge to thread his fingers in hers, to reassure her, seized him.

Javi's breathing slowed.

"Okay. Now. When I say a body part, I want you to squeeze it hard, then relax it."

"With my hands?"

"No. Just use your muscles."

He guided Javi through the relaxation technique he'd learned while on his first tour of duty in Afghanistan. It'd helped him get through those dangerous months, and sometimes, it even helped him sleep…or doze… at least.

"Your head…" he concluded, after having Javi work his way up from his toes, tensing, then releasing the muscle groups. He felt rather than saw Sofia's eyes on him.

"I can't squeeze my head," Javi said with a giggle. Out of the corner of his eye, he caught Sofia's relieved smile and returned it.

"That must mean you're a knucklehead," he joked, and to his relief, Javi emerged from behind the couch.

He shook his finger at James. "I heard that."

"Well. At least that means you don't have cotton between your ears."

Javi giggled again and wriggled free of his mother's embrace.

"Do you want to check out Justin's hunk-a-junk with me?" he asked, an urge to connect with Javi taking hold.

"Okay."

A small hand slipped into his and a feeling of protectiveness surged. Such a trusting gesture. Tender. Vulnerable. A child's faith could slay the most stalwart dragon, he marveled, and he felt the walls he'd built up about the boy begin to crumble.

He led Javi out on the porch and Sofia followed.

"Thank you," she said to him softly, a heartbreaking smile on her face. A sliver of pink gum showed above her top teeth.

Justin leaned out of the driver's-side window of a rust-brown, banged-up Chevy Impala, the number 212 spray painted on its side. The engine rumbled in the night air. James's nostrils stung from the spewing exhaust.

"Ma! You coming? I need to get moving if I'm going to take out Daryl Loveland in the first round."

Joy's hand fluttered to her hair, her necklace. "Actually, I don't think I'll go out after all."

James exchanged concerned glances with his siblings behind his mother's back. She'd seemed so animated before.

"Suit yourself. Hey, kid." Justin beckoned Javi. "Want a ride before I head to the demolition derby?"

His teeth flashed stark white against his dark beard, his grin more pirate than rancher. Justin's many speeding tickets, accident reports and wrecks came to mind.

"No," James insisted. He met his family's surprised stares, chin raised. Heedless Justin was the last person he trusted to drive Javi. "I'll take him."

"Do you want to go, honey? You don't have to." Sofia brushed back Javi's hair. James's heart somersaulted at the tender gesture.

Javi nodded, his eyes on the muscle car.

"Want me to go with you?"

Javi peered down at his hand clasped in James's and shook his head. "Can I ride up front?"

"Yes. But only because I'm going to go very slow, and you're wearing a seat belt." He met Sofia's eye. "Okay, Mom?"

She smiled tightly. "Just don't go far."

"We won't. Let's go, Javi."

And a moment later, he guided the Impala down one of the dirt roads that separated pastures. The sports coupe growled and whined, bouncing over potholes, kicking up clouds of white snow, dust and pebbles. His thoughts and feelings swirled around his head like quicksilver, unpredictable and reluctant to coalesce. As he drove alongside barbed wire fences and stared at the white-crusted land illuminated by his headlights, he allowed himself to think about Jesse. Was Javi really Jesse's son? And if so, had he disavowed the child? Why?

Although he didn't imagine he'd ever have children, he knew he'd never turn his back on his own. He'd always take responsibility and protect what was his.

He shut down the traitorous thought of his brother. Believing Javi was Jesse's son meant accepting his sibling had acted worse than he'd imagined, hurting not just his family, but inflicting pain on an innocent child. On Sofia.

He cast a sideways glance down at the wide-eyed boy beside him. Javi huddled in the passenger seat, fidgeting with the large seat belt that crossed his lap. Cool air streamed in through the open window and he breathed in the bovine scent that mingled with the hay they'd tossed out to the livestock earlier.

Javi was quiet. Too quiet. Concern rose. "Want me to turn around?"

"No."

"Where do you want to go?"

Another moment of silence. Then, "Home."

"You miss your family." It was more statement than question.

Javi shook his head. "I don't have any."

"No grandparents?" Was Sofia an orphan? If so, then who'd raised her? Curiosity rose, swift and urgent.

"Joy. I mean, Grandma's my first one besides Mama. Do you think she likes me?"

"Yes," he said, his voice gruff. Encouraging Javi to feel a part of the family was wrong until he had proof he was truly a Cade. Yet his convictions dwindled in the face of this child's wish to belong.

"No one ever likes me except Mama."

"I'm sure that's not true." James turned down a left loop that would carry them back to the house. A row of wind turbines rotated slowly on a distant hill.

"A lady behind a desk once called me a waste of space."

James's fingers tightened around the cracked

leather steering wheel. "That was a bad thing to say."

"Mama said her panty hose were too tight."

That pulled a laugh right out of him.

"What's panty hose?"

Before James could think of how to explain, Javi asked, "Was Daddy bad?"

James's throat swelled. "Jesse tried his best. He was a good man, but he sometimes did wrong things."

"Mama says he went up."

James pressed on the brake when a ginger cat broke from some brush and scuttled across the road. "That's true."

"You only get to go up if you're good," Javi said to his clasped hands.

James flipped off his lights as they neared the glowing ranch house. "That's why it's important to be on our best behavior."

"But it's hard," moaned Javi.

He grinned and ruffled the boy's hair. "Yes, it is."

They pulled up to the front porch and there stood Sofia, just where they'd left her, as if she'd been frozen in place.

She yanked open the door the moment they rolled to a stop.

"Javi!" She swung him up into her arms. "I missed you."

James joined them as she set Javi on his feet.

"Look what just got delivered!" Joy strode down the steps with a wallet held out toward Sofia.

"Who?" Sofia grasped the small clutch bag that served as her wallet then opened it and peered inside.

"A neighbor. He was having coffee at the diner when they found it wedged between the booth and the wall. He dropped it off on his way home."

If Sofia had her wallet, did she have drugs inside—her reason for not going to the police?

"May I see that?"

Everyone's heads snapped up, and Jewel's glare stung like a slap.

"Back off, bro," snarled Justin.

James ignored his brother and arched an eyebrow at Sofia, waiting.

"Mama?" Javi quavered, backing up and pressing his head against his mother's legs.

"It's okay, babe." She handed over the wallet without looking at James, her mouth in a tight line. "See?"

Feeling like a jerk, but knowing someone had to be the bad guy to protect the family, he opened it. He ran his fingers along every seam, looking for secret compartments the way Jesse's addiction had taught him. Then he pulled out money, Sofia's driver's license, a benefits card and a birth certificate.

"Well, I'll be," his mother exclaimed as she moved close and peered down at the document. "That's…that's Jesse's signature."

James stared at a birth certificate for one Javi Andrew Cade, father: Jesse Andrew Cade.

His eyes rose and met Sofia's.

Jesse had signed Javi's birth certificate.

For a long while, James lingered on the porch once the others had gone inside, marveling.

He had a nephew.

Jesse had a son.

The Cades hadn't completely lost Jesse.

The realization burned through James, turning his insides to ash. He would guard his brother's child with his life. Javi was a Cade, and family looked out for each other.

Sofia's past addiction, her secrecy, placed his nephew in jeopardy. Traveling to Portland with only a job lead and neither family nor connections for support made her and Javi's situation even more precarious.

He had to find a way to help.

There was still plenty to doubt about Sofia Gallardo. Given his unwelcome feelings for her, having her close would be a challenge.

But he was glad she'd be sticking around after all.

CHAPTER SIX

"WHAT'S THIS?"

Sofia glowered down at the yellow notepad sheet James handed her a few days later. The kitchen window beside her glowed with the dawning sun. On the stove, yellow-orange flames curled beneath a teakettle.

"A schedule." He shoved first one arm, then the other into his flannel-lined jean jacket.

"A schedule..."

"Your To Do list." He grabbed a rancher's hat from a peg by the door, donned it and pulled the brim low over his deep brown eyes. His long eyelashes curled thick and dark.

A small stream of white began pulsing from the kettle. "Duties?"

"Tasks. You've had a job before..."

"I've had several," she snapped, her temper rising at the insinuation along with the whistling kettle.

Deeper still, she stung at the remembered shame of being laid off from low-level positions when businesses no longer needed seasonal workers, closed their operations or downsized and kept only their most qualified help. High school dropouts with felony records were always expendable. Plus, "sketchy" workers like her seemed to require an extra layer of oversight since her supervisors always breathed down her neck, eager to jump on the first mistake. They made it clear she couldn't be trusted on her own...shouldn't be given any real responsibility.

When no one had faith in you, how could you have faith in yourself? You heard something often enough, you started believing it was true.

She whisked the kettle off the stove and poured the steaming liquid into two mugs set on the countertop.

"Glad to hear it," he murmured after buttoning his coat and scooping up his keys. His piercing stare made her squirm as though he saw straight through to every one of her failings. "The tasks are ordered and the start and finish times will keep you on track."

"Is this a bathroom break?" she asked faintly, scanning the list. She dunked the tea bags, squeezed them then tossed them out.

"Ten twenty and three forty-five." His chest puffed a bit.

"And Javi and I are supposed to have tuna fish for lunch with mini carrots and a banana?" she forced out, choking. Javi hated carrots and tuna fish.

Recalling how Joy took her tea, she measured a bit of sugar and milk into one of the mugs and stirred it, leaving the other black for herself.

"Substitute the fruit for an apple if you like, but carrots are important for Javi's eyesight. And omega-3 is good for his immune system."

"Thank you, but I believe I know best when it comes to *my* son." She wanted better nutrition for Javi, but she didn't need a parenting lesson from King James along with it. Sheesh.

Talk about micromanaging. She tossed the spoon in the sink, where it clattered, making James wince. His controlling nature was worse than she'd thought, and now it extended to Javi.

He rinsed the spoon and placed it in the dishwasher. "He's my nephew."

"Yeah, for two seconds. I've been managing him just fine on my own for six years."

"And now you have help."

"If I need some, I'll ask," she huffed, his interference feeling like judgment, accessing her deepest, darkest fear—that she wasn't the best parent for Javi.

Joy's light steps sounded on the stairs, then stopped.

"Oh. Dear. James. What have you done?"

She appeared paler than usual, Sofia noticed, and her concern for Joy cooled her temper. Dressed in a dark brown sweater that accentuated her silver hair and a pair of tan slacks, she looked as muted as her expression.

James advanced. "Do you have everything, Ma?"

"Never mind that. Why does Sofia look fit to be tied?"

"Not at all, Joy." Sofia used as normal a tone as she could manage. With Joy's wrist operation looming in a couple of hours, the woman didn't need to be stressed. "Here's your tea."

James stepped between them, frowning. "She can't have tea. No food or water after midnight."

Sofia flushed. "Right."

"It was on the instructions." He pointed to the pre-op orders held to the fridge with a magnet. "Did you read them?"

Heat rose in her cheeks. Reading had never been a strength of hers. Or instructions. They hemmed her in, giving her no autonomy. Her muscles clenched. At least here, where drugs weren't so accessible, she could resist this building tension.

"James, stop. Sofia. My apologies for my protective son. Believe it or not, it's coming from a good place."

"Beats me where that is, though," Jared drawled, suddenly appearing. With his dark hair slicked back, his jaw smooth-shaved, his plaid shirt contrasting with his golden-brown eyes, he looked like some movie-star impression of a cowboy. Way too put together for first thing in the morning. Not roughrider and scruffy the way she liked.

Her eyes flew to James's shadowed jaw, then dropped.

"Overcontrolling is more like. Morning, everyone." Jewel hugged her scowling brother, then bussed her mother on the cheek. She had her dark hair back in a single French braid and a denim shirt tucked into worn jeans. "I'll have that tea if no one else is."

"Oh, sure."

The porch door wrenched open. It emitted a gust of cold air and a bedraggled Justin,

wearing the clothes he'd had on yesterday…
and pretty much every day: a wrinkled black
shirt, dark jeans and scuffed black boots.

"Look what the cat dragged in," Jared
drawled. "Nice bruise."

Justin slouched across the room, lanky,
wiry as an apostrophe mark, his square-
shouldered, loose-limbed gait oddly graceful, his dark beard a little menacing. At least
it took away from his disconcerting resemblance to his twin. While Jesse had always
been cheerful and exuberant, dark, silent Justin…well… Justin brooded. "You should see
the other guy."

"Was it Daryl Loveland?" Jewel asked,
sounding eager. Bloodthirsty, even…

"Yep." Justin's grunt held a load of deep
satisfaction.

"Did you win?" Jared slipped on a curved
brown cowboy hat that looked like it'd just
come out of its wrapper. In fact, every shiny
inch of him seemed like it was wrapped in
cellophane, Sofia mused, wondering if he just
naturally repelled all stains, wrinkling or fading. Maybe life didn't want to muss all that
perfection.

Justin let out a breath. "Almost."

Joy fiddled with the cross at her neck. "I don't like those fights."

"Fights?" Sofia asked.

"Barn-boxing," Jewel contributed, grabbing a blueberry muffin from the plate Sofia set out. "Every weekend the local boys get together for matchups. No gloves. No rules. Cage fighting, country-style."

"It's dangerous," Joy worried. Her brow furrowed.

"And irresponsible," James grumbled, drumming his fingers on the table.

"Don't know why you kids need to keep fussing over those Lovelands." Joy shook her head at Jared.

Jared spread his hands. "Don't look at me."

"He's a lover, not a fighter." Jewel elbowed Jared, who gave an exaggerated wince.

"Love is all you need," Jared declared, rubbing his side.

"Tell that to your brother, please, before he gets himself killed," pleaded Joy.

"Isn't that the plan?" huffed Jewel around a mouthful of muffin.

Justin's defiant expression turned contrite. "Sorry, Ma." After pouring himself a cup of coffee, he leaned against the door frame as though he needed the house to hold him up. "Won't do it again."

"Till next weekend." Jewel laughed and her brothers joined in, except James, whose eyes, now shadowed and concerned, lingered on his agitated mother.

"Bleh. This tastes like tar." Justin poured his coffee down the drain. "Must be James made it again."

Sofia nodded. It'd already been brewing when she'd come downstairs.

"He's the only one who can drink it that strong," Jewel filled her in, breaking off another bite of muffin. "The rest of us just have to suffer."

"Or beat him to the coffee machine," Justin griped.

"You'd have to get up before dawn to do it," Jared added.

"How about a Keurig? A catering company I worked for had one," Sofia offered.

Joy nodded. "I've heard of that. Fancy coffees."

"We're not fancy," James protested.

Jewel, Jared and Justin rolled their eyes at each other. "You just don't like change," Jewel teased her brother. "We'd still be using horse and buggies if it were up to you."

"Less pollution," James said mildly.

"They have all kinds of flavors," Sofia supplied, warming to her theme. She'd loved that catering job. "Like peppermint stick or caramel vanilla cream."

"That sounds delicious." Joy smiled. "And I don't even like coffee."

"You'll like this kind, and best of all…" Sofia paused and met James's eye. He appeared to be listening closely, not dismissing her. "You can each make your own cup separately."

"Sounds perfect." Jewel gave Sofia an approving nod, then turned to James. "What do you say, moneybags?"

"I say it's time to get Mom to the hospital," James answered, noncommittal. He helped Joy into her wool coat, and something about the careful way he handed over her matching hat, scarf and purse tugged at Sofia. When was the last time anyone had fussed over her? Taken care of her?

Jesse had almost been like another child, given the constant attention he'd needed. And the workers at juvie hadn't been nurturing. As for her father, he'd demanded her obedience without giving much in return. She supposed she'd pretty much always had to take care of herself. And Javi. Speaking of whom…

"Wait for me!" Her son jumped from somewhere midway down the stairs, miraculously managed to stay on his feet, then flung his arms around Joy's legs. "Are you coming back?"

Joy hugged him and closed her eyes briefly. "In a couple of days."

"Can I visit you in the hospital?"

"If your mama says yes."

Sofia nodded. She avoided places with tempting medication, but perhaps Jewel could take Javi. He and Joy had grown so attached.

What would happen when she took Javi away for good?

"Javi. I'd like you to go up the stairs, then come down again correctly," James ordered when Javi and Joy untangled themselves.

Sofia froze at his strict tone. It reminded her of her father. She could hear him as she'd practiced piano for hours:

Start over, Sofia.

No, not that way.

Begin again.

Do it right.

You're making mistakes on purpose.

Now you're just trying to make me angry.

Repeat. Repeat. Repeat.

This is a waste of my time.

Translation: *she* was a waste of time.

Jared and Jewel exchanged a swift glance behind James's back. Justin scowled and pushed off the wall.

"Yes, sir!" Javi hustled off before Sofia could call him back.

"One step at a time. Careful. No jumping."

Exuberant Javi carefully placed one foot after the other until he reached the floor again.

"Better." One of James's rare smiles appeared, and he ruffled her son's hair. Javi beamed up at him, delighted.

Confusion warred inside. She didn't want Javi chasing after James's approval the way she'd done with her father. He'd withheld and bestowed his approval arbitrarily, crushing her spirit. Next chance she got, she'd tell James to stop ordering her child around.

He was taking his uncle responsibilities too far.

"Safety first," Justin mocked and Jared grinned.

"Good one, Evel Knievel, coming from you," Jewel sputtered.

"Get to work, knuckleheads," James said,

his lips quirking the slightest bit as he pointed to the clock.

Jared slid on his coat and eased open the door. "Better not piss off the boss."

"Someone grab my time card," Jared joked.

"Don't forget to kiss Ma," James ordered.

"As if we would," Jewel protested, then bussed her big brother on the cheek first. "Hang in there, James."

After a flurry of hugs, ending with one from Justin that seemed to squeeze the air right out of Joy, the siblings tumbled outside, leaving the room in silence.

"Thanks again." Joy squeezed Sofia's hands. "I can't tell you how much it means to me. You and Javi... I'm just glad to know you'll still be here when I get back."

"Of course."

"We're not going nowhere!" Javi proclaimed.

"Anywhere," James corrected.

"Anywhere," Javi repeated, stoutly.

"Not for a while," Sofia amended and regret forked inside at Javi's downcast expression. Would she be able to give him as warm and supportive a home, a family, as this?

"How long?" Javi's thumb rose to his down-turned mouth.

"Five weeks and four days," James put in, taking Sofia by surprise. Was he keeping track? He gently lowered Javi's finger, hugged him, then opened the door and turned. "I'll call when Ma's out of surgery."

"What time?" she asked.

"It's on the schedule." He whisked his mother outside.

Of course it is, she thought, sinking into a chair, the paper clasped in her hand.

Where was time on this list for living, though, she wondered. With all his attention spent taking care of everyone and everything, when did James ever have time for himself?

TWO DAYS LATER, James cupped Sofia's elbow and steered her away from his snoozing mother's bed. It'd been a long, anxious forty-eight hours spent traveling back and forth to the hospital. The familiar ache in his jaw from his over-clenching, a childhood habit that had returned after Jesse's death, throbbed.

"Her pain meds should be wearing off in a couple of hours. When she wakes, give her two of these painkillers and replace her ice pack. She'll also need her blood pressure medication, and the doctor says we can resume her steroids as well today. It's all on the instruction list."

He pointed to the yellow sheet atop a bureau, but Sofia stared only at the bottles.

"I can't." Sofia backed up and out of the doorway.

He followed her into the hall. "We need to keep on top of her pain, and I won't be around to ensure she takes them while on the range."

"We need to find another way." Her skin looked bleached beside the full dark hair curling around her heart-shaped face. And her eyes. So big and dark and…and…panicked.

"What's going on, Sofia?"

"It's just…just…"

Javi appeared at the top of the stairs, flushed, an apple in his hand.

"I got this for Grandmother so the doctor stays away."

"Good thinking, bud." He smiled at the kid who seemed to live to help. "But Grandma's sleeping. Just leave it by her bed."

"On it!"

James snapped his arm out straight to check Javi's forward scramble. "Slowly. Quietly."

Javi nodded and tiptoed forward a couple of paces. "Like this?" he stage-whispered.

James nodded and Sofia frowned as Javi disappeared inside the room.

"I don't want you ordering him around."

"I'm giving him direction."

"You're controlling him."

"Maybe he needs a bit more of that…"

Sofia's eyes glinted, the left one squinting hard the way it did when she got really angry. "I'm his parent."

"When you're living in my house, it's my rules."

"My child, my rules," she insisted, her nostrils flaring.

"When you're in Portland, you'll call the shots." An emptiness unfurled inside, dark and cold, as he imagined Cade Ranch without her and Javi.

Javi emerged and tiptoed back to James's side. "We can't go. I have to stay until I make Grandma better."

Sofia squatted down to her son's height. "Honey. The grown-ups will take care of Grandma. And you're not responsible for saving everyone."

"Superheroes save everybody."

"I know, but you're not a—"

"Javi, will you fetch a glass of water for Grandma?" James interrupted. He thought about Jesse. Growing up, he'd been obsessed with Superman. Like Javi, he'd wanted to save everyone and everything—especially animals back when he'd wanted to be a veterinarian—anyone but himself.

Guilt panged in the region of his heart. Was he being tough on Javi as he'd been on Jesse? Maybe he needed to lighten up a bit and spend more time with the boy. "She might wake up later and feel thirsty."

Sofia raised her chin. "No, Javi."

He skidded to a stop at the top of the stairs and twisted around, puzzled. "How come?"

"Because I said so." A pained expression tightened Sofia's delicate features.

He stared at her, slack-jawed. She'd never used such a harsh tone with Javi before—at least not since arriving at the ranch. Children needed a firm hand, boundaries and rules, yet it didn't seem right coming from free-spirited Sofia.

"Can I get her juice?" Javi wheedled, sounding just like Jesse when he'd charmed the pants off just about everyone. It went straight to James's heart. Thawed it, too.

Javi and Jesse had a lot in common, James noticed lately. Even his strictness with Javi echoed the way he'd felt forced to treat his out-of-control younger brother. Jesse, like Javi, liked to cut loose and have fun, something James struggled to do. He'd been harsh with Jesse, but maybe, with Javi, he had a second chance...one he'd be double the fool for missing.

Sofia blew out a breath. "Okay. Juice."

Javi vanished down the stairs and Sofia studied her feet, which were bare beneath the hem of her full skirt, James noticed, each toenail painted a different color, as if she couldn't make up her mind and had used them all.

How had he and Sofia descended into a civil war over Javi?

He thrust the pills at her. "Can you manage this while I'm doing my chores?"

Her mouth worked and her eyelashes fluttered, then dropped to her cheeks, obscuring her eyes. "I can't be around pills. They're—they're not good for me."

He studied her, puzzled. Then it hit him. *Pow.* Painkillers. Oxys. Jesse had become addicted to them while recuperating from a sports injury. The realization was followed quickly by another understanding, an affirmation of his earlier assessment of Sofia.

As a former addict, she couldn't be trusted.

No doubt she'd worked hard to turn her life around. And she had plenty of good reasons not to slip again, the most important one being her son. Yet addiction had been more powerful than Jesse's best intentions. It flared without warning and required vigilance and support to prevent.

And Jesse had had lots of support.

Except from him that one, critical time…

"You said you've been clean for six years," he said, though he knew sobriety was precarious and didn't obey any laws of time. Six months, six years, six decades. It was always a threat.

"Shhhhhh…" She pulled him farther down the hall and lowered her voice. "I don't want Javi to hear."

His gaze darted to the staircase. "He doesn't know?"

Javi was young, granted, but if no one in Portland knew about Sofia's addiction, who would spot warning signs if she relapsed? Besides, keeping secrets from family was the closed-off, dark environment that had allowed Jesse's addiction to fester and return. Over and over.

White appeared all around Sofia's irises.

"No. And he never will. I'm not that person anymore."

"It's always who you are. Don't they tell you that in NA?"

"I don't go to meetings," she said, fierce.

He pocketed the bottles and studied her. "None recently?"

"Ever. Once I left rehab, that part of my life ended."

His concern deepened. "It's not that easy."

"Not if *you* won't let it go," she declared, then thumped down the stairs after her son.

So now he was to blame?

Jesse had accused him of the same thing.

His fingers fidgeted with the medicine's childproof cap. He wished all their lives were tamperproof; he now had more questions and concerns about Sofia than ever.

CHAPTER SEVEN

"WHAT ARE YOU two doing?" Sofia asked James and Javi the following night.

Damp hair pulled into a ponytail, body encased in one of Jewel's T-shirts (Keep Calm and Cowgirl Up) and a pair of yoga pants, Sofia felt clean and comfy following her late shower. For the moment, the nagging thoughts about Joy's oxycodone, so excruciatingly close she could hardly breathe, receded.

Beneath a circle of light, James and Javi hovered over a folding table. It occupied a living room corner and held four piles of jigsaw puzzle pieces. Several feet away, a fire crackled in the massive two-story fireplace, where a large red stocking with a glittery *J* now hung.

Had the Cades decided to celebrate the holidays? A rush of pleasure lit her up inside. Javi might have his first real, family Christmas after all. The mellow scent of burning hickory wood wafted through the house and a sense of peace stole through her, fresh and sweet. Another smell, peppermint-fresh, accompanied the faint hiss of pouring water from the kitchen. She peered across the open space and noticed a new machine on the counter.

"Is that a Keurig?"

James continued staring down at the puzzle pieces, red rising in his cheeks. "Salesman said it's the top of the line."

"Thank you, James." She pressed a hand to her heart, touched.

"It was on sale," he added, gruff, shrugging away her gratitude. Prickly, bristly man. He didn't fool her. His tough facade had a few cracks.

"We're building Gotham City and Uncle James hung my stocking!"

James's hand settled on Javi's shoulder when he nearly upended the table. She strolled closer and flushed when James's dark eyes rose and lingered on her face before they dropped again. He'd shaved since dinner, she noticed.

And, sheesh, that fire suddenly felt uncomfortably warm.

"Gotham City?"

"A puzzle of it. James bought it for me 'cause I like Batman."

"I hope you said thank you."

"I forgot."

Sofia cleared her throat. "Then you say…"

"Sorry?"

"No, you say thank…"

"Thank you, Uncle James!" Javi interrupted, then threw his arms around James.

James's lip quirk drew her gaze like a magnet. "You think this is for you?" he scoffed after Javi collapsed in his seat. "I'm just letting you play with *my* puzzle."

"Heeeeyyyyy." Javi's protest ended in a giggle. James's deep chuckle erupted and Sofia's laugh followed, the moment contagious, as addicting as any drug she'd ever taken. Better. Their mingling laughter felt like water on parched soil. It cascaded over her years of single-parenting, and she blossomed in this small, child-rearing moment shared with another.

Never in a million years would she ever have imagined it would be with—of all people—Jesse's brother.

"So it's Batman this week," Sofia said when they quieted, gazing at James, who'd glued his eyes to the puzzle again. How kind of him to notice Javi liked superheroes and treat him to this gift. "What happened to Superman?"

"He's on the naughty list."

A movement on the hearth caught her eye. The family cat, an outrageously fat tabby named Clint, kept trying and failing to roll over on his back to soak up the heat. A vase full of red-and-white-striped candy canes, white-painted pine boughs and artificial red holly berry sprigs graced a rough wooden trestle table in front of massive windows flanked by mismatched chairs. "What'd he do?"

"Crashed his car like Justin!"

She and James swapped another quick smile, and she strolled closer. At this distance, she could smell whatever soap or aftershave James had used tonight, something subtle and spicy, and a hint of fresh outdoors.

"Remember, black pieces on the black pile."

At James's instruction, Javi stopped jamming his piece into another and dropped it on a stack of similarly colored ones. "When do we get to make the city?"

"Once we sort it all."

Sofia picked up a flat chocolate chip cookie

from a batch she'd attempted this morning. She'd fudged a bit over the baking soda versus baking powder. But it still tasted good, she thought, taking a bite, savoring the rich, chocolate chips and crispy, slightly burned-tasting edges.

She eyed the huge number of pieces in the box. They'd take hours to organize. Days. What fun was that? Especially to a little kid? Plus, who knew if they'd even finish it before she and Javi left?

"Can I help?" Sofia asked.

James eyed her warily. "Sure."

"Thanks." She leaned over and dumped the box's contents onto the table.

Javi laughed, and James's mouth dropped open. Sofia grinned at his helpless, dumbfounded silent question. It was such a human reaction for the controlled man—the controlled man who was charming her. Plus, it didn't hurt that the deep red of his shirt highlighted his eyes and those impossibly long lashes. "Now let's solve this thing."

Before James could speak, Jewel appeared on the landing above. "Has anyone seen Ma's medication?"

James's expression sharpened. "Which one?"

"The oxycodone. She took it before dinner, but I can't find it now."

"Be right up." James cast a narrow-eyed look at Sofia, then strode away, taking the steps two at a time.

"Is Uncle James mad?" Javi chewed on the edge of a puzzle piece. "Did I do something bad?"

"No, honey." It worried her to see how much James affected her son, making him worry about not measuring up. "He just wants to find those pills."

"Where's he looking?"

"Everywhere. I'm sure he'll find them. Don't worry."

"Can I go to bed?" Javi jumped to his feet.

"Now?" She glanced at the large grand-father clock in the opposite corner. Seven forty-five. Since when had Javi ever volun-tarily gone to bed before nine? James must be really upsetting him.

Javi tugged at her hand. "Please."

Thirty minutes later, she eased out of their room and nearly bumped into a pacing James.

"Is Javi asleep? I need to search your room." The silent accusation on James's face shot her full of shame. He suspected she'd taken the missing pills.

But you have been fantasizing about them. Admit it.

She muted her inner voice and stood her ground. "He's sleeping."

His exhalation flared his nostrils. "Did—"

"Doctor Fleming called in another prescription." Jewel pocketed her phone as she emerged from Joy's room. "I'm heading out to pick it up." She jingled a set of keys, then tromped down the stairs.

"Let's talk outside. I don't want Javi hearing us."

James nodded, his mouth set in a grim line. "Grab your coat and meet me on the porch."

"Fine." Sofia followed James, fuming. She would never—ever—steal pills.

But you did once. More than once. You have the mug shots to prove it.

Out on the porch, she shivered in the frigid air and zipped closed her borrowed jacket. Someone had looped lit garland around the long railing and swirled it up posts bedecked with red velvet bows. The joyful atmosphere couldn't have contrasted more with her despair.

"Sofia?" James asked, his voice gentler than she'd expected. "Did you take the pills?"

"No." Anxiety turned to an itch along

Sofia's throat. She scratched at her neck, feeling acutely vulnerable beneath his penetrating gaze. Deep down, she knew how easy it was to slide back into addiction. But now she had Javi. Wanting to stay straight for him meant she had something—someone— that she would never sacrifice for drugs. He would always keep her sober.

She hoped. Prayed, even, if that was what the silent, one-word plea that often rose within her was...

Please. Please. Please.

"Why am I having a hard time believing you?"

"Because you see what you want to see," she said tiredly, pushing back the hair from her eyes. She realized just now that she was trembling.

"And what's that?"

"An addict. A thief. Someone who'd throw everything away—my work, my pride, my self-respect—for the next fix." To her shame, she nearly sobbed out that last word. "And that used to be true, but I'm not that person anymore, only you'll never see it. Just like you didn't with Jesse."

He stepped back, stricken. Bands of moonlight streaked through a cloud-covered onyx sky, illuminating his pinched brow, his tense mouth, leaving his nose and chin in darkness. In his eyes, she saw a despair so deep it reminded her that they were alike in a way, time not healing anything, only teaching them how to live with the pain.

"I love—loved my brother."

"Loving someone and believing in them isn't the same thing," she said, thinking of her father.

A muscle jumped in his jaw, and he jerked his gaze out to the mountains. His broad shoulders sloped downward.

Regret drew her close, and she placed a hand on his tense bicep. "I know Jesse loved you, too."

His head snapped in her direction. "Did he tell you that?"

"He talked about all of you. Called you the Rocky Mountain cowboys. Said you could ride right over mountaintops and high-five the sky."

"But I didn't save him," James said obliquely and the bruise in his voice made her wince. "The night he died, he called me for a ride. He'd finished his latest rehab a few days before, and Ma had been twisting herself inside out that he hadn't come home yet. She worried he'd fallen off the wagon, and my older brother, Jack, was out looking for Jesse when he phoned."

"Had he relapsed?"

Instead of answering, James gripped the railing and his knuckles were white beneath the glowing Christmas lights. A moment later he continued, "I'll never know."

"What do you mean?"

"It means I cared more about protecting Ma and the family than looking out for Jesse."

"I don't understand."

He bent his head and his anguished eyes rose. "I told him I wouldn't pick him up unless he promised he'd never do drugs again."

"And did he?"

"He said he'd try, but that…that wasn't good enough for *me*." He spit the last word as though it disgusted him. As though he made himself sick.

"Oh, James. I'm so sorry!"

His long eyelashes blinked fast as he fought the emotion straining his face. "Don't be sorry for me. Don't ever be sorry for *me*."

There it was again. The self-loathing she recognized too well. The ferocity of his tone was the sound of a wounded animal who wanted to die alone, in peace. On his terms.

"I never told anyone that before." He let out a shaky breath and the admission touched her. Deeply. James wasn't alone when it came to feeling guilty over Jesse's fate.

"I didn't save Jesse, either."

He peered at her gravely and silence expanded between them, filled with their fears and misgivings.

"I kicked Jesse out on Javi's first birthday." She shivered at a cold breeze stirring the nearby spruce. The wind chimes on the corner of the porch tinkled.

"Why?"

"I don't know if you want to hear this."

"I do." Near the railing, their hands touched, the barest brushing of skin on skin. "Trust me," he said in a way that made her skin prickle and breathing difficult. He'd opened up to her and taken a chance. She could do the same.

"Okay." She inhaled a large gulp of air, exhaled, then began. "Javi was a colicky baby. He cried nonstop. I don't think I slept more than a couple of hours a night that first year. It's probably why I have insomnia now."

That and your addiction nightmares...

She pushed aside the thought and continued, "It was tough on Jesse."

The tender look in James's eyes, all the more disarming for its rare appearance in such a strict man, encouraged her to keep going. She didn't want to hurt him, but he needed to know.

"I made him take turns with Javi, even when I saw it was getting to him."

"And it wasn't wearing on you?"

"I'm Javi's mom."

"And Jesse was his dad," he said, tone firm. The assertion caught her off guard. That was true, but to hear it from another, to have someone say, "You know, you got dealt a tough hand," it meant something. Like James, she didn't want anyone's pity. Never had. But she did crave understanding and James was giving her that. Big-time.

"True. But he struggled with it. I should have seen it, but I was so focused on Javi that I didn't notice the warning signs until it was too late."

"What happened?"

"We didn't have much. Jesse got occasional construction work. I had a part-time job in a convenience store. Sometimes we cut it so close we had to decide between food or diapers. But I kept squirreling some away because I really wanted to buy Javi a present for his first birthday."

"What was it?"

"He was really interested in that cartoon train. Thomas the Tank Engine. A lady in my building, she had a whole set of them that she was willing to sell. A couple of days before Javi's birthday, when I finally had enough, I went to get the money and it was gone."

"Jesse."

"I didn't think so at first. But then he didn't come home that night. Or the next. Not until Javi's birthday, when I found him passed out on the stoop."

James stared up at the sky. "Poor Javi." Then, beneath his breath, she thought she heard him say, "Poor Jesse."

"He was supposed to buy the cake and some groceries. But since we didn't have any food, we went to the soup kitchen and celebrated there. They put a candle in some applesauce for Javi."

He touched her hair, let a few strands coil around his finger. "I'm sorry. You deserved better. You and Javi. I would never have walked away."

She breathed that in for a moment. Let it dissolve in her bloodstream. Did she deserve better? After all the bad she'd done in life, she wasn't so sure.

"Don't apologize. It wasn't your fault. It's just…I wanted you to know that I didn't give Jesse another chance, either. Even when he begged me. I've never told anyone else that, either."

For a moment, their breaths synchronized, white puffs of air mingling between them.

"Did he want to get sober?"

"He said it was a mistake, that he wouldn't relapse again, but I refused to listen. Bottom line, I didn't want drugs around my baby."

James nodded. "You were right to protect Javi."

His support bolstered her, encouraging her to open up more. "Javi's the reason I'm sober. I gave up everything for drugs, but I'd never sacrifice him."

"You didn't get sober for yourself?"

"Excuse me?"

"If you didn't have Javi, would you still be an addict?"

The question hung there between them and a chill, arctic air rose along her spine. She'd never considered that before, but hearing it out loud, it sounded like a real possibility.

"I didn't take Joy's pills."

"I hope not."

Just like that, the intimacy of their shared connection faded. How close she'd come to completely lowering her guard with James. He'd almost made her believe she was someone better than she'd been, that she could be more, even here on Cade Ranch. It was an absurd, immature reaction, overblown given her reality, but still it hit her hard, wounded deep. "You don't believe me?"

"I want to, but I'm as protective of my loved ones as you are."

"We'll be gone in a few weeks. No harm will come to your family."

"Javi *is* my family."

She gasped. "You think I'm a threat to Javi?"

His silence said it all.

As much as it thrilled her to hear Javi claimed as a relative, to know he belonged to an honest, respectable family like the Cades, James's wariness crushed her flat. Another judgmental outsider looking in. Same as always.

If Javi stayed with her, he'd never have a good family like the Cades. Would he be better off if she left him here and traveled alone to Portland? She slammed the door on the emerging answer. No. She would never leave her child.

"You're going to a distant city without support." James rubbed his hands together and blew on them. "You won't have anyone to check on you and your sobriety."

"I don't need anyone, and I don't want reminders of that time in my life."

"And I won't chance another relapsing addict breaking my mother's heart. Until we find those pills, I'd like you to attend NA meetings as a precaution. Show me your sobriety matters to you and you're taking it seriously."

"Here?" Her heart began to pound. She'd be expected to talk about herself at a Narcotics Anonymous meeting. If she did that, she'd be haunted by the ghost of her Christmases past everywhere she turned.

"We have a meeting each week in Carbondale. Jesse attended a few. I'll find out when it happens and take you to it."

"No way." He didn't believe or trust her, so why would she think he wanted to help her?

Because James takes care of everyone, a

voice whispered, *just like Javi... Maybe even you, too.*

"This isn't negotiable."

"That 'when you're under my roof' thing again? You know, you can't have it both ways, sensitive one minute, heavy-handed the next. Your contradictions make my head spin."

He closed his eyes for a moment, then said, "My grandmother called me an acquired taste, and that was the nicest thing anyone's ever said about my personality. Ask Jewel. She swears my name is beside the definition for *bossy* in the dictionary."

Despite everything, she chuckled. At least he was honest about it. Maybe she should be, too. "Controlling men, like my father, are triggers for my addiction," she confessed.

When he opened his eyes, they appeared unguarded, open, raw and luminous. "I'm sorry, Sofia. It's a part of me I—I need to work on. But this isn't about me. Or you. It's about Javi."

She turned slightly and peered up at him. His proximity unnerved her; looking directly into his eyes made her feel vulnerable. Her breathing was a flutter in her chest.

"I need to know you're going to be all right before you leave," he continued in his deep voice. "I hope you'd want that, too, if not for your own sake, then your son's."

He tromped down the steps and into the night, leaving her to stare after him in wonder.

CHAPTER EIGHT

"SOFIA, IS IT?"

Sofia nodded and seated herself in the chair the attorney indicated a few days later. He was a portly, fastidious man with a luxuriant head of silver hair and a perfect set of teeth revealed in an officious smile. All around her, book-lined shelves rose from the floor to the ceiling. So many stories... She marveled. What number of them could she read if she tried?

Not a lot, she bet. Not all the way through. Not every long word crammed so tightly into pages that her head would swim and her eyes cross. Reading had always made Sofia restless. Her legs would start to twitch impatiently after the first page, one of the many reasons, along with her dismal attendance record and her arrest, that she hadn't finished high school.

She lifted her chin and did her best not to look intimidated. It was important to seem like she belonged in a smart, educated place like this. It practically reeked of expensive leather, imported wood and privilege, the kind of environment she imagined she would work in when she finally took the receptionist position awaiting her in Portland.

This wasn't a place for people who'd messed up.

Out of the corner of her eye, she saw James's fingers flex on his thighs, one of them jiggling up and down. To her right, Joy perched on the edge of her seat, her bandaged wrist tucked inside a navy sling that exactly matched the formal suit she'd donned for no particular reason that Sofia could determine.

In fact, Joy had been mysterious about her reasons for insisting that Sofia and James accompany her to the Cade family attorney's office today when she'd spoken to them about it over breakfast. While attending a meeting without knowing its purpose worried Sofia, she couldn't refuse, considering Joy's kindness and generosity with Javi.

"Can I have my secretary get anyone coffee?"

"None for me," James refused, an edge to his voice. Sofia slid him a sidelong glance. With his hat off, his rugged profile contrasted with the wood paneling beyond it. Tan and firm, he was sternly handsome with that chin jut that always seemed to creep right under her skin before he even opened his mouth.

Which he hadn't done much of lately, she reflected, since their tense exchange the other night. Mostly, he'd been keeping to himself and spent his free time working with Javi on the puzzle. To her surprise, Javi had woken early the next morning and restored the piles she'd destroyed.

Unwilling to argue, she'd let it go. Seeing Javi focus on a long-term project like she'd never been able to do soothed her. It lowered her trepidation about James's controlling ways. Strangely, Javi responded well to James's boundaries and restrictions, maybe even thrived a bit.

Was James a better influence on her son than she was?

And was there a chance this impromptu meeting had to do with the missing oxycodone? James had suggested she was a threat to Javi. What if Joy thought so, too? Could this have something to do with guardianship?

Her stomach muscles tensed.

No. She was just letting her insecurities get

the better of her. Not to mention the stress of attending an NA meeting later tonight.

"If Pete wouldn't mind, I'd like tea." Joy's features softened when her eyes settled on Sofia. "Would you like some, dear?"

"No. No, thanks."

With her nerves making her insides jump, Sofia was sure she wouldn't be able to keep anything down. A moment later, the lawyer, a Mr. Sloan, Esq., finished relaying the drink order to his secretary, folded his arms against his keg of a stomach and leaned back in his chair.

"Joy. Would you care to begin?" he asked.

"Thanks, but if you don't mind, I'm not sure I can explain it as well as you."

"Well, that's kind of you to say. I'll do my best. James, your mother has requested that we reopen Jesse's estate."

James's chair creaked as he leaned forward. "Why's that?"

Sofia cast a quick glance at Joy, who reached out, without turning, and squeezed her cold hand.

"It's my understanding your family has located Jesse's heir."

Sofia's mouth dried right up. She couldn't swallow if she wanted to. In fact, suddenly, she felt as though she might be sick. What did this have to do with Javi?

James met her eyes briefly, then whipped his head back. "Yes. My nephew, Javi."

At that moment, a light knock sounded on the door and Mr. Sloan called out permission to enter. The secretary, a thin, bespectacled man with a too-short tie, whisked inside bearing a tray. Steam curled from the ceramic cups and a honey-lemon aroma made her breathe deep.

"Over there, Pete. Thanks."

She pressed her shaking lips together, in an agony of waiting as Joy and Mr. Sloan fixed their tea, then settled back in their chairs.

Two sips and a long *ahhhhhh* later, Mr. Sloan set down his mug and steepled his thick fingers on the desk.

"Given this new information, we need to reevaluate the distribution of Jesse's assets."

James stared at him and silence fell, thick and heavy. It lined her throat so she felt as if she might choke a little. What assets? Like her, Jesse had never been able to hold a job for long. Was this about a coin collection from when he was a kid or something?

"I agree," James said. He crossed his arms over his chest.

"Good to hear." Mr. Sloan paused and beamed so hard at Joy she squirmed a bit and shuffled her navy heels beneath her chair. "Joy was worried you might have some objections."

"To…" James frowned and scratched his cheek.

"Jesse's share in the ranch, the ten percent each of your father's descendants inherited when he passed, reverted to your mother on his death. We'd like to transfer those shares into a trust for Javi if none of the children object. Joy plans on talking to the rest of your siblings tonight at dinner, but she felt—" He spread his hands and a tight smile wrestled with the heavy flesh of his face. "Well, she felt that you might have the most questions."

The room seemed to spin around Sofia and black crept in on the edges of her vision. Joy's hand pressed hers again and Sofia squeezed her eyes shut, sure she might faint as she tried wrapping her head around this. Javi. Heir to a portion of a huge cattle ranch. It was everything she'd ever wanted for him. All that she wished she could give him…only…she could never stay here.

How could he have it without her?

How could she stay if it only kept her bogged down in her past?

A future, one that Javi inhabited without her, rose in her mind, threatening. She could not—would not—ever be separated from her child. But even if he came with her to Portland as planned, which he would, he'd always have a tie here to Cade Ranch. It was a world she couldn't be a part of, and one day, he'd leave her to return to it.

If she tried keeping him from it, he'd only resent her. He wouldn't be proud of her the way she needed him to be…though he would be proud of being a Cade. Was that more important?

It was all she could do not to bury her aching head in her hands.

James shifted beside her. "So how does this work?"

"Your mother will relinquish Jesse's shares and they'll revert into a trust I'll create for Javi."

"After my surgery, I started thinking how I won't be around forever. I want to make things right for Javi, in case anything happened to me," Joy said.

"Nothing's happening to you, Ma," James

said, firm, then, "And who will be the trustee?"

"We were thinking." The lawyer tugged at his bow tie a bit. "We were thinking that—"

"I want Sofia to be the trustee," Joy interrupted.

At James's harsh intake of air, she released Sofia's hand and angled around in her chair. Sofia froze in place. Even her lungs locked up and the blood in her veins seized.

Trustee? It sounded daunting. Way, way over her head and ability.

Who was she after all? She ran her fingers over the ridged track marks on her arm. A former addict, a convicted felon, a high school dropout. Not member-of-the-board material.

"Absolutely not," James thundered. "What experience does she have with a trust like this? We're talking shares in the ranch. Sitting in on board meetings. Voting on business decisions."

Sofia opened her mouth to agree but something in the absolute terms he used nettled her. Hadn't that been the way her father, her teachers, her ex-employers always talked about her, over her, as if she was of no consequence, as if she hadn't any ability to control anything or be responsible for anyone, least of all herself?

"Why don't we hear what Sofia has to say?" Joy prompted.

Sofia stared down at her clasped hands. She'd be in way over her head at those meetings. What if she messed things up for Javi and made bad decisions that affected his inheritance?

"I might not be the best choice since I'll be leaving for Portland in a few weeks."

"You don't have to live in the vicinity to serve as trustee," Mr. Sloan asserted.

"And I think you'd be a fine addition to our family board meetings." Joy cocked her head. "A different point of view. When you leave, we can conference call you in."

James stood. "I'm formally submitting my name for consideration as trustee."

"We're hoping to avoid going to court."

"If you're serious about that, then appoint me. Javi's future hinges on how this trust is handled. Not only that, with Sofia as a voting member of our board, we'd be giving an outsider input into our family business."

Hurt swept through Sofia. She would always be the outsider looking in with the Cades. Yet Javi was a Cade, and *they* were family. As his mom, she had as much motivation to ensure his best interest as the Cades. She was Javi's family and that mattered, too.

"Sofia?" Joy asked gently. "What are your thoughts?"

She locked her shaking knees, stood and extended her hand to Mr. Sloan. "I accept."

THE SHARP EDGE of a cracked plastic chair dug into Sofia's spine later that night. Sitting up straight when she wanted to slouch, she kept her eyes on her lap. She didn't look up as others shuffled into the NA meeting and took seats in the arranged circle.

A light smattering of chitchat rose. An artificial Christmas tree, bedecked in red and white lights, twinkled in the corner. The smell of freshly brewed coffee filled the warm space, the atmosphere thick and humid despite the snow that had started falling when she and James drove into Carbondale after dinner.

Was he waiting outside like her personal parole officer?

It bugged her that he hadn't trusted her to drive herself, but she hadn't wanted to argue in front of Javi. Keeping him in the dark about her whereabouts right now was most important. She didn't like lying to him, and it irked her how James had put her in this position with his crazy insistence that she attend tonight. This meeting was a complete waste of time. She'd managed to stay sober for six years without NA meetings. Once she escaped to Portland, she would finally erase this bad chapter in her life for good.

Now she'd have to listen to everyone else's issues and try really, really hard not to think of her own past.

"Is this seat taken?" someone asked beside her. Someone male. Young. Maybe a teen, given the crack in his voice. Sofia slid her eyes to the left and nodded, eyeing the clean-cut kid who looked like he should be in a college interview, not here with the rest of life's losers.

He wore a white-and-blue-striped shirt that had sleeves rolled up to his elbows. It tucked into a pair of khaki pants. The creases looked so sharp that she guessed they were newly bought, maybe for this occasion. Only a varsity letterman jacket slung over one shoulder and his shoes, bright red basketball sneakers, gave a nod to his age. They shuffled slightly and she shrugged.

"Take it."

"Thanks."

"I'm Sofia."

"Riker."

He flung himself into the chair, then slid down so far his long legs jutted nearly halfway into the circle. He inserted wireless earbuds, crammed his phone in his pocket and gave her a sheepish, lopsided smile when he caught her stare. Despite her nerves, she smiled back. He looked so young yet so bored. As if he'd already fast-forwarded through his life, saw how it ended and was now just skimming over the highlights.

Riker's eyes closed and he rested his chin on his chest. If only she could tune out like that. She certainly had plenty else to focus on, given what had happened in the attorney's office. It still hadn't fully hit her yet. Javi's future was secured. He'd never be homeless again, now that he'd own a part of Cade Ranch. And she, at least until the judge heard the case that James demanded, was his trustee.

"Sorry, everyone," said a tall African American man, waving his phone. "That was Mr. Sampson saying he has car trouble and won't be attending tonight's meeting."

He slid his chair a bit to the left, then sat. "First of all, I want to thank everyone for coming out tonight. The weather isn't looking great, and I appreciate your commitment to this program."

Sofia dropped her gaze when his eyes landed on her.

"My name's Anthony and I'll be leading the group for the next few weeks."

"Did Kim have her baby?" someone asked, a wire-thin man with teeth too large for his lips to cover.

"A little girl on Wednesday. She says hi and she sent pictures you can look at on my cell." Anthony passed his phone to the person on his right.

"Now. Kim and I don't do things the same way, but we still follow the principles of the twelve-step program, and I'm going to be here for you during the season. As many of you know, this can be the hardest time of all for addiction."

A chorus of yeses rose.

"First," Anthony said, "I'm going to tell you a little about myself so we can get comfortable with each other."

Sofia arched her back slightly, trying to escape the dig of her cracked chair. Comfortable? There wasn't a chance of that happening tonight.

Anthony spread his hands wide and his open, unassuming expression had her staring straight at him again. "You're looking at a man that used to be very successful at one time. I started off as a laborer. Moved up to being a contractor and then a developer, building houses, making other people's dreams come true. So. You know. Along with that, I started making good money. Six-figure income. Had me a beautiful wife. Four beautiful sons. I thought I was untouchable. Building houses. Making my family's dreams come true. And with all that success, I started ego-tripping. And within that ego-tripping, I got introduced to crack. You know…you would figure that after all that hard work that I had put in to become a successful businessman that I wouldn't have gotten involved with drugs. Right?"

Several of the members nodded slowly.

"Just goes to show," Anthony continued with a shake of his head. "Happens to anybody."

Not her, Sofia vowed to herself. Never ever again. She didn't need this meeting to know that.

Anthony leaned forward and pressed his hands into his knees. "When I tried crack the very first time, it was like no experience I'd ever had. Man. I showed that thing more love than I gave my family."

Sofia thought of her father. He'd never been particularly interested in her love, only her obedience. If he'd wanted affection, would she have given it? Did she love her dad?

An ache in her heart whispered the answer.

Once. She'd clung to him as a child and tried to please him until years later, she'd learned there was no pleasing him. She'd realized that she would always be more of a disappointment than a daughter, a bitter replacement for the woman he'd truly loved and lost, so she'd given up.

When she'd stolen money from a neighbor and been sentenced to a week in jail and six months on house arrest, he'd made his position clear by refusing to let her come home again. She'd finished her sentence in juvie, then hit the streets, completely on her own, with heroin the only escape, the only love in her life.

And maybe that had been better. No one to disappoint except herself…and now Javi. A breath she hadn't known she held whistled through her tight lips. She couldn't mess up. Not as a mom and now not as trustee to his inheritance. Maybe James had a point and she should just let him take over. Only not as parent…not a guardian…

"Didn't plan on my wife leaving with our four kids." She tuned back in and heard Anthony say, "It got so bad. So bad. That me, the guy who was building homes for other people… I became homeless. Wife gone. Kids gone. Income gone." He counted on his fingers.

A strong wind rattled the windowpanes to her right. When she glanced at the dark glass, her pale, pinched face stared back at her. She recognized the reflection as the one she'd glimpsed in storefronts while she'd walked the streets, obsessed with getting her next fix, oblivious to the weather, to anything but finding more pills. But that person didn't exist any longer. So why was she still here, right here in that window? Sofia whirled back around.

"Home gone. Car gone. Everything. Just gone." Anthony's voice rose in a crescendo. "It got real crazy. You know? I'm thankful that God didn't let me die out there that way. That wasn't His will. But without pain there is no gain. I also thank God for this NA program. It constantly teaches me how to be honest with myself and be okay with expressing to you what needs to be talked about."

Sofia dug her nails into her palms. She wasn't okay with talking about it and couldn't understand this compulsion to rehash the past. Wasn't it far worse to wallow in ancient history than to simply let it go and step away, clean and free?

Anthony's gaze settled on her. "I know some of you are new. It might be a little difficult and that's why I wanted to open up and share some of the struggles I've been through. So once again, I want to thank y'all for coming out. Thank you for letting me share."

Sofia joined the other members in saying "Thank you" or "Thank you for sharing."

Silence fell and a woman who looked to be ten or so years older than Sofia waved. She wore a pretty yellow shirt that flowed over a pregnant belly and her fine brown hair was tucked behind ears glinting with small diamond studs.

"Good evening, everybody. My name is Leigh and I'm an addict."

Sofia blinked at her. Leigh could have been a local librarian. A bake-off contestant. PTA president. Never would she have thought *addict* if she'd met Leigh on the street. And hearing her call herself an addict was jarring. There had to be a better term for people who'd put it behind them.

"Hey, Leigh."

"What's up, Leigh?"

"Good to see you, Leigh."

Leigh waited a moment for the group to quiet, then said, "Sex, cocaine, alcohol are my drugs of choice. You know, I typically use the same excuse for why I did what I did—I didn't have a mother or any type of female figure around as an example. But I'm not going to let the anger that sometimes rises up inside me, or the hole in my soul, control me any longer."

Sofia stared. Those seemed like good, reasonable excuses for why Leigh had turned to drugs. In fact, they weren't all that different from her own.

Leigh rested her hands on her belly. "Today I'm not going to let it win. I am going to accept the fact that I made those choices. I took those drugs. And I am a woman and a role model to myself and this little one." She patted her bump. "Thank y'all for letting me share."

"Thanks for sharing," Sofia murmured

along with the rest of the group, her mind in a whirl.

What good was this kind of therapy if they dismissed the real reasons that drove them to take drugs? Without understanding triggers, like her father's rigid ways, you couldn't avoid them or put them in perspective. She was glad she hadn't come to NA meetings all these years. It would have been a waste of time. Clearly.

She glanced at the teenage boy and caught his smirk and eye roll, but somehow couldn't return it. Sure. This was lame. But a part of her saw that it was also really, really brave. She couldn't dismiss it totally, as much as she wished she were anywhere else.

"Hello, everybody," said an elderly woman across from her. With her neatly clipped gray hair and the pearls around her neck, she looked ready for a church social, not an NA meeting. Sofia tried hiding her surprise when the woman smiled directly at her.

"I'm Pam, and I'm an addict."

The group greeted her.

"About five years ago, I had a hip replaced. The doctor sent me home with hydrocodone. Said I could take as much as I needed for pain and to call him for a refill when I needed it. Anytime."

She paused and her smile revealed two deep dimples. A round of ironic laughter circled the room and Sofia nearly joined in. A prescription-happy doctor was an addict's best friend and worst enemy. She'd taken advantage of enough to know, starting with a legitimate sprained ankle where she'd begged for pain pills long after the bruising and swelling had disappeared. It was one of several "injuries" she'd faked for months at a time to get more pills.

"I felt so good when I took my pain meds. Soon nothing mattered except feeling that way. Then I lost control. I didn't care about my family. I shut them out. Stopped seeing my friends. Didn't even finish the quilt I'd been making for my daughter's family. It had all my grandkids' blankets sewn into squares. But that didn't matter to me anymore. I was one hundred percent selfish. I didn't care about anything else or anyone else. All I cared about was taking pills or drinking. I hit rock bottom when my daughter found me passed out. Overdosed."

Her voice cracked and dried up and Sofia's

heart went right out to her. She would die if Javi ever saw her like that.

Pam blew her nose, pocketed her tissue and sat a bit straighter. "It was the best thing that ever happened to me."

Sofia blinked at her. What?

"Looking back, I realized that I've always had a problem with alcohol. I spent most of my time as a mother with a glass of wine in my hand, though I went through plenty of bottles of vodka, too. People can't smell it on your breath," she said, almost conspiratorially. A few members nodded along. "Rehab, this program, showed me who I really was. Am. And I'm proud to celebrate one year straight today."

She held up a yellow chip with the number one and everyone burst out cheering and applauding. "Thank you for letting me share with you today."

Twenty minutes later, after other members spoke, their group leader asked, "Anyone else like to share? New members?"

The collective weight of everyone's stares pressed her back in her seat. She peeked at her neighbor, but he still had his eyes closed and looked oblivious. Shoot. She didn't want to say anything.

"We'd like to welcome you," Anthony prompted.

"Sofia. Sofia Gallardo. I was an addict a long time ago. Six years."

"Was?" Anthony questioned.

"I've never used since then."

"Never been tempted?"

She opened her mouth to deny it but nothing came out.

"Then, darlin'," Anthony said slowly after a pause, "you've come to the right place."

CHAPTER NINE

COLD WAFTED THROUGH the equipment barn that housed the ranch's boardroom later that week. Outside, the sun began to set; pink light filled the high-set windows and encircled Sofia. With the air soft and gold around her, highlighting her tan skin and dark hair, she couldn't have looked more beautiful, James thought. Or more nervous.

Her clasped hands moved restlessly atop the rectangular table in front of her. Her teeth bit down on her bottom lip and her forehead had a slight sheen despite the chill draft curling around their feet. Seeing her so nervous at her first Cade Ranch board meeting bothered him, but she'd insisted on attending even though her trustee status wasn't official.

"Here's the list of our upcoming major purchases for vote," he heard Jewel say. As her voice droned, James watched Jared nod along, one eye on his iPhone, while Ma took notes with her good hand. Justin watched, silent and motionless, with half-slit eyes that had fooled plenty of his former teachers and pastors into thinking he was awake.

"Another drive-through gate to replace North D, two heated waterers, calf bottle feeders," Jewel listed in a scratchy voice. Her freckled skin looked pale and the tip of her nose was red and rough. She'd been battling a cold these past few days, and by that he meant ignoring, since he had yet to convince her to stay out of the saddle and in bed.

"Manure spreader needs replacing," Justin added, then dropped his chin to his clavicle and his black hat dipped low over his brow. He had his legs stretched out in front of him and his hands clasped comfortably across his stomach, his head angled back as if he were napping on an invisible pillow.

"Right. The rest is just routine supplies without any real increases over last month," Jewel continued and James tuned back out as she ran down the list he'd approved yesterday. His thoughts drifted to Sofia.

When they held the hearing to appoint the trust's manager in a couple of weeks, he had no doubt he'd be named trustee. Sofia hadn't been able to hold down a job or a place to live in the six years following her rehab. As for her sobriety, it still held a question mark given the missing pills.

Worry about her possibly having taken the drugs consumed him, especially as he watched his mother blossom a little more every day under Sofia's care.

Could her renewed happiness fall apart?

Yes. Easily. He needed to know where those pills went.

The fact that Sofia had attended two NA meetings this week alleviated his concerns, some, and he gave her a lot of credit and respect for following through. Was he naive in hoping the pills were simply misplaced?

He wanted to believe in Sofia.

Very much.

That fact grew more and more undeniable. He caught himself straying from his daily schedule to linger over breakfast, helping her with dishes, inviting her to join him and Javi in finishing the puzzle for probably no better reason than the excuse to talk to her.

When she met his eye across the table, her cheeks pinked, matching the color of the silky shirt he glimpsed beneath a blue blazer. A beauty mark dotted the satin skin above the left side of her mouth. She'd trapped her normally unruly curls into one long French braid that revealed the perfect oval of her face, and though it was a nice look, he found himself wishing for her usual wild tangle of hair that seemed to defy her efforts to control it.

"What about my new saddle request?" he heard Jared ask. "We've tabled it for a couple of months now."

"There's nothing wrong with your saddle except a little wear and tear," James said, offhanded. Jared always wanted the latest and greatest.

"The cinch straps need replacing. Stirrups, too."

"Then order them." James waved his hand. "Topic tabled."

"Noted." Joy's pen flew across her notepad. A single ray of sunlight bounced off the wire frame of her glasses like the pop of a camera flash.

Sofia nodded along, as though granting her approval, her body language stiffer than he'd ever seen it. Were they intimidating her? He hoped not. But she was in over her head, and no matter how businesslike she dressed, she couldn't erase her lack of ranch experience. She'd given him the briefest of nods when he'd hurried to join her this afternoon on their walk to the board meeting, hoping to reassure her.

This distance from Sofia should suit him, but it didn't. A part of him, he had to admit, missed their flare-ups, this brittle politeness wearing on him.

He often found himself watching her from afar as she hustled around the house, anticipating his mother's needs with tea, ice, magazines, brewing up the best coffee he'd ever had from the Keurig machine, even though their old machine had worked just fine for over a decade. But he had to admit he was partial to some peppermint Christmas blend.

As for Sofia's forays into unpronounceable French recipes this week after she'd watched a movie about Julia Child, they'd been hit-or-miss. Inedible when they went wrong but otherworldly good when she succeeded and focused long enough not to burn the house down.

Yes. Lots of things, little and big, had changed with unconventional Sofia taking over for his mother. He was starting to see that different didn't always mean bad, at least when it came to coffee and baked scrambled eggs now called quiche.

"New business," announced Jared.

"We got another request to use our ranch for a wedding reception," Joy said, looking hopeful. She removed her glasses and her eyes shone bright and tender, like emerging leaves in spring. It came back to him in that moment just how much she loved weddings. Little else, except his cousin Beth's recent nuptials on the property and now Javi and Sofia's visit, had captured her interest these past two years.

Jewel made a face. "No, thanks. Beth's was enough. All that tulle. I had a rash for weeks." She shuddered.

"You're just allergic to weddings," Jared teased.

She coughed into the crook of her arm. "Maybe, but there's even less of a chance you'll get married before me."

"Be that as it may," Joy said without looking up. She cleaned her glasses with the hem of her floral shirt. "Since their wedding video got some kind of virus..."

"Viral, Ma," Justin said. "It went viral."

Sofia looked around the room. "What was on the video?"

"Google 'goats battle bridesmaids for bouquet.' I think we're the first one to come up." James felt himself smile at Sofia's snort of a laugh. It did something funny to him. As if someone had carbonated his blood a bit. Made it fizz.

"It got almost five hundred thousand views," Jared bragged.

"I wouldn't mind renting out the old barn from time to time." Joy replaced her glasses. "It's nice to see young couples in love."

He caught his mother's speculative stare and forced his gaze from Sofia to the snow-covered pastures outside and the cattle scuffing through it to graze. "Plus, we could use the extra income. We're getting by, sure, but long-term, we need to look at new revenue sources if the ranch is going to remain viable."

"We don't want strangers all over the place." His voice felt heavy in his mouth, weighing down his tongue. No other possibilities than their current way of life were worth considering. The extra income would relieve his occasional worry about bills each month, but he'd rather the devil he knew than the one he didn't. "Besides, who has time to help oversee it?"

Silence fell and he caught something bright spark in Sofia's eyes before she shuttered them. What had he glimpsed? If he had to name it, he'd say *yearning*.

"I worked as a caterer for a wedding planning business once," Sofia said. "It's a lot of work. Details. Organization. It's not something you can do part-time."

"I suppose you're right. Let's table that for now." Joy sighed.

"Jack and Dani could get married here," Justin said, referring to their older brother and his new girlfriend. "Bet they're engaged by Christmas."

"You're on," Jewel responded. "Fifty says Jack's too busy to get married now that he's a deputy sheriff."

"But he sure does love Dani," Jared observed. "We should throw our annual Cade Christmas party again and invite them with all the neighbors—except the Lovelands, of course—like we used to. He could pop the question here."

James put up a hand to silence his brother. "We stopped hosting years ago. And you know why." He shot his siblings a quelling look.

"But maybe it's time to move on," Jared said, defensive. "We've got new family members now. The neighbors should meet Javi and Sofia."

"Ma? What would you like?" James asked, gentle. He didn't want to see his mother hurt reliving their generations-long tradition without Jesse. Yet Jared had a point. It would fill him with pride to introduce his nephew to their neighbors. Well. Most of their neighbors, since the Lovelands were never included on the guest list.

"I'd like to show off my grandson," Joy said after a brief, stricken silence. "But I can't do much party planning with my wrist still healing." She cleared her throat and waved an open envelope. "Next order of business is this letter from Boyd Loveland. He wants to renegotiate access through our property to the Crystal River."

James stiffened at their archenemies' mention. "May I see that?"

Joy nodded and passed over the letter. As he scanned, Jewel exclaimed, "We shouldn't let them on our land at all."

"We don't negotiate with terrorists," Justin drawled. "Next."

James's eyes traveled over a paragraph of the usual arguments: the land settlement act that had divided up property in western states like Colorado hadn't fairly distributed water access. Second, Boyd argued, the river was public property and shouldn't be blocked by private owners of surrounding land. Third, Boyd concluded, recent increases in temperatures combined with drier summers made it challenging for ranches like the Lovelands' since they had to travel miles out of their way to access the Crystal River.

"I heard they're on the brink of foreclosure," Jared disclosed.

"Where'd you hear that?" The paper in James's hand rustled as he set it on the table.

"I have my sources."

"Yeah, Melody at First National Bank…" Jewel's tease turned into a long string of coughs.

"Is that true, Jared?" asked Joy, her tone sharp. Three shallow lines furrowed her forehead, like ripples on the bottom of a brook.

"Nah." Jared's wide shoulders lifted, then fell. "Nothing serious."

"She means about the foreclosure, idiot," Justin said to the ceiling, his exasperated voice gruff with humor.

"Everyone isn't obsessed with your dating life, Jared," Jewel added with an affectionate smirk.

"Speak for yourselves." Jared laughed. "As far as the foreclosure, I don't think Melody would lie. Plus, she revealed it by accident, then made me swear not to repeat it."

"Way to keep your promises, dude." Justin flicked the brim of his hat so it angled back; his glinting eyes caught the last of the fading light.

"All I'm saying is that it wouldn't kill us to help a little." Jared flipped his hands palmside up to the ceiling. "Giving them some access, like when we're in higher pastures over the summer. Little chance of their Brahmans breeding with our longhorns then."

"Right." Jewel dabbed at her nose. "Because a Loveland would never try taking advantage of a female on our property..."

James joined his siblings in a collective groan.

"What's the feud about exactly?" asked Sofia.

"Murder."

"Theft."

"Kidnapping."

He and his siblings spoke at once, and Sofia's eyes widened.

"Let me tell it." Jewel leaned forward so that her elbows rested on the table and her two braids swung forward over her jean jacket. "You see, our great-great-great-great-grandfather came out west from Chicago as a prospector."

"There were gold and sapphire mines in the Yugo Valley," James clarified and his chest got a strange lightness inside it when Sofia nodded, smiling at him with the strip of pink gum showing above her white teeth.

"Let *me* tell it," Jewel ordered. "He left behind his mother, Cora, to make his way in the world."

"Then he struck it rich," interjected Jared. "Hit a hot streak that panned him enough gold to buy this place and a sapphire so big he sent it to Germany to be cut by one of those famous jewelers."

"Forty karats." Justin whistled. "Imagine how much it'd be worth today?"

"It was fifty karats and it was cut in France, not Germany," Jewel interrupted, her voice growing hoarse and irritated. "Now let me tell it. Ugh. Why did God invent brothers?"

"To teach us patience," Joy ventured.

Jewel rolled her eyes. "Exactly. Anyway. He had it made into a brooch he named Cora's Tear for all the crying his mother did while she worried over him alone in the Wild West.

After she passed, it went to her granddaughter and so on. A tradition. The oldest Cade daughter always inherited Cora's Tear."

"I'd like to see you wearing it," Justin said with a smirk.

"Yeah. Pinned right at the top of none of those dresses you own." Jared's laugh broke off when Jewel faked a shoulder jab. When he relaxed and straightened, Jewel walloped him good.

He had to hand it to his little sister, James thought, full of admiration. Growing up with five brothers, she more than held her own, outdid them, in fact, on a regular basis. He pretty much spoke for all his male siblings in saying he was also just a tiny bit afraid of her.

"It doesn't matter anyway." Jewel blew her nose again.

"What happened to it?" Sofia asked.

"The Lovelands stole it," Justin grumbled, sounding murderous. His dark eyebrows plunged low and his deep-set eyes sank further.

"There isn't real proof," Joy insisted.

"Sure there is," James said. "Our great-great-great-aunt, Maggie Cade, was betrothed to marry Clyde Farthington the Third, a wealthy speculator and the best catch in the county. But the day before Maggie's wedding, she turned up dead at the bottom of a ravine, Cora's Tear gone, and the only one around, Everett Loveland. He must have tricked her into running off with him like that, then killed her to get the sapphire."

"What'd Everett have to say on the matter?" Sofia asked, rapt. Her large brown eyes were wide and round, the glow in them revealing golden flecks he hadn't noticed before.

He forced his gaze out the window and caught the last gasp of the sun before it slipped over the Rockies. "Everett couldn't say anything since Maggie's brothers strung him up on the spot."

"Without a trial? Aren't we innocent until proven guilty?" Sofia's face paled.

Joy reached out and patted her hand. "Of course, dear."

"Plus, the doctor said she was pregnant." Jewel's tone turned dismissive. She tossed another tissue on her growing pile. "I would have liked the story better if Maggie had just run off with Cora's Tear so she didn't have to marry anybody."

"No surprise there." Jared winked at her.

"I pity the poor guy who tries dragging

you down the aisle." Justin tsked, his eyes gleaming.

"Not a chance." Jewel's vow veered into a cough.

"Unless it's Heath Loveland," added Jared, his lips twitching.

"Shut it, Jared."

"Ooooohhhh, sensitive much?"

"Jewel, put your arm down." James waited until his sibling lowered her hand. "Anyway, there's no logical reason why Maggie Cade would have run off with the youngest Loveland son since he had no prospects."

"Love," Sofia murmured, her voice wistful as a heartbreak.

She'd loved his brother once. What would it feel like to have someone like Sofia love him? She'd impressed James today when she'd come to the Cade board meeting despite being unsure of herself. That took guts—and he admired courage in anyone. Respected her for it. Cared…? Did he care for her?

His breath lodged in the base of his throat. He shoved the impossible thought aside, and his heart, the only part of him that seemed to be capable of movement now, beat with a heavy thud that sounded in his ear.

Didn't he need to know, with one hundred

percent faith, that she hadn't stolen the drugs before he developed feelings for Sofia?

His eyes drifted over her again and his heart twanged as hard as a banjo string. Sofia said loving someone and believing in them wasn't the same thing. Was she right?

Sofia cleared her throat. "Maybe she loved Everett."

Jared nodded. "Could be. Women do crazy things when they're in love."

"You should know," Jewel teased.

Justin shrugged. "He never sticks around long enough to find out."

"So that's the Cade-Loveland feud?" Sofia asked.

"In a nutshell," Joy said. "When the Lovelands found out the Cades had hung their boy, they captured the Cade boys and brought them to the sheriff."

"That ended it…?"

"Nah." A clanking of boot spurs sounded as Justin uncrossed his ankles and straightened. "See, the sheriff was also a Cade and a really heavy sleeper as it turns out. He didn't hear a thing when his cousins broke out of jail."

"Imagine." Jewel chuckled.

"And he wasn't too interested in hunting

down the escapees who were hiding out in the area, harassing the Lovelands' cattle and stopping deliveries to the ranch."

"They became outlaws?" Sofia queried.

"Peacekeepers," James clarified, suddenly feeling on the defensive. "The Lovelands never did return Cora's Tear, which makes that entire family a bunch of thieves."

Sofia tilted her head. "So it never turned up?"

"No. They claim they never had it, but they won't let us search their property for it."

"But if they had the priceless jewel, wouldn't they have sold it to help their ranch?" Sofia asked, her tone light, reasonable.

The group quieted. His siblings looked at one another. Then Jewel shrugged. "It's a famous piece. It's not like they could sell it easy... But who knows with them. Plus, they had a suspicious business bump shortly thereafter."

"And that was just the beginning of the dispute," Jared added. "They wouldn't give us Cora's Tear or let us on their land to find it, so we stopped letting them cross into ours. Ever since, they've had to drive their herds miles out of their way north, making them lose cattle and causing their ranch to struggle all these years."

"They brought that on themselves," Jewel grumped from behind another tissue.

Justin whistled. "Stubborn, sneaky—"

"What if they paid you?" Sofia eyed them. The chatter died down, and James blinked at her.

"What if you charged them money like rent? This could be another source of revenue and you'd earn back the money you say they owe you for Cora's Tear."

"Only if we charged them hundreds of thousands a year." Justin popped a toothpick in his mouth.

"What?"

"That brooch would be worth about three to four million dollars now," Jewel said in hushed tones.

Sofia pursed her lips. "Well, I don't see how the Lovelands could have it, then. If they're in foreclosure, they'd use it."

"And not worry about going to jail?" James asked, impressed by her rational ideas. Sofia was intelligent. If drugs hadn't hijacked her life, how far would she have gone toward realizing her dreams? He imagined very far, and regret seized him for what might have been for bright, clever Sofia.

"Sometimes you have bigger things to worry about—like whether or not you'll eat, have a place to sleep," Sofia murmured, and he wondered again about her fear of going to the Carbondale police to report her wallet. Had she committed crimes? A common occurrence, he knew from Jesse, when addicts desperately sought their next fix. His concern deepened. He made a mental note to ask her tonight on the way to her NA meeting.

"Sofia's right." Joy stared directly at each of them, her back straight. It'd been a long time since he'd seen her so interested...so involved in a meeting...not since Jesse. "This feud's gone on long enough. Let's allow them to come on the property. It's the neighborly thing to do."

"Like that time they dammed up the river and we nearly lost our cattle?" James demanded. Ma's enthusiasm was great, but he wasn't about to forget decades' worth of bad Loveland behavior.

"They were desperate," Sofia said quietly, almost to herself.

"Or the times they trespassed and let their cattle impregnate ours," Jewel said, as forcefully as she could now that her voice had nearly disappeared from her coughing.

"When you don't have any place to turn, sometimes you go the wrong way." Sofia's lips turned down at the corners.

"Doing the right thing isn't a choice," James insisted, though it was hard to take this line with Sofia when, more and more, he found himself wanting to simply reassure her that everything would be okay. That he'd make sure of it. For her and Javi.

"Doing the right thing isn't always easy, either." Sofia's eyes narrowed and her long eyelashes obscured their expression.

"Maybe we should vote." Joy tucked both sides of her hair behind her ears, then raised her hand. "All those in favor of allowing the Lovelands access to the river through our property when our herd is in its summer pasture, raise your hand."

After a moment, Jared lifted his hand and said, "On the condition that some of the additional funds go into updating our saddles. They're older than our ranch."

"Anyone else?" His mother checked.

Sofia's hand rose.

"Tie," Joy declared, looking far too pleased to finally have another voting member on her side. Usually she and Jared, who typically voted together, lost to James and Justin and Jewel. "According to the bylaws—"

"We'll table it and take another vote next week." James rubbed the back of his tense neck. "Except it isn't really a tie since Sofia's not a voting member of the board."

"She's Javi's trustee," Joy insisted. "That won't change because of your legal challenge."

"As Sofia pointed out, she's leaving in a few weeks." James bit the inside of his cheek to keep the worry from showing on his face. His mother had begun to emerge from her depression, and he didn't want to dampen the moment.

"But I'm here now." Sofia's arched brow and squinty left eye seemed like a declaration of war. "In fact, I'd like to move that we vote on Jared's saddle replacement request again, whether or not we grant the Lovelands water access."

This time, Justin joined his mother, Jared and Sofia in voting to add a new saddle to this month's expenditures.

What was the saying, he wondered, as the meeting adjourned and they headed out into the cold.

All's fair in love and war.
Not that love had anything to do with it.
Did it?

CHAPTER TEN

"That one!"

Sofia stopped in the calf-high snow a few days later and followed Javi's point to a mammoth fir tree. The cold morning air in this remote forest at Mount Sopris's base had her shivering a bit and she rubbed her mitten-covered hands together. How long had they been hiking? An hour? Two? The tips of her ears ached, for goodness' sake. As for her toes, they'd lost feeling a long time ago.

James halted as well and the hacksaw he carried swung beside his knee. Wearing brown boots, dark denim jeans and a plaid jacket that brought out the rich brown of his eyes and his rugged features, he looked like a handsome outdoorsman. Tough, proud and unbroken, as though his spine, his limbs, his square jaw had been forged from the very bedrock of these mountains. She couldn't entirely blame the high altitude for her breathlessness whenever he glanced her way. In fact, she'd even struggled a bit to focus on the task at hand: finding Javi his very first Christmas tree.

She still couldn't get over that it had been James's suggestion. He'd been so thoughtful with Javi this past week. More often than she liked, she caught herself wishing he would let down his guard with her a bit. With the missing pills still a source of contention between them, though, she doubted it would ever happen. And that might be for the best. She spent too much time dwelling on Jesse's older brother who, even if he wasn't so controlling, was off-limits. She couldn't betray Jesse's memory with his brother...

"It's too big," she called, eyeing the tree.

Though it was pretty. Blue-green, snowy, tier-on-tier boughs fanned out from a slender top to a full graceful bottom that swept the white snowdrifts. Last night, a storm had howled down off the mountains and dumped over a foot of snow on Carbondale.

Today there was little evidence of the blizzard. The sun shone bright in an azure-blue sky and cloud wisps curled on the horizon like an afterthought. A cardinal settled on one of the balsams in the glade, followed by two more. Scarlet against silver-gray-blue-white. It felt like she'd stepped right into a holiday card. Even the air, pine-scented and fresh-scrubbed, smelled like Christmas.

"Twelve feet," James speculated, his voice a deep rumble that vibrated in the frigid air between them. "Manageable."

"I can help, Uncle James."

Out of the corner of her eye, she spied James's one-sided dimple dent his cheek in an indulgent smile. Of course Javi would offer to help. Yet she wished sometimes that he didn't feel like he needed to prove himself all the time. That he didn't have to be extra good, go the extra mile to make up for all the events in his life that had taught him to believe he didn't matter.

Though he had the Cades now, who clearly thought the world of him, especially James. He spent every free moment he had with her son, teaching him how to ride a horse, instructing him on ranch work, the kind of cowboy skills she'd once dreamed of Javi learning back when she and Jesse had still been together.

"It's a deal." James advanced on the tree, his head cocked as he assessed.

"How will we carry it?" Sofia wondered out loud as she watched Javi flop backward and begin scissoring his arms and legs to create a snow angel.

"I brought a tarp." James angled his chin to his shoulder, indicating the bulging backpack he carried.

"A tarp that carries trees?" she couldn't help but tease. For a moment, the tension between them eased.

His dark eyes danced a little. "It's not a magic carpet."

Javi leaped to his feet, spread his arms wide and began zooming around the small clearing. He belted a lyric she recognized from *Aladdin*, one of the animated movies she'd taken him to see at their public library in Albuquerque. "Come on, Mama! Uncle James!"

His trill sent the cardinals winging back into deep woods, and her stiff cheeks creaked into a smile. *Oh. Why not?* This was Javi's first real Christmas and she'd make the most of it. Who knew what their situation would be like next year?

She raced after her child, arms flung wide open, singing the next line in a shaky soprano. To her surprise, James tramped up, swung Javi up off his feet and held him aloft, airplane style. The two turned in a dizzying circle that got faster and faster until James took one step too far to the left, overcorrected to his right and stumbled into Sofia.

They all went down in the icy powder, shrieking with laughter. Javi raced away screeching, and somehow James's face ended up just inches from hers. Their merriment subsided, then transformed into something more serious as some unidentifiable emotion crackled between them. Her heart thundered.

"Stop making googly eyes." Javi pounded on James's shoulder, breaking them out of their brief trance. "Google eyes. Google eyes!"

"Javi, stop." Instead of listening to her, he raced away, screeching.

Sofia pushed to her knees. Her arm, however, sank elbow-deep into a depression. When she looked up, James loomed over her, hand extended. A thrill shot up her arm when their fingers touched, an electric shock that traveled through the wool of her mittens. Her cheeks grew warm when his steady tug brought her back on her feet and suddenly toe to toe with him, their faces so close the tips of their noses brushed. She felt his breath on her eyelashes.

"Sorry," she said, breathless. She might

have stumbled if his arm hadn't snaked out and caught her, firm, around the waist.

"I'm not," he murmured, his lips almost a breath away from hers. He touched her cheek and his dark eyes burned with a tender passion she'd never seen before. Something unfurled inside the scraped interior of her heart.

"Googly eyes! Googly eyes!" Javi returned, chanting and laughing.

Google eyes, indeed, she thought, breaking away from the man who'd just made the world drop out from under her. Lord. Had he almost kissed her?

"What do we do now?" Javi asked, his words accompanied by a plume of white air. Over his shoulder, Sofia watched a cluster of leafless young birches bend, whiplike, in a gust off the summit.

"Well. There is a proper way to do this," James intoned.

Sofia tried and failed to stop her eye roll. Please. Could they not, just once, do something spontaneous? Where was the *Aladdin* singer from a moment ago? The tender man who'd melted her? He was complex and full of contradictions… If they made a live-action film of *Shrek*, prickly, stubborn, secretly soft-hearted James would be perfect for the lead. Her mouth hitched up on one side.

Javi stopped running and planted himself in front of James. The kid practically looked ready to salute.

"We've got to sing 'Tannenbaum' first," James said and her mouth dropped open.

"That's my rule," she confessed.

"You have rules?" He arched a brow, a wry twist to his lips. "Looks like we're more alike than I thought."

"Looks like," she murmured. Seeing James so relaxed and cheerful attracted her to him in ways she could never have imagined when they'd first met. And after that almost kiss…

"What's a tannenbaum?" Javi's brown eyes, a slightly darker shade than James's, sparkled and popped.

"Another word for Christmas tree," James answered. "You've never sung that Christmas carol?"

Javi scrunched his face at her. "Did I, Mama?"

"Sort of. Remember?" She hummed the tune to "O Christmas Tree."

James's eyes met hers over Javi's head and something about the warm, appreciative way that he studied her made her knees dip.

"Uh-uh." Javi buried his face in the tree. "This smells good."

"When your daddy was little, your age…" James began.

"I'm not little," Javi protested, emerging.

James nodded, eyes serious, mouth twitching. "No. But your daddy was. Anyway, our father used to have all of us hold hands, make a circle around the tree, then sing."

"Grandma, too?"

"Yes. And your grandfather. He couldn't sing a lick, but he sang that song with us every year. He even sang some of it in German like his father taught him."

The sad expression on his face moved her. He'd never talked about his father, but it looked like he'd had a good relationship. One that he missed.

Did she miss *her* father?

In moments like this, she had to admit that she did just a bit.

"Mama doesn't have a daddy," Javi offered.

"It's hard not having a dad. I don't have mine anymore."

"Me, neither." Javi wrapped his arms around James's leg and stared up at him, a worshipful, enraptured look on his face that made her heart strain in her chest. Oh, how she wished she could have given him a father...

"We should make a club! The No Daddy Club."

Sofia adjusted Javi's slipping knit cap. "That sounds a little sad, Javi."

"I think it's a great idea," James said. "We can do things to honor our fathers so they always stay with us." He tapped his chest. "Right here."

Javi pressed his hand to his heart, looking concerned. "He can't fit. Is he heavy?"

"No, honey. Daddy went up. Remember? He's light now. Like a cloud."

Javi squinted up at the streaks of white overhead. "So daddies can fly?"

"Absolutely," James affirmed. His definiteness got her thinking about the mother who'd passed before she could know her. What would her mother think of her life's choices?

She hoped, when it came to Javi at least, that she'd approve.

"This one's for Daddy." Javi yanked James's hand and nearly pulled him off his feet. James just had time to grab her hand and the three of them galloped around the tree, a human chain, then skidded to a stop, breathlessly laughing.

"Uncle James, hit it!"

"O Tannenbaum." The deep clarity of James's bass singing voice, melodic and actually quite beautiful, filled the open-aired space.

"O Christmas tree," she joined in, crooning through smiling lips. Hand in hand, they sang the carol.

"O Christmas tree, you bring me lots of presents," Javi belted with his trademark lyric substituting.

He'd learned from the best, she thought, thinking of the creative license she took now and then since she never could get an entire song straight. When the final words of the carol eluded her, she simply went with "O Christmas tree, you are so charming."

"Unchanging," James corrected, his mouth hooking up at the corners in a gorgeous half smile. At the tender affection in his eyes, a war of emotions, vulnerability and exhilaration, erupted.

"Are we a family?" Javi asked.

Sofia felt James's hand tighten around hers. Their near kiss had changed things between them, created an intimacy that she needed to guard against. "Yes."

Her heart picked up speed and she forced herself to let go and put some space between them. James seemed to be stealing the air

from her lungs, the thoughts from her head
and the barriers she'd erected from around her
heart. For a moment, vertigo whirled inside
her so that it felt as if she stood on a precipice,
about to tumble, head over heels.

"What's next, Uncle James?"

"The next step is…" James dropped his
backpack to the ground. To her astonishment,
he produced a thermos and three Styrofoam
cups. "Hot chocolate."

"With marshmallows?"

James paused in pouring and pursed his
lips. "Might have forgotten them, buddy.
Sorry."

"It wasn't on your list?" she asked, then
smiled at the stunned expression that crossed
his face.

"I didn't make one," he admitted, abashed.

Her heart softened. Was he finally lowering his strict standards? Did she have anything to do with it?

"Looks like you went off-grid. Must be my
bad influence…" Sofia teased.

"I wouldn't call it bad." He grinned back
at her, their eyes locking.

"Is it ready?" Javi leaned over and sniffed
the chocolate with a red-tipped nose.

James shook his head and blew on the

steaming brown surface. He would make someone a good father someday, she mused. While *she* didn't like being micromanaged, watching Javi with James proved that boundaries did work for some kids.

A moment later, she breathed in the rich, chocolaty smell, then sipped the warm, sweet fluid.

"Did you use the Keurig?"

James nodded.

"Hmmmmmmmmmm… You weren't too keen on it when I first mentioned it."

"Let's just say…" He lowered his cup and met her eyes over the brim. "That some of the changes around here are starting to grow on me."

A FLUSH SPREAD up Sofia's neck and pooled in her cheeks. Her teeth appeared on the full bottom lip that he'd nearly kissed just moments ago. Her long lashes fell and obscured her eyes. They had little flecks of green to break up the brown color, he'd observed under the bright sun today.

In fact, he'd been noticing a lot about Sofia lately. Much that he liked, despite the lingering concern about the missing pills. He thrust aside the worry. Today was about Javi. About family. He wouldn't ruin this incredible day. Nearly kissing Sofia, despite everything that stood between them, had felt right. No. That wasn't the word. It'd felt *meant*.

In the distance, a snowmobile engine whined and he pictured Justin plowing through the fresh powder, immune to the risks of speeding around hairpin turns thousands of feet above sea level.

"What do we do next, Uncle James?"

He shoved aside the allure of her soft lips, gathered the empty cups, stored them, then held up the hacksaw. "We cut the tree."

Javi's eyes widened. "That'll hurt it!"

Sofia put a hand on Javi's arm. Her dark hair curled out from beneath her red wool cap. In her white jacket, fitted jeans and boots, she'd never looked prettier. "Trees can't feel."

"Yes, they do!"

"Honey, it's just a tree. Plus, now it'll get to be a Christmas tree. That's special."

"Will it die?"

When Sofia paused, James jumped in. "Yes. But not right away. Not until we throw it out."

Javi grabbed one of the boughs. "Can we bring it back?"

"No, honey. It doesn't work that way."

Sofia knelt in the snow in front of her son and placed a kiss on the tip of his nose.

James's heart zoomed in his chest at the tender gesture, his reservations about Sofia fading to dust. She loved her son. Absolutely. Unselfishly. The struggles she'd forged through on her own, without family, her determination to serve on the Cade Ranch board, her follow-through on attending NA meetings, even her sobriety, weren't actions she took for herself. She'd made that clear. Yet the fact that she did them anyway, for her child's sake, deeply impressed him and touched him. There was a lot to like about Sofia. Love even...

"Then I don't want it." Javi sniffled.

"But you said you wanted a Christmas tree."

"We can't take it from its family." Javi pointed at the surrounding pines, spruce and firs.

A crazy, complicated tangle of feelings rose in his chest. For a kid who'd never had much family, or maybe because he'd never had it, he treasured it most of all. Deserved it. Was there a chance Sofia might consider leaving Javi here on Cade Ranch when she left for Portland? They could keep him until she was settled and have more time to bond and cement their ties. Now that he'd discovered Javi, James had made a place for him in his heart, and he couldn't imagine their family without him. Or Sofia.

"But…"

Javi flung his arms out. "I'm saving the tree. Like Batman."

"Oh, honey." Sofia sighed a long, white exclamation of air. She held out one of Javi's gloves that had slipped off. "You don't have to rescue everything."

"Batman would."

James stored the hacksaw in his pack and approached Javi. "Your father could never bring himself to kill anything, either."

Sofia brushed at Javi's damp cheeks. His lashes, wet and clumped, rose. "Nothing?"

"Nope. Not even a spider. Whenever we'd spot one, he'd holler for us not to kill it so he could trap it and set it outside."

"Daddy was a hero."

"Yes. Yes, he was. He wanted to be a veterinarian and rescue all animals." James's throat swelled right along with his heart, an aching pressure. In this moment, he remembered his little brother the savior, not the addict. How easily one aspect of a person could overshadow the rest if you let it, he thought, his eyes alighting on Sofia.

He'd been hard on her, too quick to accuse when the pills went missing—he now saw that. His suspicious nature blinded him to the possibility that Sofia's former addiction didn't automatically make her guilty. There was much more to her than her past. "Let's leave the tree right here."

"Then it can't be a Christmas tree." Javi angled his head to look up the length of it.

"Yes, it can," James insisted, thinking of an old tradition his mother had taught him and his siblings. "We'll make some ornaments at home. The kind birds and squirrels can eat."

"They can eat it?"

"Yep. I'll show you."

A few hours later, he, Sofia and Javi sat in the kitchen. Newspaper covered the long table along with pinecones. On the stove, Tuscan bean soup bubbled, spewing a rich, buttery aroma that had his stomach grumbling. Sofia had moved on from her French cooking obsession after watching *Roman Holiday* and promised (threatened?) Italian cuisine like none of them had ever tasted.

He grinned a bit to himself at that. On Sunday, she'd offered to make them homemade pizza while they watched the football game. Good thing he had Domino's on speed dial.

"Smells good, Sofia."

Her head snapped up. "You think so? I didn't have fresh basil, but I rubbed the dried flakes to bring out the flavor."

"Where'd you learn to do that?"

"The catering company I worked for. They didn't let me cook, but I used to watch the chefs, wishing I could be one someday."

"I believe you can."

Her eyes searched his, as if she didn't trust her ears.

"I do," he insisted. "You're smart, hard-working and—uh—creative."

One side of her mouth hitched up. "The duck à la grapefruit wasn't my finest moment."

"But who else would have thought of it?"

"No one, thank *God*."

Their shared laugh felt like sinking into a warm tub, a comforting homecoming.

"Is this right?" Javi held up a pinecone he'd smeared with peanut butter.

The spread rose so far up the cone that it'd make a huge, sticky mess when they attached it to the tree. Javi had also missed a few spots, leaving the pinecone bare in places so it couldn't be evenly coated with birdseed.

He opened his mouth to correct Javi then heard himself say, instead, "Good job, buddy."

Sofia's slightly gummy smile brightened the air around him, and he found himself smiling right back until Javi yelled, "Googly eyes!"

From the mouths of babes, his mother always used to say to his father whenever he or one of his siblings said something that made them laugh. He supposed Javi had it right. He was staring a little too long at Sofia, listening a bit too close, lingering longer than he should, but he couldn't help himself. Gone was his ironclad control. She was kryptonite to his self-discipline. Worse, he wasn't sure he minded anymore.

He even found himself looking forward to seeing whatever unconventional dish she'd make for dinner. Burned, undercooked, overspiced, bland as cardboard… The anticipation and surprise kept things interesting. And no denying, he liked coming home to Sofia and Javi. Would he miss Sofia as much as Javi when they left? Lie in bed, thinking about her soft lips and that smile that lit him up from the inside?

He watched her out of the corner of his eye as she painstakingly sprinkled birdseed all around her pinecone. Without her, life would settle back to its quiet, ordinary routine. Not a comforting thought like it had once been, he realized. A narrow world by comparison. It tipped him sideways to imagine the house, his family and himself without them.

Suddenly, he had so much feeling trapped within his chest, he had to take shallow breaths while he waited for it to subside.

"I'm glad we didn't kill our Christmas tree." Javi paused in his work to lift a baleful Clint onto the table. "Oof. You're heavy."

Clint's short, stubby tail, a comical proportion given his huge girth, flicked in rebuke. Then he flopped on his side, lifted his head in a futile attempt to lick his basketball of a stomach and dropped his head back to the table. His paws batted at the birdseed rolling on the table.

Sofia scratched Clint behind the ear. "Now the tree can give presents to the rest of the forest."

"What about me?" Javi turned with the birdseed bag he'd picked up. In a pinging shower, the pellets poured to the floor. James and Sofia hurried to pick up the mess. "Do

I still get presents? Santa only leaves them under trees."

"Well. We'll get an artificial one. So that counts." James grabbed a broom and handed Sofia the dustpan.

"What if I'm on the naughty list?"

Sofia looked up sharply from where she crouched on the ground.

The broom made a swishing sound as James flicked the mess into the dustpan. "You're not on the naughty list."

"Of course not, honey," Sofia chimed in. She dumped the seed into the garbage.

"If you're a liar, Santa puts you on the naughty list." Javi's lower lip trembled.

Sofia swept him in her arms. "You never lie, Javi."

"What about taking stuff?"

Sofia kissed the top of his head. "My Batman would never steal."

Javi squirmed free, dropped his brow to the table and covered his head with his arms. When his muffled voice emerged, they had to step close to hear him.

"I took Grandma's pills."

CHAPTER ELEVEN

"Poor Javi." Joy sighed. "He really didn't mean any harm."

Sofia nodded, then flicked on her turn signal and waited beneath a blinking red light at the intersection. Sleet pinged against her windshield and hood, a hollow, ominous sound with the world a swirling, writhing black mass beyond her headlight beams. Her insides twisted along with it, turning round and round as she replayed Javi's confession about the missing medicine from earlier this afternoon.

Javi had lied and stolen.

Like mother like son?

No.

He was nothing like her and never would be, she vowed. His motive had been to protect her. Although he didn't know about her addiction, he'd gleaned from conversations that she thought pills were dangerous. He'd wanted to save her and that admission both touched and hurt her most of all. Her little man, the superhero who would save the world if he could, had tried to rescue her. She was the mom. The strong one. She never wanted him to worry about anything, least of all her.

"I hate leaving him." Sofia cranked the wheel and eased off the gas as the truck slid in the turn as she headed into town. She should have stayed home from tonight's NA meeting. In fact, since Javi's revelation exonerated her, she no longer had to honor James's attendance request. Yet she'd come anyway. Why?

"Me, too." Joy brushed the snow that had fallen on her navy wool dress coat and stamped her boots on the rubber floor mats. "But he only wanted James to stay with him."

"They're close," Sofia said without taking her eyes off the treacherous road. The thin scrape of white atop the shining tarmac suggested the sanders hadn't passed through in a while. She pressed the snow button on the dash to give the tires more weight and traction.

"Careful on the speed. Looks like black ice." Joy pulled off her leather gloves and folded them on her lap. "It does me good seeing James and Javi together."

"I thought he'd be furious about the pills." Sofia gripped the wheel and concentrated on keeping them on the road. When she flipped on the defroster, a blast of stale warm air roared from the vents.

"I'm not. For all James's bluster, he's got a big heart. In fact, he's the biggest softy of all my children and a huge pushover where Javi's concerned...and you."

"Me?" Sofia squeaked.

"We've been asking for a new coffee maker for years. You mention it once, and it's on the counter the next morning."

"Oh... I..." Sofia clamped her babbling mouth shut. Could she sound any more awkward and inarticulate? Ever since their almost kiss, her thoughts and feelings for James had been a tangled knot. "Maybe it was on sale?"

"Like the chrysanthemum centerpiece that appeared the day after you mentioned they were your favorite flower? Or the steam iron you vowed got rid of wrinkles better? And what about how he replaced all our cleaning products with the environmentally safe brands you recommended? He's changing, Sofia. Willing to try new things, and it's because of you."

"You mean Javi."

"I don't think I do," Joy replied, her tone sounding slightly amused and a little too knowing for comfort.

Did Joy sense anything between them? Every time Sofia caught James looking at her lately, she grew warm and flustered. "But I... ah... I mean...he's just being nice."

"I can say a lot of good things about my son, but nice isn't one of them. He's a proud man. And decent. Moral through and through. But he's also stubborn and closed off. A lot in life has made him that way, his father for one."

Sofia peered into the whirling white murk, trying to distinguish the rapidly disappearing median. "James loved him."

"Oh. It was a complicated relationship. My husband considered feelings a weakness and he wanted his children to be tough. Working these mountains requires a mental and emotional fortitude they wouldn't get if we spoiled them, he always said...and though I didn't quite agree, I knew he meant well. He loved our children. I just wished he could have actually told them that now and again. It would have gone a long way. Especially with James, who hero-worshipped his dad."

Understanding and empathy welled inside

her. She knew how it felt to chase after the shadow of a parent's love.

"Sometimes I wonder if people who love easily don't love as deep," Joy observed. "Maybe it's because they don't have as much to lose? Haven't invested as much? James. Now, once he lets someone in, he doesn't hold back. I think that's why he's as closed off as he is. We always guard that part of ourselves that's the most vulnerable. For James, that's his heart."

Sofia's mouth opened and closed. What to say? She wished she could be loved absolutely by someone, but she was too flawed, too scarred, too full of past mistakes to ever inspire those kinds of feelings. Someday, when she reinvented herself, she might be worthy. Sofia 2.0. A new person without the blemish of her past to hold her back from love.

"Sometimes I think Javi will be the only person to ever love me," she confessed, then nearly clapped her hand over her mouth. Why had she said that out loud? Joy's motherly caring inspired Sofia to open up. "If he ever finds out about my past..."

"It wouldn't change a thing." Joy leaned forward and swiped at the condensation misting the glass in front of the steering wheel.

Sofia's pressed lips couldn't fully contain the wounded sound that welled in her throat. It escaped in a pained groan.

"Oh, honey. I'm sorry. But please believe me." Joy patted Sofia's hair, her arm, her knee… The act drew a bit of the pain from her heart. Joy meant well and cared about her. It was a strange feeling. A wonderful one. Was this how it felt to have a mom?

Sofia slowed down as the back of a snow-plow loomed ahead. Fans of white sprayed from its right-angled blade landed on drifts now swallowing up the guardrails. The grating sound of metal on ice mixed with the rough whoosh, whoosh, whoosh of her wiper blades. "I don't want Javi looking at me like I'm some—some—"

"Addict?"

She pumped her brakes as the plow slowed, then curved in a broad arc onto a white-covered side street. "That's not who I am." Yet the anguish in her voice said something else entirely.

"Honey, you'll always be an addict." Sofia cringed inside the down jacket that Joy patted. "One of my biggest regrets with Jesse was how I always tried carrying on like normal, thinking if I gave him the same loving home as always, he'd come to his senses and become himself again."

Sofia startled. Wasn't that what she was trying to do with her own life? Portland would give her a chance at a normal existence without reminders of who she'd been.

"You loved him, Joy." She blinked her eyes against the stinging rush rising inside them.

"Yes. But he also needed my understanding. My unconditional love. He needed me to love and support him for who he was, not who I wanted him to be. I never accepted that side of him, and he must have felt so lonely."

"You were doing your best," Sofia murmured, thinking of herself and how lonely she'd been as an addict, a sensation she could only escape with the next hit. Would she feel lonely again when Javi grew up and moved out? Would her addiction return to fill the void without, as James put it, Javi to stay sober for?

Joy pressed the end of her scarf to each eye while her other hand kept pat-pat-patting away at any part of Sofia it could reach.

"I was being selfish, honey. Jesse had changed and I wouldn't change with him. I lied to myself and acted like his time in rehab was just him leaving home for a spell.

And when he was passed out, I told myself he was sick and made him soup. When he came home, I never asked any questions. The less said, the quicker we could move on. Pretend like it didn't happen. Stuck my head right in the sand and lost my baby because of it."

Joy dropped her head in her hands and her shoulders shook.

"Oh, Joy. No. No. It's not your fault." Sofia wished for a safe spot to pull over but the road's shoulders were piling up with snow right out into the lane.

"It is my fault. I'm his mother and I failed him. There just isn't anything worse you can do in life than fail your own children."

The air in the car pressed humid and close.

"Jesse wouldn't blame you, Joy."

She lifted her head and pressed her scarf to her damp cheeks. "He wouldn't. But that doesn't make it any less true. But now that you're here, I have a second chance to get this right."

Sofia's heart thumped. Javi had brought Joy out of her grief. Would she fall back into her depression when they left for Portland? And what about her own feelings? She hated thinking about leaving a place, a group of people that were becoming more and more dear to her…a family.

"I'm so grateful for everything you're doing for Javi." Sofia gently pressed the brake, careful not to lock up as the wind swept a wide swath of snow from one side of the road to the other.

"I wasn't talking about Javi."

Sofia flicked her a surprised sideways glance. "What?"

"You're my second chance, Sofia. I can get this right by showing you that I care and accept you for who you are. Yes. Part of that person is an addict. And that might be the part of you I care about most since it's the part that's the hardest to love and the most deserving. If I'd loved Jesse—all of Jesse—that way, maybe he wouldn't have hidden himself from me."

Sofia felt a strange numb sensation begin in her feet, steal up her legs, then into her chest and heart, stopping it momentarily.

"You love me?"

No one had ever loved her for her…all of her.

"I do. And Javi does, too. Don't ever hide any bit of yourself. Be proud of your struggles, your failures. They make you who you are, a better, stronger person."

"I don't always feel strong." Her gut clenched at the admission. She needed to believe in her own invincibility. Never wanted to think of the chinks in her armor. She ran from anyone or anything that shone too bright a light on those weaknesses.

Like James.

Yet he'd almost kissed her, and somehow, in that moment, she'd felt worthy of it.

Was she deserving of love? Acceptance?

"None of us do." Joy was back to patting, this time Sofia's shoulder and arm. "That's why we have each other. Have you ever heard of the poem 'Footprints in the Sand'?"

Sofia shook her head. Hazard lights flashed red from a car that had swerved off the road. Its hood was buried in the drift and the driver stood outside with a phone pressed to his ear. He waved them on when Sofia turned on her blinker to pull over. A tow truck's yellow light appeared in her rearview mirror and she eased her foot off the brake.

"It's a religious poem, but you don't have to be religious to find meaning in it," Joy continued once they passed the accident. "It's about a man who has a dream about his life.

In each scene, he sees two sets of prints, his and God's. Yet during the lowest times in his life, he sees only one set. When he asks God why, God says, 'It's because I carried you then.'"

Sofia's heart thudded. "That's beautiful."

"A family is like that. We're strongest when we go through tough times together, holding each other, lifting one another up. When Jesse struggled, I didn't walk beside him or carry him like I should have. I just waited on the other end of the beach for him to come back to me. I'll never make that mistake again."

Sofia chanced a quick hand off the wheel to squeeze Joy's hand. "Is that why you came to the NA meeting with me tonight?"

"Yes. That and there's a grief support group that meets at the same time. I've been meaning to go but kept putting it off, thinking my sorrow would go away on its own. Seeing you get help has inspired me."

"*I* inspired *you*?"

"Yes."

"I don't even want to go to these meetings."

Joy pointed to the building that suddenly loomed ahead in the white shower. "But here you are."

Sofia braked, rolled to a halt, then turned

the key. The engine ticked to a stop. All was quiet except the pelting ice and Joy's quiet breathing beside her.

"Yes," Sofia said at last. "Here I am."

After a quick hug, they parted ways and Sofia took her seat inside the meeting room. She listened to her group leader's opening comments and couldn't stop her knee from jittering up and down.

"Who would like to begin?" he asked.

Sofia's hand shot up. "I'd like to introduce myself." She tried not to flinch at the avalanche of attention descending on her. "Again."

The teenage boy beside her cracked open one eye, then the other and slid up in his seat. She took a big breath and said:

"My name is Sofia Gallardo…and I'm an addict."

"WHAT ARE YOU DOING?"

James startled and the train engine he held dropped onto tracks that now nearly circled the entire living room. The last remnants of the evening's fire glowed in charred embers deep inside the hearth and its warmth curled in the snug room. Bing Crosby crooned about a white Christmas from wall speakers, a popcorn maker sizzled with heating oil on the kitchen counter and Clint lay on an easy chair, his massive head between his tiny paws, eyes half-slit and watchful for any signs of forthcoming food or affection. On the mantel, a pair of green balsam-scented candles glowed.

Sofia stood at the base of the stairs in an old-fashioned white nightgown straight out of some Charles Dickens Christmas movie. With her hair loose and curling over her shoulders, the firelight flickering over her beautiful face, she knocked the air clean out of him. Yet it wasn't just her looks that swelled his tongue and evaporated his words.

She hadn't stolen the pills. That was part of it. Just a part. Big picture—she'd still attended her NA meeting. And she had returned home different somehow, lighter if that made sense, her smiles coming a little easier, freer and even sometimes straight at him. It messed with his heart so it skittered like a newborn colt, wobbly and off balance.

It was an inconvenient feeling that stuck with him since their near kiss on the mountainside. He'd done his best to avoid her and now here she was, materializing like she'd stepped straight out of one of his dreams.

"Is this for Javi?"

He nodded and inhaled the vanilla scent rising from her as she drew close. "You mentioned he liked trains."

"This is—this is amazing." The soft awe in her voice filled him with pride.

"We had the set as kids. Javi was still upset when he went to bed, so I thought I'd surprise him with this when he woke up."

"He'll love it." She clapped her hands together and the sparkle in her brown eyes made his pulse pick up speed. "Thank you, James."

"For?"

"Treating him like a father would. He's never had that before."

James ducked his head. "I didn't expect to have that bond with him. Sometimes it makes me feel guilty, though."

"Because of Jesse?"

"Yes. Javi's his son."

"And he's your nephew. That's special, too. So—can I help?"

"Well. There's a specific order to it…"

She rolled her eyes and the now-familiar exasperation she usually wore teased a laugh from him. "Of course there is," she said.

An explosion of popping kernels sounded from the kitchen. "Don't touch anything," he warned, then strode away. Working quickly, he cut some butter into a bowl and melted it inside the microwave. When the popper quieted, he unplugged it, then dumped the fluffy white pieces into a red-and-white-striped movie-theater replica tub. He salted and buttered it, sneaked a handful of the rich, crunchy treat, then added more salt.

"Do you want anything to drink?" he called.

"Is there eggnog left?"

"I'll check."

The fridge's cool air rushed against his heated skin. If he had any sanity whatsoever, he'd make his excuses and retreat to his cabin. Being with Sofia late at night, alone, with his heart so raw and exposed it practically beat outside of his body, was asking for trouble. He couldn't deny his growing feelings or the complications they caused.

Sofia was Javi's mother. Jesse's ex. Giving in to any feelings he had was out of the question. Jesse should be here celebrating Christmas with his son and the mother of his child. Not James. He'd safeguard what had once been Jesse's but wouldn't cross the line and become the father he longed to be to Javi.

As for Sofia, what did he want to be to her?

He poured two glasses of the nutmeg-scented eggnog, sprinkled cinnamon on top the way Sofia had shown him earlier and suppressed his traitorous thoughts. Acting on his emotions would be disloyal. Unbrotherly... The final act of betrayal for a sibling who had deserved so much more from him.

He would only ever be an uncle to Javi and maybe, just maybe, an ally to Sofia, someone to guide her, especially if she insisted on battling him for stewardship of Javi's trust. While she'd made strides when it came to facing her addiction, she still lacked the experience, the discipline and the respect for the proper way of doing things needed for the position. Hopefully the upcoming case's judge, an old friend, would rule in his favor.

After loading a tray with the popcorn and drinks, he returned to the living room, then pulled up short. The eggnog sloshed up and over the sides of the glasses. A few popcorn pieces tumbled to the floor.

"What did you do?"

Sofia sat back on her heels and a completely unrepentant smile flashed, a line of pink gum appearing. "Made a few improvements."

"Improvements?" In a couple of strides, he

reached the tree-stump coffee table, set down the tray and joined her by the chaos that had once been his neat and orderly village.

"Where's the depot?"

"Over there. It's more fun to have it in the center of town. Lots of hustle and bustle."

He swallowed that down. Everyone knew a train station sat at the edge of town. Although it did look colorful where she'd placed it. And having several access points to different town tracks made for some extra play opportunities.

"What happened to the skating rink?"

"Now, that had to go outside of the village. It gives the people an excuse to use the train. See?"

And sure enough, a couple of figures waved from the slightly gaudy red, green and gold–painted Christmas caboose, part of the train that now encircled the pond. She'd also moved the hot-chocolate stand and the sliding hill there as well.

He wanted to argue but couldn't dredge up a single line that wouldn't sound petty. Just because something deviated from the way it had always been didn't mean it wasn't right. Wasn't better, in fact. How much he might miss, he mused, by refusing to consider different options.

"Where's the tree lot?"

To his surprise, her face flushed a bit and her eyes fled his. She nodded at a trio of figurines before a large blue-green tree that resembled the one they'd nearly cut down yesterday. A young boy held hands with his mother and father, their smiling faces angled down at their child.

"What do you think?" she asked with a catch in her voice.

He stepped close and laced his fingers in hers.

"I think I love it."

CHAPTER TWELVE

"You do?"

James turned and his other hand enfolded hers so that they faced one another in the soft blink of Christmas lights. The iPod shuffled to "Baby, It's Cold Outside" and she shivered. Not from the waterfall of white still flowing from the black sky outside, but from the storm within. It felt like someone released a million butterflies inside her heart.

"I do," he rasped. His brown eyes searched hers and she swayed toward him.

He smelled of fresh mountain air, pine and streams, snow-covered valleys and blue-sky horizons. Of the infiniteness of space and possibilities existing in this rugged outback, where the biggest discovery tonight was within herself...and now this. Them. An incredible joyful sense of being, of unity, that only existed when they occupied the same space. Breathed the same air. Shared the same thoughts.

What was he thinking?

"I should go back to bed," she whispered. Her stomach jumped when his thumbs skimmed over the sensitive flesh of her palms.

"Don't," he murmured, his voice tattered at the edges, the controlled, clipped tone gone. "Stay." He released her hand and slid his fingers through her hair. "Stay with me."

"I—I—" She struggled to regain her voice but it disintegrated, disappearing under the onslaught of sensations bombarding her. James stroked a finger down her cheek. "Yes." She sighed, melting inside. "I'll stay."

He encircled her waist and her head tipped back. He brought his lips close and the warm, sweet curls of his breath brushed against her skin. "You're beautiful."

"No." She pressed her eyes closed.

"Yes," he insisted and then a strange thing happened. Instead of kissing her, he guided her down next to him on the couch. Lifting her hand, he brushed her fingertips with his lips in a delicious caress that traveled in an electric rush to her toes. Then his mouth trailed to the inside of her wrist and lingered at the vulnerable spot, making the flesh over her bones shake.

"You smell good," he murmured against her skin.

"So do you," she gasped.

As he kissed his way up her forearm, her breath grew labored, the air impossible for her lungs to hold, as she responded to his gentle onslaught. When his mouth stopped on her track marks, she stiffened against him, hating the reminder of who she'd once been. Not the kind of woman who should be with a man like James. An upstanding man who'd never made any real mistakes in life, not like her, not like she still could...

"*These* are beautiful," he whispered against her scarred skin before kissing there. His lips paid homage to every ridge as though they were precious to him and her heart clenched along with the rest of her, in an agony of want and of wishing for what could never be.

"James," she protested. She lifted her lids and glimpsed the top of his dark head bent over her. He rolled his eyes up without lifting his face and the disoriented heat in them made her unravel, too. This undone James was ten times harder to resist than his usual controlled self. "Don't."

He sat up, swept his arm around her shoulders and guided her against the warm, muscular length of his chest. His heart hammered against hers. "Don't what?"

"Don't…" Her voice faltered. "Don't kiss me there."

"How about here?" he murmured before his lips claimed hers in a joining so sweet she nearly cried. The teasing pressure drove her wild and she opened her mouth, allowing his tongue to glide over hers in a slow rub that singed her. She couldn't get enough of the earthy-spicy taste of him.

"Yes," she gasped, her eyes drifting shut again.

He kissed her ardently and pressed her back against the couch, lifting her legs so they lay beside him. Her nightgown rose slightly and her knee brushed against the smooth, worn denim covering his leg. Every drop of her blood rushed in her veins where they beat beneath the surface of her heated skin.

The world spun when he left her lips to sample her neck and then lower, sliding down its length to the hollow valley at the base of her throat where his tongue smoothed over her thrumming pulse. Her fingers bored into his shoulders. When her body arched against his, his low groan vibrated against her skin.

She was losing control, but what scared

her more was that James, the voice of reason, logic, order, seemed to have completely lost his as well.

"James," she gasped. "James."

"Ummmmmmm?" He nipped at her collarbone and his broad hands gripped her waist.

"James, stop."

She felt him stiffen above her and his crazy long eyelashes brushed her skin as he blinked. A moment later, he shook his head and sat up, bringing her with him before releasing her. Never had she seen him look so vulnerable, dazed even.

"I'm sorry. This is just… It's just…" The iPod shuffled again and she froze when Rascal Flatts began singing "I'll Be Home for Christmas."

"That's Jesse's…"

"Favorite song," James finished for her; the open expression he'd worn fell away and disappeared. He'd closed himself off again and disappointment surged.

But that was what she wanted, wasn't it? She couldn't let herself fall for someone like James who would expect more than she might ever be able to give, someone who would always remind her of her past.

Besides, he was Jesse's brother. She just

couldn't. What kind of horrible person would kick Jesse out, deny him his son, then take up with his brother after Jesse's death? Kissing James in Jesse's house was as bad as dancing on his grave. She didn't deserve this kind of happiness when she'd denied Jesse that chance.

And hadn't she loved Jesse?

Yes. Of course she had.

But deep down she knew her feelings for him had never been as intense, as complicated as those she experienced every time James's soulful eyes landed on her.

Was she falling for him?

He edged away. The eggnog shook slightly as he lifted a glass to his lips and downed half of it in one long gulp.

"I'm sorry," she began. "It's just…"

He shook off the hand she'd placed on his arm. "No need to explain. We let the moment get to us. That's all. It was a mistake. One we shouldn't repeat."

No. She wanted to cry. She wanted to repeat it. Wanted to hold him. Kiss him. But neither of them was capable of being the person the other needed.

"I learned something tonight, at NA."

He set down his glass. "I'm glad you went."

"Me, too." She felt herself glow at the warm appreciation, the respect flickering in his gorgeous eyes. "I realized that there's someone I need to get to know before Javi and I leave for Portland."

"Who's that?"

"Myself."

He nodded and the dying fire popped in the quiet swelling between them. When she shivered, he grabbed a red wool afghan off the back of the couch and tucked it around her. His fingers fumbled a bit as he crisscrossed the ends and she nearly drowned at the longing on his face.

"I'd like to get to know her, too." His deep voice sounded so sincere she ached. "Before you go, I mean."

"Right." She spied the popcorn and the need to break this tension seized her. "Like… I bet you didn't know I could do this."

She tossed a kernel up in the air, stuck out her tongue and caught it neatly. His long eyelashes fluttered before a big, walloping grin broke out across his handsome face.

"Impressive. But can you do this?" He crossed his eyes, then stuck out a curled tongue to touch the tip of his nose.

A snort-laugh escaped her. James was fun.

Funny. He made her laugh, open up, cry. Lots of things, including making her feel safe. In another place, a different time, she wondered if he could be a friend…but then she shut down the thought. She'd never had a real friend, not anyone outside of her old drug life.

"Yeah? Try this." She patted her belly and rubbed the top of her head.

He chuckled. "You're supposed to rub your stomach and pat your head, idiot," he said affectionately, demonstrating.

"Now you're just showing off." She rolled her eyes.

His dark, dreamy gaze gleamed at her. "Is it working?"

"Not really," she teased, but it was, *it was*.

"Didn't think so."

Clint's ears twitched at the sound of their mingled laughter. The way James's rugged features lit up, Sofia observed, it transformed him from a gruff, hard-bitten ranch manager to a gentleman cowboy.

"Why did you say these were beautiful?" she asked, surprising herself as she extended her arm. The room fell silent save for an instrumental version of "Silent Night."

His smile evaporated and he shuffled his feet. They watched roly-poly Clint lurch onto his paws, drop to the ground then stalk to the fire, stubby tail flicking.

"You don't have to answer that," she rushed in when the silence swelled and stretched to its breaking point. "I'm not sure why I asked. Like you said. That was a mistake."

James's chest lifted in a deep inhalation and his deep brown eyes searched hers. "Guess what I meant is—is that your pretty face isn't all that makes you beautiful."

She blushed at the compliment.

"Those marks. They show you're a survivor. That you've been tested. That you're strong and that—that's beautiful to me."

Sofia's heart leaped into a gallop and she leaned toward James again, pulled by an irresistible force.

"Jesse didn't survive," he continued, his voice raw and his eyes sad.

"But he tried. He did what he could."

James stroked a finger down the side of her face, a touch so gentle, so magical, it could have been a butterfly's wing.

"Mama! Is it Christmas?"

She and James stood so quickly their knees knocked together. Javi flew down the steps in a blur of red and launched himself into James's arms before he hit the landing.

"Hey, buddy. What did we say about the stairs?" James chided. Her gaze swerved to his and she couldn't quite read his expression.

"Sorry, Uncle James." When Javi squirmed, James set him down and her son scrambled back up to repeat a more sedate descent.

"Was I good?"

"You're always good, honey." Sofia bent to press a kiss to his cheek but he ducked out of the way. Funny how he'd started acting like he didn't want her to give him any affection except when they were in private now.

"Santa doesn't think so." Javi pointed at the large, empty stocking that hung from the chimney. "He didn't bring me any presents."

"That's because it's not Christmas yet, silly," Sofia clarified. "And we don't have a tree."

"Then how come you and Uncle James are up?"

"Yeah. How come you two are up?" drawled Jewel from above. At her arched brow and knowing look, Sofia's toes curled beneath her nightgown's hem.

"Up to no good, I bet," Jared said with a wink as he entered the house. Cold air rushed in on his heels and swept through the room before he shut the door against it.

"What's going on?" Joy appeared beside Jewel, her hair flattened on one side of her face.

Sofia cringed. How this must look.

"Nothing, Ma," James called, back in control again. "Sofia and I were just setting up the train."

"Is *that* what you call it?" Jewel smirked.

"A train! Whoopeeee!" Javi leaped at the tracks with a bounce that would have demolished them if not for James's lightning-fast kid reflexes. He caught Javi around the middle.

"Not yet, bud. Sleep first. Play in the morning. Deal?"

Javi's cheeks blew with the force of his sigh. "Is that being good?"

"Very good."

"Okay. Uncle James? Can you tuck me in with Mama?"

"If your mom says it's okay."

She nodded, touched at the bond between her son and this incredible man. Jewel, Joy and Jared called good-night as she and James walked up the stairs, each holding one of Javi's hands. At the top, Javi paused.

"Do you love me, Uncle James?"

"Yes," James said, his voice gruff. "I love you."

"Are you like a daddy?"

James pulled Javi close. "Yes." The single syllable was fierce and packed with emotion.

Javi hugged James's knees and Sofia's heart skipped at the tenderness on James's face. "Santa gave me what I wanted."

Her heart clenched. She wanted to give Javi a parent, a family to be proud of so badly. Could that person be James rather than her after all?

James angled his head and their eyes met.

Javi had what he wanted, but what about her and James?

What did they want?

"THAT ONE!"

James followed Javi's pointed finger to a ten-foot white artificial tree strung with pink and purple twinkle lights and clear glass ornaments. Sandwiched between a string of traditional Christmas trees bedecked in traditional red, green and gold, it stuck out like an Elvis impersonator officiating a Quaker wedding.

Winter-clad groups passed by. Some stopped to drop their auction tickets in one tree's bucket or another while a few lingered to stay inside before Carbondale's Festival of Lights parade began.

"You sure?" Jared absently waved to a couple of hollering women. Spit-shined in a new brown Stetson, and tooled leather boots so clean they begged the question if Jared had levitated instead of walked here, his younger brother looked more than ready to mingle at Carbondale's annual holiday event.

"Yep." Javi nodded emphatically. "Her name's MaeBelle."

"MaeBelle?" Jewel asked. Her brow scrunched.

Tonight, she'd tamed down her tomboy look a smidge, James noticed. Her trademark braids still swung against her shoulders, but she'd done something different to her face, he mused. Makeup? Seemed unlikely given she didn't own any. Yet how to account for the hectic blush that turned the skin between her freckles a bright pink? Then he noticed Heath Loveland, Jewel's old classmate. The tall, lithe cowboy shoved off from a nearby wooden pillar and ambled outdoors, Jewel's eyes tracking him every bit of the way.

Interesting. He and his brothers loved teasing their hotheaded sister over the manufactured crush. Jewel's reaction, however, sometimes made him wonder if they might have hit the truth after all.

Did she have a thing for Heath, the soft-spoken singing cowboy of the Loveland clan? He couldn't be more opposite from tough-talking, bold, impetuous Jewel. Sometimes opposites attracted, though.

A relationship between a Cade and a Love-land wouldn't ever be possible, of course. It was as unlikely as something happening be-tween him and Sofia, despite last night's dev-astating kiss, which left him sleepless and thinking of little else.

A group of singers launched into an a cap-pella version of "The First Noel" and their five-part harmony filled the gingerbread-scented air.

He glanced over at Sofia. She'd done some-thing pretty to her hair tonight. A headband pulled it off her oval face, leaving dark curls to dangle around her ears and frame her deli-cate features. In gray dress slacks and a white cashmere sweater with a silver scarf twined around her neck, she resembled one of the Christmas angels that adorned his church's front lawn. His gaze dropped to her rosy lips and the beauty mark above them and his body tightened just thinking about kissing her again. Right there.

Last night, the intimate feel of her warm and soft in his arms, the rightness of it, had blown him away.

But none of it could be.

Not with Jesse's specter growing stronger as the holiday approached, reminding them both of their shared guilt. They wouldn't cross the line and betray Jesse. As for his family, he couldn't imagine what they would think. His siblings had given him heck in the barns today about getting caught with Sofia last night. Going forward, he'd ensure they never had cause to speculate about her again.

Besides, her impressive steps to address her addiction didn't erase her history as a drug user. After Jesse, James refused to open himself up to living that roller coaster of heartbreak, mistrust and despair again. What shook him most about Sofia, however, was how easily he lost his self-control around her. Logic and order stopped mattering and it scared him.

A lot.

Jewel stepped behind Javi and rested her hands on his shoulders. "MaeBelle, huh? How do you know that's what she's called?"

"'Cause she's got bells. See?" Javi pointed at the strings of glitter-covered bells encircling the gaudy tree.

Jewel nodded solemnly. "All right. I'll put my tickets in for MaeBelle. Anyone else?"

Justin detached himself from the dark corner he'd slouched into when they'd entered the pavilion. He wore his usual head-to-toe black and a swarthy scowl, and the crowd scrambled out of the way of his stalking, slightly menacing gait. "Let's win this thing."

The Cades dropped all their tickets into the white tree's bucket. What a crazy thing to bring into their home. Not expected or normal. Did that have to be a bad thing? No. Not necessarily. Closing himself off from anything different also meant missing amazing experiences, like showcasing a disco ball tree in his family home. James's mouth quirked up—like teaching his nephew how to saddle a horse, or kissing a beautiful woman, one he was coming to care for deeply.

He pressed back the traitorous thought and focused on the fun night ahead.

"Can I get more cookies, Mama?"

"I don't think you have room in your bag." Sofia brushed a couple of crumbs off Javi's cheek.

The cookie walk, a town-wide Christmas cookie exchange, loaded up residents with enough baked goods to last until the New Year. Booths ran the length of the pavilion. Just outside stood a makeshift petting zoo, complete with reindeer.

"I've got room." James held up his bag.

Javi studied the laden tables. "Can I get some of the chocolate kiss ones?"

Sofia's eyes fled James's and he felt a smile come on. "The peanut butter one with the Hershey's in the middle?"

Javi tugged at his hand. "Come on!"

A little while later, James found himself alone with Javi and Sofia inside the old-time train depot that now housed Carbondale's town hall and post office. Jewel had splintered off to join some of her barrel-racing friends. The parade's Miss Snowflake had claimed Jared and hustled him away. Justin. Well. Justin lurked somewhere, James supposed, somewhere he'd find trouble no doubt. As for his mother—where had she gone?

Well. He couldn't manage all of them every minute, nor should he have to. The rebellious thought released some of the tension in his shoulders and his body relaxed beside Sofia.

He breathed in her vanilla sugar cookie smell and his pulse picked up speed.

He'd give anything to hold her again.

"Do you need any help, honey?" Sofia asked.

"Can I draw what I want?" Javi stopped scribbling on the fancy red-and-green-bordered paper the town provided for kids to write letters to Santa.

"I'm sure. You'll just need to sign your name so he knows who it's from."

"Javi Cade with a *J* and a *C*," Javi proclaimed, the pride in his voice making James's heart swell. It seemed like forever ago that he'd questioned whether Javi was a Cade. Now Javi seemed woven into the fabric of their lives and James couldn't imagine his family without him.

Sofia, too.

In just three weeks, they'd leave for Portland. The dismal thought tolled inside his empty spaces, echoing.

"Is this right, Uncle James?"

He peered down at the paper. Javi had drawn a mother, father and son, their hands joined. They stood before a massive tree topped with what looked like a unicorn head as a topper.

Sofia's quick breath of air voiced the shock reverberating inside of him. Javi wanted a family. Specifically, given the coloring and size he'd given each figure, Javi wanted the three of them to be that family. Technically the male figure could have been Jesse, but a part of James, a big part, wanted it to be him.

Javi had asked if he was like a daddy. The love he felt for this boy surpassed anything he'd ever felt before, save the moment his lips had touched Sofia's. He wished he could be Javi's father. But for his careless actions, though, Jesse would be—should be—the one having that honor.

"Yes. Yes, it's right," he said.

"Mama?"

Sofia's wide eyes darted anywhere but at him. "I—I— Yes. It looks very good."

Her lashes rose and suddenly he found himself gazing directly into her warm brown eyes. Did she believe they looked good as a family or was she just humoring Javi?

It shouldn't matter.

But it did.

"How do I spell *please*?" Javi asked.

"P-L-E-A-S-E," Sofia announced.

"I'm writing it three times so it comes true."

"Javi. You know we're going to Portland in a few weeks, right?"

Javi shrugged his shoulders and didn't raise his bent head. The knuckles around the pencil clamped inside his fist blanched.

Sofia widened her eyes at James and mouthed, "Help." James returned her stare but remained motionless. Sofia needed to be honest with her son about her addiction and how it played into her decisions, like moving them to Portland.

"How do I write *thank you*?"

James spelled it out carefully. If he could have a Christmas wish, what would it be? He eyed Sofia, then Javi. In a perfect world, he knew exactly what he'd wish for.

"All set?" Sofia asked when Javi dropped his pencil and kissed the paper.

"That's for good luck. And this." He pulled some holly berries from his coat and added them to the envelope with the letter. "I saved some from when we met Grandma."

"It's not really about luck, honey. Santa can't make everything come true."

Javi's nose flared and he angled his face toward James. "You said Santa made miracles."

Sofia's eyebrows rose.

"He does," James confirmed, knowing he

was raising expectations but unable to crush this little boy's dream. "Let's head outside for a spot on the street. The parade starts soon."

Brightly clad crowds thronged the thoroughfare and it took some searching for James to locate a spot with a clear view. They stopped beneath a wreath-decorated light post and squeezed in with the other townsfolk.

"I can't see," Javi cried, straining on his tiptoes.

"Here." James swung the child up on his shoulders, like he saw other fathers doing, like his own dad had done, and a fierce pride seized him. For a moment, he let himself imagine that he, Sofia and Javi were a family, free of the weight of a past that pulled them down and kept them apart.

"There's Grandma!" Javi shouted.

James peered, scanning, then spotted his mother talking with—of all people—Boyd Loveland? What? They didn't seem to be arguing. In fact, the way Boyd was smiling, the way his mother's eyelashes were fluttering, the conversation seemed a little too chummy for his liking.

"Ma!" he called and she startled, looking guilty, and then spotted a waving Javi. After a quick word to Boyd and a pat on his arm, she hurried across the street to join them as the first marching band approached. The bass drummers beat a pounding rhythm, followed by snares and then blaring French horns.

"Oh. I must have lost track of you earlier," Joy said, looking and sounding flustered. Over her shoulder, a lit float decorated in white cotton and featuring penguin-costumed riders appeared. "Did you write your letter to Santa?"

"I drew him a picture."

"Well, that's even better!"

"Is that the same man you were talking to at your grief support meeting?" Sofia asked Joy, surprising him.

Javi hooted and jumped a bit on James's shoulders when an enormous, flashing gift box rolled by accompanied by elves.

James strained to hear his mother over the cheering crowd and the orchestrated Christmas tunes. It looked like she nodded.

"Why were you talking to him, Ma?"

"What?" his mother asked.

Hadn't there been a story once about Boyd Loveland and his mother dating back in high school? He'd never paid it much mind, but given his mother's sparkling eyes and wide smile, he wondered.

"Why were you talking to him?"

A hail of miniature candy canes rained down on them from a Christmas tree float ridden by a waving Miss Snowflake and, somehow, Jared.

"We got kicked out of the meeting," she shouted back through cupped hands around her mouth.

"They were talking too much and the moderator had to ask them to leave," Sofia hollered in his ear. The swirl of noise around them grew deafening.

"Just like in high school." His mother giggled.

Giggled.

His brows lowered. "Steer clear of him."

Boyd Loveland had made his first wife so miserable, some whispered, she'd committed suicide. Others repeated the unproved theory he'd killed her for her trust fund and gotten away with murder. Years ago, news stations flooded Carbondale to get the scoop on the notorious death of their popular state senator's only daughter. Whatever the truth, Boyd had a messy past and a more uncertain future.

His mother pointed at her ear. "Can't hear you," she shouted and she and Sofia dissolved into more laughter, which only got him fuming.

Was Sofia egging his mother into a relationship with a Loveland? He was fine with some changes, harmless ones, he supposed—Keurig machines and meals that defied explanation, let alone recipe names. But that... that kind of disarray took things to another level entirely.

Maybe it was a good thing Sofia and Javi were leaving soon, he thought several minutes later as the final float glided by, a Santa and his reindeer rising from a mountaintop.

Then life would return to normal.

But normal and good weren't always the same thing, he was learning.

"We won! We won!" chanted Jewel, joining them in the thinning crowds. She waved a ticket. "We won MaeBelle and it was Javi's ticket that got pulled."

James grabbed Javi before he flung himself bodily to the ground.

"Yay!" Javi thrust two candy canes over his head at the rising moon. "See, Mama, miracles are real."

Sofia nodded and she offered James a pained smile. "Sometimes." She took Javi's hand and led him back to the pavilion. James followed, his mind in turmoil.

As much as he wished, wanted Sofia to

stay, the sooner she left, the better. Not only for his peace of mind but for his family's.

A leather-clad Justin appeared, the top of the white-frosted tree bundled under one arm. Jared materialized and he and James hefted the bottom half to carry it to their parked pickup.

Javi skipped ahead, jabbering a mile a minute to a grinning Jewel. His mother stared off at the moon, seemingly lost in her thoughts. As for Sofia, she lagged, her stricken expression mirroring the twist of emotions bottled up inside him.

They'd just won…so why did it feel like he'd lost…or was about to?

CHAPTER THIRTEEN

"IT'S A MOVIE!" Sofia shouted at a gesturing Joy.

Sandwiched between Javi and James on the couch as the family played charades, her lap weighed down by a purring, comatose Clint, Sofia had never felt happier in her entire life. Or more content. The nervous fear about her addiction had quieted because of her work at NA meetings and the support of these wonderful Cades. Even better—and maybe most incredibly of all—she finally had a place where she belonged.

At least for a few more weeks.

Would her life in Portland be as full and secure?

From an iPod player, Bing Crosby crooned about silver bells while a train whizzed through the miniature Christmas village arranged around the room. A pine-scented candle flickered beside an oversize red poinsettia that'd been delivered this morning from an anonymous source that had made Joy blush and James frown. The white artificial tree they'd won at the Festival of Lights yesterday rotated on a mechanized stand before the window bank. The tree was full of glittery tinsel and psychedelic colors, and Justin warned them not to stare at it directly in case they lost a few brain cells.

No one had any real quarrel with that.

Joy stood in front of the hearth and held up a single finger. In a bright red sweater that matched her lipstick, ceramic bangles and her gray skirt's piping, she was practically unrecognizable from the pale-faced woman they'd met in the cemetery a couple of weeks ago.

Earlier this evening she'd glowed as she'd talked to Boyd Loveland after the grief support group. When Sofia overheard the words "thank you" and "poinsettia," she'd hesitated to break up what looked like a budding romance between the two. Instead, she'd waited patiently, then a little less patiently, then kind of impatiently until Joy glanced over a half hour later and noticed her lurking by the car.

"Sorry about that," Joy had apologized, flushed and slightly out of breath, on the car ride home.

"No apology needed," Sofia had reassured her. "It's wonderful to see you smiling. Happy. You've really changed from the woman who used to struggle to get out of bed in the morning."

Joy's hand had squeezed her arm. "We've all changed. For the better."

JESSE, IF YOU'RE listening, thank you for making this possible, she thought, and her eyes jumped to James. Ever since their kiss, she'd been thinking about him nonstop. He'd held her that night as if she were the most cherished person in the world, like he'd never wanted to let her go. When he'd confessed his feelings about her needle marks, her heart had opened wide for him.

He saw her as a survivor, not a victim, a woman who'd been tested and become a better, stronger person. All her life, she'd believed herself at fate's mercy, a motherless child unloved by a closed-off father, an addict whose habit had cost her a high school diploma and earned her a felony record, two strikes that prevented her from having a real career and a respectable life to provide for her son.

James helped her see that she could be anyone and do anything. She wished she could be his girlfriend, a real partner.

She clapped a mental hand over those runaway thoughts. If not for Jesse, she wouldn't be here. She had no right, no call, to be thinking about his brother. James might not be a threat to her sobriety anymore, but valid reasons to steer clear of a romance with him still existed.

"ONE WORD!" CALLED JEWEL. She sat crosslegged on a patterned rug and leaned forward, elbows resting on her worn jeans. Her jaw jutted forward and her freckled features appeared a bit pinched and intense, as did the rest of the family members' faces. Cade Christmas charades was a blood sport, not the quaint tradition Sofia had imagined when James suggested it after dinner.

Joy nodded and pushed up her slipping glasses.

"What Christmas movies are only one word?" mused Jared from his perch on the edge of an armchair. In a pressed brown dress shirt and dark jeans, his thick, impeccable hair slicked back, he looked like he should be *in* the movies, not guessing their names. James's rugged profile snared her attention again. Funny how all the girls fawned over Jared at the Festival of Lights when, to her, James was the best-looking Cade.

A picture of Jesse, front and center on the mantel, caught her eye and she flushed with shame. His flashbulb smile and dimples nearly turned the photo into 3-D. Once, she'd thought Jesse the handsomest man she'd ever met.

But she'd known him as a young man, and James, well, James had the kind of weathered strength, quiet confidence and life experience that carved character in a face. The pain he'd suffered had left its mark in the faint grooves around his mouth and the trace of lines on his forehead. Sometimes she itched to smooth them away when he looked to be worrying over something. Oftentimes, though, she figured she and Javi were the cause of those anxieties.

Would he be happier when they left for Portland?

Would she?

"Scrooged," Justin called as he emerged from the kitchen wearing an incongruous frilly pink apron over his faded black T-shirt, dusty black jeans and boots so worn the color blended with the wood flooring. The rich scent of

roasted nuts preceded him. When he plunked the bowl down on the coffee table, he backed away fast to avoid Jewel and Jared's pounce.

Joy shook her head hard and the smooth silvery strands of her bob swished across her pretty face.

"Stop hogging all the hazelnuts," Jewel growled.

"You snooze, you lose." Jared cracked open a nut and popped it into his mouth.

"Can I try some?" asked Javi.

James carefully opened an almond and passed it over. "They're like the ones in those cookie bars."

Joy tugged on her ear.

"Sounds like…" Jewel mumbled around a mouthful of pecan bits.

Joy pointed at the hearth behind her. A green, lit garland looped across the length of its mantel, and stockings for each family member dangled from metal hooks. Sofia's heart expanded when she took in the red-and-green-plaid one James purchased for her at the Festival of Lights.

What to make of that?

He wanted to include her.

And it meant a lot.

Gruff, guarded James had a tender, generous heart she found harder to resist every day. Was she falling for him? If so, the sooner she and Javi left for Portland, the better for all concerned.

"Sounds like mantel," Jared mused aloud. "Santle…?"

"You dork." Jewel laughed with more affection than anything else. For all their teasing, the Cades adored each other. Sofia had never met a closer family. "Leave the thinking to the professionals, pretty boy."

Justin guffawed and James chuckled, too. Jared rolled his eyes. "I'll take that as a compliment."

Joy pointed again. A log popped and a shot of red-yellow-orange flame rose inside the chimney.

"*Grease*!" called Jewel.

"That's not even a Christmas movie." James cracked another almond for Javi and tsked at his sister.

Jewel's thin brows knit. "They didn't do a holiday version of that?"

"Those were the Mary-Kate and Ashley Olsen movies," Jared teased.

Jewel winged a pillow at him. "I never watched those."

"Keep saying it and maybe someone will believe you," Justin insisted. He chomped down on a walnut and the shell splintered in his teeth.

"Who owns the box of those DVDs up in the attic? If not you, then who, Jewel?" James smiled and when his warm, amused eyes fell on Sofia, she grinned right back, the blood in her veins popping and sparkling like champagne, his effect on her just as intoxicating.

"Justin was the one who made me watch them," protested Jewel.

"I broke my arm that summer. What else was I supposed to do?" Justin shrugged, looking completely unrepentant, tough and uncompromising, quite a feat for a cowboy rocking a frilly apron and fangirling over tween flicks. "Plus, they're very talented actresses," he intoned. Solemn.

Everyone hooted at that.

Joy wagged her finger again and the group sobered and quieted. This was, after all, a life-and-death contest.

"Okay. One word. Sounds like…" James mused aloud. He handed Javi another nut without taking his eyes off his mother. "Sounds like…shelf?"

Joy nodded vigorously.

"Shelf…shelf… *Elf*!" Jared hollered and the rest of the group groaned.

"You got it," Joy crowed. She collapsed into the chair behind Jewel and squeezed her daughter's shoulders. "Jared wins."

"Ugh. He *always* wins. I demand a rematch." Jewel leaned her cheek against her mother's hand and gazed up at her with so much love that Sofia blinked fast and pinned her stinging eyes to the ceiling.

The phone rang and Jewel grabbed the cordless off its handset. "Hello? Yes. She's here. Sofia. It's for you."

"Hi, Sofia, this is Dr. Trombley calling. I wanted to quickly touch base with you about your arrival date in Portland."

"Hi, Dr. Trombley." The Cades fell silent, their faces varying from curiosity to outright dismay. James and Joy stared at her with downturned lips, their bodies rigid. "I was hoping to start after the holidays. Would that work for you?"

"Absolutely. My wife's expecting, as you know, and she's ready to leave the front desk as soon as you can make it. Also, my friend has a one-bedroom loft that's available to rent if you'd be interested."

"Rent?" she echoed faintly. James's eyes burned into hers.

"Or do you already have a place lined up?"

the doctor asked. "It's rent-controlled, and since I can guarantee your employment, my friend only needs a one-month deposit, which I'd be happy to take care of for you."

"That's so kind of you…"

"Just paying it forward. I was raised by a single mother. I know how hard it can be without support."

Sofia felt the collective weight of the Cades' stares, *their* support… She wasn't alone here.

"Thank you, Doctor. That sounds wonderful. I'll see you in the New Year, then. Happy holidays." She set down the phone.

"Good news?" Jewel asked.

"Yes," Sofia said slowly, dragging the words off her tongue. She felt James's eyes on her. "My job's waiting and so is a place to stay."

"Good news." Jared clapped James on the back. "Right, bro?"

James forced a smile that didn't reach his eyes. "I'm glad for you, Sofia." Then he hurried into the kitchen.

"Now…about that rematch," Jewel said.

Jared rose. "Can't. I've got plans."

"Who's the hot date?" Jewel nudged him with her boot as he traipsed by. "Miss Snowflake?"

For some reason, that made Jared's stride falter. "No. It's Amberley."

"Well, hell's bells. Why didn't you invite her over here?" Jewel demanded. "She was my friend first."

"She's your only female friend—admit it."

Jewel ducked her head. "Me and pedicure parties don't exactly go together."

"They're both barrel racers," James informed Sofia, returning from the kitchen and settling beside her again. "Jewel's been jealous of Amberley since she lost the state championship to her years ago."

"That's a flat-out lie!" Jewel declared. Heated.

Jared grabbed his brown hat off a hook. "Night, all." A blast of cold air ripped inside as he eased open the door and headed out.

"Still don't know why he didn't invite her over," Jewel groused. She snatched the nutcracker from Justin and plunked down beside the bowl again.

"'Cause maybe he wanted to be alone with her," Joy observed quietly. "Here, Clint." Clint's ears flicked at her coaxing call. With a curled-tongue yawn, he stretched forward, flopped to the ground and lurched Joy's way.

"Alone? Those two? Whatever for?"

James met Sofia's eye for a beat too long. Heat flared in her cheeks, then blazed when she noticed Joy's, Jewel's and Justin's speculative gazes on them both.

"Well. There's this little thing called the birds and the bees." One side of Justin's mouth cranked up in his marauding pirate smile.

James clamped his hands over Javi's ears. "Little pitchers…"

Justin shrugged. Jewel frowned. "Amberley's got more sense than to join Jared's girl-of-the-month club."

Joy rubbed Clint's ears. "The right gal could make him give up all of that. Amberley's special."

"We should invite all our neighbors over." Jewel sat up straight and her braids whipped as she looked around the group. "Have our annual Christmas party again this year."

"We talked about it at the board meeting. You know why we stopped putting it on." James's gaze settled on Jesse's picture.

Jewel bit her lip and nodded. "Sure. Sorry, Ma."

"I'd love to have it again," Joy said, her face buried in the side of Clint's neck.

"I want a party!" Javi leaped off the couch and slid in his stocking feet to the disco tree. "Do we get to dance?"

"Lots." Joy joined him and took his hand

in hers. She twirled him around and around. "And we sing."

"Tons of eating, too," Jewel added. She dropped into Javi's spot on the couch and propped her feet on the coffee table. "Ma used to make ten different kinds of Christmas cookies. It's Carbondale's event of the season. Used to be, anyways."

"We need to introduce Javi to everyone," Justin added.

"It's not possible," James said. Stern. "Ma can't put on an event that big with her wrist still healing."

Joy's and Javi's faces wore matching expressions of disappointment. "It'd be a big undertaking," Joy said, slowly, her eyes on Sofia as she spoke. "Invitations to address. Shopping to do. Decorating. Cooking. Baking."

Sofia's heart pounded against her eardrums. She'd love to help and give this wonderful family a party to remember. An event that Javi would never forget, either. Could she do it? She'd never been able to see a large project through before. Anytime she'd tried, she'd ended up feeling like a bigger failure than ever.

But NA had taught her not to fear setbacks or hide from defeat. Making mistakes was how she learned. Real problems arose when you didn't try at all.

"I'll do it," she volunteered, then smiled wide, with more confidence than she felt in the face of James's sudden, fierce frown.

"SOFIA?" JAMES PROMPTED AGAIN and she looked up from the notepad she'd been clutching since her offer yesterday to resurrect the family Christmas party.

"I'm sorry. What was the question?"

Sofia's dark brows slanted together over long-lashed eyes. Her golden skin, highlighted by a cream cowl-neck sweater, glowed with some internal light of its own. She drew his eyes, his thoughts, his heart—he'd admit it—like a moth seeking warmth on a cold, chill night.

"We were asking if you'd completed an expenditure budget for the holiday party," James asked. He rolled the pen in front of him on the boardroom meeting table, back and forth, back and forth, anything to keep himself from staring too long at Sofia, especially since his family now seemed to be catching on to his growing feelings.

"An expenditure budget? Like a shopping list?"

He closed his eyes briefly. Putting on a party for over a hundred neighbors in just a week was no easy feat, especially for someone with little experience. Why hadn't he spoken up when she'd offered to take over the party planning last night?

Because you've grown to trust her, a voice inside whispered.

You want to see her succeed.

If she failed, would the progress she'd made disappear? Gone was the insecure woman who'd flailed against any suggestion or criticism. In her place stood a woman whose growing confidence, strength and steadiness disarmed and enchanted him. He didn't worry anymore about her going to Portland in terms of providing a stable home for Javi.

No.

His worries about her departure stemmed from a selfish motivation.

He wanted her and Javi here.

Period.

They'd become family to him. Yet he wasn't in any position to convince Sofia to stay when every minute alone with her tempted him to give in to his growing affection. He'd refused his brother's pleas to come home. The last person who should ever benefit from Jesse's tragedy was him.

Despite the below-freezing temperature outdoors, a laboring woodstove in the corner kept the air crackling hot. He yanked the collar of his thermal shirt away from his warm neck.

"An expenditure budget means prices for each of the items you need to purchase," his mother said. "I can help you with that."

Sofia's shoulders lowered and she let out a breath. "Thank you." She reached across the table for the pitcher of sweet tea that sat beside an enormous box of chocolates and poured herself a glass. The fluid spilled a bit down the side of her glass, he noticed, her hands shaky.

"What about decorations?" Crinkling sounded as Jared, a fast-food junkie, peeled back the wrapper from a cheeseburger. "Need any help there? I can get anything you need."

"I could use a hand setting up, but I believe Joy mentioned decorations in the attic."

Joy nodded. "And my recipes. I still need to get those out for you."

Jewel sighed heavily. "I can help bake."

At the loud chorus of noes, Jewel slunk

down in her chair and crossed her arms over her chest. "Well, don't say I didn't offer."

"Duly warned," James drawled, enjoying how easy it was to rile his spitfire sister, especially when he sat a safe distance away.

Jared tipped his hat. "The fire department thanks you for staying out of the kitchen."

"And the ER's also grateful since we won't be showing up with food poisoning." Justin smirked.

Lightning fast, she swatted each brother in the shoulder and their laughter turned into *ow*s.

In the bright day outside the window, the wind was picking up. It sounded like wide country wind, barreling down long, straight miles with nothing to stand in its way, as if the ranch was standing high in the middle of empty nowhere. Yet here with his family, with Sofia, he felt like he was exactly where he wanted to be.

"Speaking of punch," Jewel continued with only the slightest twist to her mouth, "I can handle that."

"Sure looks that way," Justin grumbled, rubbing his arm.

Well. Served him right, James thought. You messed with Jewel, you got the paws.

"That's appreciated, Jewel." Sofia turned her glass of sweet tea in her hands, watching the light play on the surface of the amber fluid.

"Jack can play Santa." His mother's eyes glowed. "He's bringing Dani home."

"Think he'll pop the question?" Jared ripped open a packet of ketchup and squirted red on the edge of his wrapper.

"He'd be an idiot to let Dani get away," Jewel vowed. Murmurs of agreement circled the table. They all liked the dude-ranch stable manager who had managed to wrangle his wandering older brother.

"How's the guest list coming?" James asked when the room quieted. "Where are we on that?"

Sofia's large eyes came up, wary. "I've been going through your Christmas card mailing list and the contacts on everyone's phones. I'll have it finalized soon."

"Don't invite all of the girls on Jared's phone," Jewel warned. She leaned across the table, studying the chocolates. After selecting one, she bit it in half, grimaced, tossed it back, then selected another.

"I second that," Jared concurred after swallowing a mouthful of burger.

"Will you run the list by me before sending invites?" James checked.

"Sure," she mumbled, sounding anything but. His concern rose. Was she getting in over her head?

"Want me to put together a party playlist?" Justin offered. He linked his fingers over his head and stretched backward, setting his chair creaking.

Sofia drew tight lines in the condensation on her glass. "Sounds great."

"Metallica isn't exactly holiday music," Jared countered. He balled up his sandwich wrapper and winged it across the room where it dropped neatly into the garbage can.

Justin lifted an eyebrow. "Speak for yourself."

"I hadn't really thought about music." Sofia flipped through what looked like pages and pages of scrawled writing. Concern pinched the corners of her eyes, and there was a seriousness to her mouth that belied her casual tone.

"And we'll need to make sure that we have some gluten-free and peanut-free options," Jewel prompted. She examined another chocolate and scraped the top with her fingernail before putting it back and reaching for another. "Who puts jelly in chocolate? Ugh. Oh. And the Harris kids are allergic to like everything, right?"

"And Mrs. Finley's lactose intolerant, so we'll need to keep that in mind with the appetizers." His mother tried to catch Sofia's eye.

Sofia nodded vigorously, shoved back her hair and scribbled fast without looking up.

"For the ham, talk to Mr. Burton. He sells fresh," Justin mumbled around the toothpick clamped between his teeth.

"Ham?" The question was natural enough, but all of a sudden her voice was full up with things James couldn't catch, and the flash of her wide eyes beneath her hair was too fast and too intent.

Jewel sniffed another chocolate piece. "Caramel!" She popped it in her mouth. "We need ham for the dinner course." Her cheeks bulged as she chewed.

"Dinner course?" Sofia echoed. The corners of her mouth drooped.

"Can't have the dessert course until we eat our supper." Ketchup dripped from one of the French fries Jared dunked, then brought to his mouth. "Right, Ma?"

"Right. Now, Sofia, I don't want you to

worry about making all ten kinds of my Christmas cookies."

"What about the rum cake?" Justin leaned forward. Everyone knew Justin loved rum cake with a passion that nearly surpassed his love for his Harley.

"And somebody needs to make the bread pudding." Jewel pointed a half-chewed chocolate. "I can—"

"Nooooooo…"

She shrugged, looking more relieved than offended. "Then put me down on the decorating committee with Jared."

Sofia nodded jerkily, as though her mind and her body had drifted apart somehow and weren't listening to one another.

"And I'll help write out the invitations," Joy contributed. Then she glanced down at her sling. "Not sure how good my writing will be, though."

"You can apply the stamps," Sofia said, her voice steady, but he could see her knee jiggling beneath the table and glimpsed the extra bit of white all around her eyes.

"How about lights…special effects?" Justin rubbed his hands together, as excited as ever about anything that might cause a major insurance claim.

"Like…?" Sofia's eyes moved to him, dark and doubtful.

"We used to have fireworks. I can get those." Jared scrounged in the bottom of his bag and fished out a couple of limp fries.

Sofia nodded and wrote. "Okay."

Though she didn't sound okay—not that his excited family, too focused on the party, noticed.

For quite some time, he'd been seized by a heightened awareness around Sofia, as if he alone observed her more closely than others. The way her left eye twitched a bit when she got nervous or upset. How her expressive hands revealed more than her words. The relieved and grateful expression she wore whenever someone approved of something she'd done or said. How she put everyone first. The lengths she took to make people happy and at ease, though she was never either of those two things herself.

"So Jared and I are decorating, Ma is doing stamps, Justin's blowing himself up." Jewel licked the chocolate from her fingers one by one, catlike. "And Sofia's doing everything else?"

Sofia swallowed hard.

"No, she's not." He spoke up and all eyes swiveled to him. "I'll be helping, too."

"And what's your job?" Jewel demanded, skeptical.

Sofia watched him, steady-eyed, her wariness gone. He admired her determination in taking on this challenge, no matter what they'd thrown her way at today's meeting.

"I'm going to do anything Sofia tells me to do."

Her surprised smile warmed him right down to his boots.

CHAPTER FOURTEEN

"WE NEED *HOW* many bags of chocolate chips?"

Sofia stopped scanning her shopping list (more of an illustrated guideline) and glanced over at James. Well over six feet, broad shoulders filling out a rugged jean jacket over endless, denim-clad legs and scuffed boots, his head encased in a dark brown cowboy hat that accentuated his handsome face, he oozed masculinity in the baking aisle's feminine midst.

Lots of appreciative female glances zoomed his way, more than a few from Sofia. With his hands shoved deep in his pockets, his weight shifting from boot to boot, his jaw tense, he appeared utterly uncomfortable surrounded by rainbow sprinkles and colored frosting tubes. Seeing über-controlled, uncompromising James out of his element softened her toward him, disarmed by discomfiture.

Not that looks were all of it. Not even close. The more she'd gotten to know James these past couple of weeks, the more she appreciated the layers beneath his hard-bitten facade. The fact that he'd followed through on his surprise offer to help yesterday and accompanied her party shopping made him someone she could count on—a man of his word. So very different from her father after all, whom she could never depend and lean on, especially in her darkest times. She'd never known a tough, loyal, principled person like James before, and she very much hoped that he might be starting to respect *her*, too.

Doubt nibbled on the edges of her happy bubble. Had he joined her simply to help or because he didn't trust her to get the job done properly on her own?

"We need ten bags of chips."

"We *don't* need ten," he refuted with the absolute certainty of a man who'd never done a day's baking in his life. His boots clomped on the store's glossy tiled floor. Overhead, long rectangle fluorescent lights cast the vast, two-story space in grayish-blue hues and a piped-in, instrumental rendition of "Rudolph the Red-Nosed Reindeer" filled the stagnant air. She shivered inside her parka every time the automatic front door swished open.

As he drew close, she breathed in his subtle

scent: leather, clean male skin and an undertone of something spicy that made her toes curl in her boots. "We need at least three bags for the chocolate chip cookies, four for dipping the almond crescents and another three for the fudge."

Tingles of awareness shot up her arm where his shoulder brushed hers. "I thought the white chips were for dipping."

"We dunk the Oreo balls in white chocolate," she said, as patiently as she could. Honestly, if not for the aggravation, she'd feel a little giddy at how the tables had turned. Suddenly, she'd become the responsible one, explaining plain facts to Mr. Authority-on-Everything James. All her life, she'd been labeled a failure, the person who didn't follow through, who left when the going got tough.

The loving, generous Cades, however, inspired her to try harder, drawing on her experience working for a catering business. Plus, with James, she had something to prove. She wanted him to see her as a capable woman he could trust. Count on. Why exactly, she hadn't a clue.

Or at least not one that she'd admit to.

Everything was set for her Portland move. With the money Sofia saved from her care-giving work with Joy, her future now promised the fresh start of her dreams. So why wasn't she more excited about it?

Her eyes drifted to James.

"Then what were the butterscotch chips for?" His thick brows met over his nose as he scanned her scribbled notes.

"Magic bars." She snapped her fingers. "Shoot. I guess I mean eleven bags of chocolate chips since we need some for those, too."

"What else is in a magic bar?" he asked, wary.

"Coconut flakes, sweetened condensed milk, graham cracker crumbs... It's all on the list."

The overhead PA system crackled and a disembodied voice asked for managerial assistance at a front register.

"This list?" He pointed a calloused finger at her scribbling and doodling.

She did her best to will the heat in her cheeks to subside. "Yes."

"Thought you were allergic to lists." One eyebrow rose.

"Maybe I've grown to appreciate them..."

He smiled slowly, eyes gleaming. "Wore you down, didn't I?"

"Like pneumonia." She sighed dramatically, full of fake despair, enjoying this developing comradery between them. "No. The plague."

They shared a laugh and then she sobered. What was she doing? She needed to resist her growing feelings for James, not flirt with him, for goodness' sake.

"Is this some kind of shorthand?"

"It's more conceptual. Kind of like a graphic novel."

Since she didn't have patience for much reading and writing, this was the best she could do...and so far, it'd worked. It might not be a traditional method, but she was finding her own way and it filled her with satisfaction. To her surprise, she liked event planning. Had she stumbled, at last, onto something she might be good at?

"You certainly got creative with the spelling. And some of these calculations are a bit off." Despite his teasing tone, she stiffened, the shame of her lack of education washing through her and dousing her budding excitement. After a moment, he waved a hand in front of her face. "Sofia?"

"I didn't graduate high school, okay?" She was done with hiding every bad thing in her past. It only festered and filled her with fear.

James gaped at her. "I—I—"

Before he could finish, a toddler careened down the aisle clutching a glass jar of maraschino cherries. "I want it!" he wailed.

"Timmy, get back here!" hollered his mother.

Instinctively, she and James fanned out, blocking the child's path. The moment he crashed headlong into James's legs, Sofia dropped to her knees and caught the jar inches from the hard floor.

"Thank you!" huffed the mother. The metallic wheels of her cart creaked and wobbled as she neared.

"No problem, ma'am." James smiled and Sofia coughed to break up the trance the woman seemed to fall into as she stared and stared and stared at the gorgeous cowboy.

Giving herself a small shake, she took Timmy's hand in hers. "You two certainly know what you're doing when it comes to kids."

She waggled her fingers at them, then strolled away, leaving them openmouthed and staring at one another. The stranger had a point, Sofia thought, and her lips lifted at the corners.

James's answering smile began on his full

lips, then traveled upward, lighting up his eyes, making them glow. Her heart squeezed. They made a good team, much better than she and Jesse had. She ducked her head and ran unseeing eyes down her list again, singed by guilt over the thought.

Despite Javi's question the other night, James would never be a father to him. That role belonged to the man she'd kicked out of her son's life without a second chance: Jesse. James was only an uncle to Javi and could be nothing to her. It just wasn't right, no matter how she wished it so.

This was the price she must pay for not facing her addiction issues until now. If she hadn't been so intent on sweeping them under the rug, she could have stood by Jesse and gotten him the help he'd needed. And if she had, he'd be here beside her instead of down deep in the earth.

Would fun-loving Jesse have made her happier? Maybe. But she'd been younger then. More carefree. Now she appreciated a mature, world-worn man like James, a cowboy who'd been tested and honed by life's hardships, like she had. Her feelings for James ran deeper and were more complicated than anything she'd felt for Jesse. James challenged her, got her thinking, made her melt and then drove her crazy…like right now, basically. He squinted down at her list and his nose flared.

"Carbondale has a place where you could get your GED," he said without looking up. "I enrolled Jesse once."

"I won't have enough time." Though she did appreciate him not judging her as she'd imagined he would. "I can look up classes in Portland."

"Okay." A sigh escaped him. "So why do we need lemon juice concentrate and fresh lemons?" he asked.

Men.

There was a world of difference. A universe, even.

"Because they're not the same thing."

"How so?"

"One's concentrated."

"Can't you just add more fresh lemon?"

She didn't even bother holding in her long sigh. "Wasn't your promise to do anything I wanted?" An elderly woman nodded politely when Sofia angled her cart to let her through.

James's lips twisted. "'Within reason' was a silent, implied caveat."

She shrugged, tossed the yellow plastic container of lemon juice in their heaped basket and wheeled the cart around a corner and down another aisle. "'If a tree falls in the woods and no one hears it,'" she quoted over her shoulder.

"So, you don't think you're overbuying?" James said, snatching a tottering box of brown sugar and sliding it deeper into the cart.

She paused to study Keurig coffee flavor packets. "One hundred guests are not going to eat chips and salsa and chocolate chip cookies all night."

"Why not?"

She shot him a disgusted look so he'd understand just how much she valued that "input."

James grabbed a carton of peppermint-flavored Keurig cups and dumped them in the cart, the irony of the pricey extravagance completely lost on him, apparently, when it came to something *he* really liked.

Sheesh.

"Look," he continued. "I know Ma usually goes all out, but this year can be different. More reasonable. You should see the amount of food she ends up giving away at the end. I'm not even sure how many people even want it since she doesn't give them a choice."

"Whatever happened to tradition? Thought you didn't like change. Oh. And that reminds me. We need to buy a bunch of plastic disposable containers."

He maneuvered himself between her reaching hand and the shelf. "Some things should be reconsidered when prudent. Are you listening?"

One side of her mouth rose. "Not really. And we're going to need another cart."

He shook his head and her heart fluttered a bit at that exasperated-amused expression that he usually wore around her. "Is that an order?"

"Yes."

"Any chance you'll consider off-brands at least?"

She mashed her grin into a frown to keep this playful moment from turning too, ah, fun—a dangerous place for her to be in with a man she needed to resist.

"This is the first time in my entire life that I'm holiday shopping and you are not ruining it for me. Besides, your mother was very specific. And the first thing she advised was not to take you with me."

"I think you're a stricter drill sergeant than

me," he observed, then headed to the front of the store.

Thirty minutes and twenty exasperated huffs from James later, they stood in front of the cashier.

"Any coupons?" the young woman asked around a wad of chewing gum.

With a flourish, Sofia produced a thick pile of clipped papers and handed them over.

"Thanks," groaned the cashier, not sounding grateful in the least.

"Where did you— How—" James headed to the end of the conveyor belt and began bagging scanned items.

"I found Sunday's paper, clipped some from there, got on the internet, visited a few sites I used to follow back when Javi and I were—were—"

She stopped, sensing the cashier's attention, realizing what she'd nearly admitted and then, suddenly, that it didn't matter. No. It did matter, in a good way. NA taught her to be proud of her struggles. They'd shaped her into the person she was growing to both like and respect.

"Back when Javi and I were homeless and broke."

The cashier's heavily made-up eyes swerved

to her and filled with tears. "I'm getting evicted," she whispered.

"I'm so sorry," Sofia murmured after a quick glance at the growing line behind them. "But it'll get better. Promise."

"That's what my dad says." The scanner beeped eleven times as she ran the chocolate chips bar code over it.

"You're moving back home with your parents?"

The cashier's jaw lifted. "Just until I'm back on my feet. I dropped out of high school but I'm going for my GED."

"Me, too. Everyone deserves a second chance," Sofia said. "We'll get it this time."

James studied her for a long moment, then nodded, and a warmth spilled from her heart and flowed to fill every inch of her.

What would she have done without the Cades? If she'd gone straight to Portland with insufficient resources, she and Javi would have struggled through another holiday. Now she could give her child the kind of Christmas she'd only ever dreamed of and it meant everything.

Even more important, if not for hard-nosed James, she wouldn't have gone to NA meetings and learned about herself and how strong she really was. He pushed her to try harder, work longer, never quit. He'd held up a mirror until she'd faced herself and changed what she saw.

She couldn't deny anymore that she'd fallen for him, no matter how hard she struggled to deny it.

Electronic beeps droned on as the cashier continued scanning and James and Sofia bagged.

Despite James's grumblings, he'd stuck by her during this marathon shopping trip, streamlining her list, organizing it in ways that didn't demean her or hijack what she'd done. Instead of her old resentment toward anyone who ordered her around, she appreciated his input. Help. Not control or a threat to her sobriety.

And even if it was, she was her own boss, the only one in the driver's seat. No one could threaten her peace of mind and sobriety except herself. If she kept vigilant, didn't bury her head in the sand as she once had, she could trust in her ability to stay clean because she mastered her destiny.

If only James could be a part of it.

Did she dare divulge her feelings in case

he might reciprocate them? Would Jesse forgive them?

"Thanks and good luck!" Sofia called to the cashier after money changed hands.

"Happy holidays!"

Out in the parking lot, James heaved open the back door of his closed-bed truck. "How much money did you just save?"

"Ninety-three dollars and fifteen cents."

He whistled. "Now, that's the kind of change I can get behind."

Unable to resist, she waved a brick of cheddar at him. "You're so cheesy."

He hefted a bottle of Pinot. "At least I don't whine about it."

Their shared chuckle ended when the family's lawyer joined them. Mr. Sloan wore a bright red knit cap with a white snowflake pattern and a matching scarf over his double-breasted gray dress coat. His black dress shoes gleamed against the snow-covered tarmac.

"Just the man I wanted to speak to."

James lifted the last bag of groceries from the cart. "How are you, Mr. Sloan?"

"Good. Good. I wondered if I might have a word in private?"

"I'll just return the cart." Sofia wheeled the apparatus around in the slushy parking lot and headed back to the grocery story, mind working overtime. Did this have to do with James's challenge to her trusteeship of Javi's share in the ranch? It seemed so long ago since he'd voiced his disapproval. Had his opinion changed?

She hurried back and overheard Mr. Sloan saying, "Then I'll tell Chuck to keep the case on the docket. See you in court."

Her heart sank.

Despite everything, James didn't trust her after all.

On the drive home, the humming of wheels on asphalt was accompanied by the occasional swish of a wiper against some flurries.

"You know that has nothing to do with what you told me in the store. Dropping out of high school and all."

Several more minutes flew by before James cleared his throat and said, gruff, "I believe you're very bright. Very caring. You just haven't had the chances others have had in life."

"I want Javi to have those chances...to have everything I didn't," she cried, her voice thick. "Before I had him, heroin was my only love. I had no one to disappoint except myself then, until I had my child."

A breath whistled through her tight lips. "So that's why I'm the best choice to safeguard his inheritance. Cade Ranch is Javi's future. Something he can be proud of. As his trustee, I'll still be a part of his life, and he'll be proud of me, too."

Her last words echoed in the cab. If James couldn't see the best in her, then so be it. His view did not—would not—affect her own. Not anymore.

He reached over and gathered her hand in his. "Your recovery is a lot to be proud of, but this isn't about you. Or us. It's about Javi."

She yanked her hand free, pressed her hot cheek against the frosted window and walled up her wounded heart. He was right. This was about Javi. But it was about them, too. She sensed him thawing toward her. He talked to her differently now, listened to her opinions, looked at her with respect.

But perhaps she no longer needed his approval. Self-respect mattered most of all. Somehow, she'd managed to survive the hardest conditions, had even raised a child the best she could. Maybe she hadn't provided all his school supplies, but she'd made sure he always attended class. She hadn't had a fridge full of groceries, or even a fridge sometimes, but she'd made sure her child ate and had a warm place to sleep.

Those weren't failings, she saw now; they were successes. Successes that proved going to Portland on her own was still the right thing to do. She would not fail, and she and Javi would have a fresh start.

As for her feelings for James, that was an ongoing battle she'd have to wage until Carbondale disappeared from her rearview mirror.

Though she suspected it might never vanish from her heart.

CHAPTER FIFTEEN

A COUPLE OF NIGHTS LATER, as Sofia stacked the last of the glasses in the dishwasher, the cordless phone on the counter rang. Joy snatched it up.

"Hello? Oh, hi, Boyd."

The girlish lilt in Joy's voice made Sofia smile. She hustled over to the drying rack, grabbed a cloth and plucked out a dripping pot. Tonight at dinner, the Cade siblings had indulged in another Loveland gripefest about cattle breaking loose again on Cade land and Travis Loveland, a county sheriff, pulling Justin over for the third time this week. Eventually the heated conversation morphed into pointed remarks about Boyd's precarious financial state and how much he'd appreciate snagging a rich widow right about now, especially after running through his affluent first wife's funds, her cause of death still a source of speculation…

It hadn't missed any of the Cade siblings'

attention that anonymous presents, like the large poinsettia and the box of Belgium chocolates, had been arriving nearly every other day, gifts that made Joy blush and her eyes glow. They strongly suspected the source and their criticisms only escalated with each delivery.

"No. I—I can't." Joy's tone grew serious. "Well. My kids aren't exactly taking to the idea of us too well."

Come on, Joy. Follow your heart. Stay strong.

Sofia stowed the dry pot and reached for a frying pan. Watching Joy and Boyd together after support groups let out filled Sofia with hope. She'd been agonizing that Joy's depression would return when she and Javi left for Portland. Seeing Joy giggle with Boyd, the two of them acting like a pair of infatuated teenagers, standing close, heads bent to almost touching, gave her faith that Joy would stop mourning and start living again for good.

"I know we talked about this, but I think we need to take things slow after all."

Don't give up, Joy.

Giving the skillet a last swipe, Sofia hung it from the pot rack above the granite island, then reached for a small saucepan. Boyd seemed like a perfectly nice guy when Joy introduced them. A man of few words, he had a firm handshake, a proud face and an open, direct stare. Most important, he made Joy happy, which ultimately should matter more to her children than keeping up some family feud. This was Carbondale, twenty-first century. Not Romeo and Juliet times. She hoped Joy wouldn't cave to the family pressure and continue to hide and discourage a man intent on wooing her.

"I want to see you. I—I miss you, too, but—" Joy turned away and Sofia heard only a jumble of words that ended in a tearful-sounding "Goodbye."

Joy joined her at the island, swiping damp cheeks. "Now. Where should I begin?"

"I think you should start by going out with Boyd."

Color flooded Joy's cheeks. "Oh. No. He wants to pick me up to go caroling tonight, but I don't think that's a good idea."

"Why not?"

"It'd cause tension with the children."

"They're hardly children, and it's your life." Sofia stored the dry pan and turned to face Joy. "Only you have the right to control it."

Boy, did it feel good saying that.

Joy closed her eyes and inhaled deeply. "You're right."

"'Do what you feel in your heart to be right—for you'll be criticized anyway,'" Sofia said, repeating a quote she'd heard in NA last week.

"Eleanor Roosevelt." Joy's lashes lifted. "She's my favorite first lady."

"Why don't *you* pick up Boyd?"

A low chuckle emerged from Joy. "Now, that'd be a twist for this old-fashioned gal."

"I kind of like it."

Her eyes twinkled. "Me, too. I'll call Boyd."

A moment later, Joy hung up the phone, her grin wide. "He said yes!" She let out a breath. "I can't believe I'm doing this."

"I'm so happy for you."

Joy picked up her cloth again. "Did I ever tell you how we met?"

"I thought it was at the support group…?"

Joy smiled and the distant look in her eye seemed to carry her back in time. "Boyd gave me my first kiss."

"No!" Sofia gasped, more fascinated than shocked.

"Yes. And don't look so scandalized. We Midwesterners know how to get up to no good sometimes." A smile the likes of which Sofia had never seen before crept across Joy's face, transforming her from mother/grandmother to a bold, audacious younger woman who might have been a hellion once upon a time. She had more in common with her troublemaker son Justin than Sofia had ever suspected.

Joy squirted cleaning fluid on the stove. "We were playing Seven Minutes in Heaven."

"Is that the game when you go into the closet?"

"Right. Basically, you spin a bottle and the person it lands on has to accompany you." Joy had her back to Sofia and her elbow jerked as she scrubbed the stove top with her good arm.

"That's it?" Sofia teased. The cabinet closed with a low thunk as she stowed the pan. Perhaps that was the Midwestern version of "up to no good."

"It?" Joy laughed, pausing, and turned. "No telling what anyone got up to in those closets. Pretty much anything. When my spin landed on the boy I'd had a crush on for years, Boyd Loveland, I was thrilled."

"So he kissed you in the closet?" Sofia fanned her hand in front of her face. "What a player."

"Boyd?" Joy rolled her eyes and returned

her attention to the stove. "Not a chance. He told me straight-out he respected me and then sat in the farthest corner."

Sofia headed to the broom closet. "So, what'd you say?"

"Told him to stop respecting me and just kiss me already." Joy returned to the sink, flipped on the faucet and ran her cloth under the stream.

With brisk sweeps, Sofia gathered the floor debris left behind from the complicated Polynesian meal she'd attempted tonight. *Attempt* being the operative word. "Did it work?"

"I might have had to force myself on him a tad."

Sofia's broom stilled in her hand. "Oh, dear." Joy was full of all kinds of wicked surprises. Up-to-no-good Midwesterners. You had to keep your eye on them, apparently. "Did you start dating?"

"A couple years later, after I wore him down." Joy winked, shut off the faucet and hung the cloth from the side of the sink.

"What broke you two up?"

Joy crouched and held the dustpan. "My husband."

"A love triangle…" The intrigue just kept

coming. Three quick sweeps and the pile of crumbs disappeared.

"He'd always been sweet on me, but I never saw him as more than a friend," Joy said over her shoulder as she dumped the dustpan's contents into the garbage. "Besides, Boyd and I were serious and I wasn't the two-timing type. Then me and Boyd went cliff jumping into a spring-fed ravine. My parents had warned me never to go up there because of the underwater rocks, but I never listened well back then. They were always lecturing me about something or another, especially about Boyd. They didn't approve of me dating an older boy. Said he was too reckless. Wild."

The mischievous smile playing on Joy's lips had Sofia guessing Boyd had been the tamer one in the relationship.

"Did you get in trouble for diving?" Sofia picked up a serving platter and ran it under the faucet again when she noticed she'd missed a couple of spots. "Did they forbid you from seeing him again?"

Disappointment deepened the faint lines around Joy's mouth. She leaned a hip on the countertop beside Sofia. "Worse. I landed wrong and broke my leg and pelvis. I was laid up in the hospital for weeks and Boyd never visited, not once. It crushed me worse than the fall."

"Why didn't he come by? Guilt?"

"I thought so, at least at first. I even wrote him letters but he never wrote back. My only visitors were my parents, a couple of girlfriends and Jason Cade."

"Your future husband."

"Right. Except I was still too hung up on Boyd to have any feelings for Jason. The day I got released, I phoned Boyd but his mother told me he'd joined the Marines and shipped out the day before."

Sofia wedged the oblong platter into the drying rack. "Without leaving word for you?"

Joy shook her head. "It hurt me bad. Over time, I picked myself up, told myself to stop pining for someone who didn't care about me and to learn to love the young man who did. When Jason proposed, I accepted."

"Then what happened?" Sofia was all ears now. Plunking her elbows on the wet countertop, she leaned in closer.

"Boyd came home on leave the following Christmas and asked if he could see me. I didn't tell anyone. Just snuck out and met him by the ravine. When I showed him my ring, he got real quiet. I asked him didn't he want to congratulate me, but he refused, claimed I broke his heart."

Sofia gaped at her. "Huh?"

Joy's eyes grew moist behind her wire-framed lenses. "When I told him he had it wrong, that he'd crushed me by not visiting, by not answering my letters, he turned white. He said the nurses told him I'd left word he wasn't allowed in and they sent back the gifts he'd left. He thought I was mad and wouldn't forgive him for egging me on at the ravine."

A short silence descended, broken by the living room's chiming grandfather clock. After a moment, Joy's chest rose with a deep breath, then, "We just stared at each other for the longest time. Not comprehending. My parents had always been protective of me. They must have wanted to keep away the man they held responsible for nearly killing their daughter."

Joy stared down at her brown suede boots; a perfect match for the belt that spanned her waist. When her eyes rose, they glittered and her eyelashes blinked fast, as if swatting back tears.

"What happened next?"

"I cried. He cried. Then he took my hands

and swore it wasn't too late for us. We could make this right. Then I threw up."

"Nerves?"

"Morning sickness." Joy nodded glumly. "And that was that. When I confessed my suspicions about a baby, Boyd got so still I thought I'd stopped his heart and killed him outright. Then he got up, wished me and Jason well and left without another word. I never spoke to him again until a couple weeks ago, at the support group."

Sofia dropped her hand on Joy's slumped shoulder. "And you got kicked out for talking too much."

"We had a lot to catch up on."

Sofia caught her in a tight hug. "Oh, Joy. You and Boyd deserve this second chance."

Joy squeezed her back and the clean, floral scent Sofia now associated with the woman rose off her neck. "Well, I had over thirty years of happiness with Jason, so maybe I've had all the joy anyone can hope for in life, but, oh, I hope, I really hope, that Boyd and I can have another chance. Deep down, I think Jason would want that for me, too. Though I just don't see how it's possible with our families so at odds. They'll never approve."

A possible solution fired through Sofia.

The Cade family holiday bash was for neighbors and the Lovelands were technically in that category… They had a right to make it onto her guest list, but more important, it would allow both sides to see how happy their parents were together. Surely that would heal this crazy feud.

She pulled back and gave Joy her most reassuring smile. Funny how just weeks ago, she believed herself at fate's mercy. Now she felt as though she could conquer the world and help Joy reignite an old love while she was at it. "Let me worry about this silly family feud, okay? Now hurry up. You've got a hot date waiting on you."

Joy shot her a tremulous smile. "Thank you, honey. I hope you know that, blood or not, near or far, I consider you my daughter. Javi isn't the only miracle that's come to me this Christmas. I love you, Sofia."

Sofia's eyes stung so hard she squeezed them shut. She'd never known a mother's love, that unconditional love she'd only heard about in songs. "I love you, too." She lifted her lids and smiled through her tears. "Now get!"

She stared after Joy long after she'd grabbed her coat and hustled away.

SEATED INSIDE A one-horse sleigh, James assessed Milly, the large white quarter horse attached to its front. His brother Jack had rescued the troubled heel horse a few months ago and brought her home to live out her life on Cade Ranch.

Yet James had sensed right off the bat that Milly longed for more human interaction. She poked her head out of her stall first thing when he entered the barn each morning. At feeding time, she'd eventually stopped shying away and had taken to brushing up against him. Taking the hint, he'd begun working with her, bringing Javi along, and the two of them had formed the kind of fierce bond that only a child and horse could make.

When Milly finally accepted a bit, he'd begun hitching her up, and now at last he had enough faith to take her, Javi and Sofia out for a spin. His heartbeat drummed in his ears when Sofia appeared through the front door, hastily zippering up the white parka that contrasted with her dark coloring. She'd been a marvel these past few days, executing party planning tasks with an efficiency he never would have expected when they'd first met. Sure, her unorthodox methods still made little sense to him, but that wasn't the point. They worked for her.

By stepping back, James allowed her to take the lead, and she more than rose to the occasion. It challenged his deepest conviction that he needed to control everyone and everything. He was only one person. Trying to be everywhere took its toll and consumed him. It left him lonely and without free time for fun, like this: taking a moonlit sleigh ride with a beautiful woman and the child he'd grown to love as his own.

"That's the North Star!" Javi shouted and Sofia passed him over to James. She angled her chin upward but the only heavenly object he had eyes for was Sofia. With her hair loose and tumbling from beneath a white knit cap, her cheeks pink and her lips rosy, he itched to sweep her into his arms, to lay her down against the fur blanket and kiss her senseless, kiss her until they both lost their minds and their hearts.

Though he knew down deep that he'd already lost his heart to her long ago, maybe from that first night they'd spoken on the porch when she'd alternated between defiance and vulnerability. He hadn't seen her as some wounded dove to rescue. No. He understood right off that, despite her hardships, she stood proud. Fierce. A woman who'd struggled all her life and never quit. A fighter in spirit and deed, and he'd grown to love that about her.

Had grown to love her.

"Uncle James has been teaching me."

"Yes, he has," Sofia murmured and her appreciative gaze fell on him, smattering the dry cracks in his heart with droplets of happiness.

James settled Javi, then reached down and helped Sofia up into her seat. Javi wedged himself between them. James threw the covering across their laps and lightly snapped the reins. Milly moved forward smoothly, the bells on her harness jingling, and the runners glided over the packed powder covering the moonlit field.

"Do you like our surprise, Mama?"

"I do."

"Uncle James said you needed a break from all of your hard work."

They exchanged smiles over Javi's head. "Thank you."

Heat crept up James's neck, despite the chill, windless night. "Also wanted to introduce you to Milly."

"Milly?" Sofia's delicate eyebrows rose.

"She's my horse!" Javi bounced up and down on the bench, then stilled. "Uncle James says I can keep her if you say so."

James maneuvered Milly around a large boulder and caught Sofia's nod out of the corner of his eye. "Of course. But you can't bring her to Portland."

"She'll be here when you visit." Despite his best efforts, James heard a tinge of desperation enter his voice. The need to know when they'd return shocked him.

In fact, he wished they'd never leave. Given his overwhelming feelings for Sofia, though, he wouldn't last much longer without speaking them and betraying Jesse. If he won Sofia's heart, it meant taking it from Jesse, who'd already lost his life because of James's poor actions.

No.

He had to keep on resisting until they left.

An owl hooted from a nearby tree and Milly's hooves pranced in the snow, the silvery notes of her swaying bells singing to the stars.

"Can we visit soon?" asked Javi. When they passed a copse of spruce trees, Javi grabbed a low-hanging branch, showering them with needles and snow, perfuming the air with the fresh, sharp scent.

"Maybe in the summer."

James's heart sank. That'd be half a year. Forever.

"But Milly's going to miss me!" James blocked Javi from grabbing at Milly's swishing tail.

"She has other horses to play with."

"She only likes me and James."

"I'll play with her," he assured the child in terms Javi could understand. Although the truth was, without regular work, Milly might slide backward again and become more reclusive than ever.

"Grandma will miss me!"

"She will."

"Uncle Jared said he's going to teach me how to tie a tie. He said I'm going to be a ladies' man."

James smiled. "I agree."

"But I don't like girls."

"You will someday, bud. Trust me." Sofia's eyes fled his and the small, sweet curve of her lips enchanted him.

"Aunt Jewel said she'd teach me to barrel race, but Justin said that's for sissies 'cause he's a bull rider. Can I ride a bull?"

"No!" James and Sofia exclaimed at once.

Javi shrugged and snuggled in deeper between them. His eyes began drifting closed. "Uncle James says Milly's a roper and he's going to teach me how to rope so we can be a team."

"I like that idea, sweetie."

"How come we have to leave, Mama?"

"I have a job in Portland."

"Can't you work here?"

"When Grandma gets better, the Cades won't need me anymore."

I'll need you, James thought.

He urged Milly up a small knoll and fought back the desire to tell her just how much the Cades would still need her. His mother hadn't spent a day in bed for weeks and he worried her progress would disappear right along with Sofia.

As for him, he'd grown to need Sofia and Javi, too. He no longer spent sleepless nights tossing and turning, agonizing over what-ifs. Instead he woke energized, excited about what the day ahead held…relying on the fact that Sofia and Javi would be a part of it.

"Will you get fired again?" Javi's quavering voice filled James with concern. No child should ever have adult worries like that. James wished he could compel Javi to stay on Cade Ranch. He'd ensure his nephew never worried about or wanted for anything again in life. And that went for Sofia, too. In a perfect world, he'd sweep her off her feet and care for her the rest of her days. She'd already survived enough hard times and deserved nothing but peace, joy and love.

Could he give those to her despite his guilt about Jesse?

James sensed Sofia retreating against the soft, padded seat back. "I won't lose my job again."

"But you always—"

"It's not going to happen," Sofia said, fierce. "Ever."

"I don't like Portland." Javi's voice grew muffled and his head lolled a bit against James's chest.

"You have to give it a chance."

"I like it here," he said through a huge yawn.

James peered at Sofia's beautiful profile as she stared at the dark outline of the mountains ahead. "I do, too."

Silence reigned for a few moments as they drifted over the snow, Milly carrying them farther and farther from civilization and into another world, one that seemed to lose the rules of his regular life and transformed the moment into something magical.

"Is he asleep?" James asked, staring down at the top of Javi's bobbing head.

"I think so. Thanks for this. It's lovely."

And it was. With the fir trees laden with snow, the white-capped mountains outlined against a star-studded sky, the ground a glittering, crystalline surface, he was more awed than ever by the land he shepherded.

For so long, he'd thought his job was to keep out others, to protect and maintain this world, this way of life, to preserve it. Yet Sofia had turned those notions, and his life, upside down and he was a better man for it. A lucky man for having Javi in his life.

And Sofia.

Did he dare share his feelings with her? Could she reciprocate them? And if so, did they deserve to find joy together, through Jesse's loss?

The questions ate at him.

"You're doing a great job organizing the party."

She turned, startled, eyes wide and unblinking. And there was something off about her mouth. The way it shook just a bit. "Thank you."

It surprised him how his simple words affected her. Didn't she believe she deserved praise? Understand how amazing, incredible, special she was?

Especially to him.

"I mean it."

Yet you still don't trust her with stewardship of Javi's trust, mocked a voice inside. Guilt cramped his gut. He'd love nothing more than to believe he could count on Sofia, but he just wasn't all the way there.

"What about the invitations?"

"Technically Christmas is celebrating Jesus's birthday, so if anyone's confused by the balloon and cake cover, they can stay home," he said stoutly.

"I wanted to be different."

He could no more stop himself from reaching out to cup her cheek than he could stop his next breath. "That's one of the things I've come to appreciate the most about you."

Dragging his hand away, he returned his attention back to Milly, who strained slightly as they climbed a steeper incline.

"You don't like different."

"I didn't know what I liked until you and Javi came along." Their breaths synchronized for a moment and frosted white in the dark air. "I thought I had everything figured out until I met you."

"And now?"

"Now I see what an idiot I can be."

"*Can* be?"

"Okay. *Am.*"

Sofia had taught him the importance of empowering people, not controlling them, of valuing them for their contributions as individuals. Others had plenty to offer, even if they didn't exactly follow his way of thinking.

"I'm no prize, either."

He could barely hear her quiet voice despite the winter hush around them.

"Why would you think that?"

"Oh. I don't know." Her red mittens flashed as she gestured. "Addiction. Joblessness. Homelessness. High school dropout. Single parent. Pick one. Any one."

"How about survivor? Outstanding parent? You're always with Javi. He knows he has a mother who loves him. That's more than a lot of kids can say."

In his peripheral vision, he caught her mouth open, then close a couple of times before she said, "My mother died when I was born, and my dad, well, he might as well have been gone, too."

She shivered. James transferred both reins to one hand to wrap an arm around her shoulders. "Tell me about him."

"Nothing about me pleased him. He wanted the perfect daughter, and when I began rebelling, he shut me out."

"How?" He pulled Milly to a halt at the top of a lookout and they gazed down at the valley below, the occasional twinkle of a house light breaking up the gloom.

"I was arrested for drug possession, and since it was my first offense, the judge wanted to be lenient. He gave me a week in jail, then house arrest for six months."

He waited when she stopped speaking. After a moment, she released a long, shuddering breath. "My dad refused to let me serve the time at home."

"He kicked you out?" He blinked at her, stunned.

"Yep. Just walked out of the courtroom without a word. I ended up in a juvenile detention center and he never visited once. The day I got released, I waited and waited on the curb for him to come pick me up. I didn't want to see him again, but where else was I supposed to go? I was just eighteen. A kid. He was the only family I had." Her voice began picking up speed, rushing, tumbling. "I'd left messages on his answering machine, so he knew what time I got out. Still. I didn't budge from that gate until one of the officers finished her shift and offered to give me a ride to a homeless shelter in Albuquerque."

He pulled her as close as he could with a snoozing Javi between them. "I'm sorry."

"I knew he was mad at me. Disappointed. Disgusted, even, but that—that was when I realized he hated me."

"*Hate* is a pretty strong word."

"I wasn't ever good enough or worthy of his love. I guess that's why I…"

"Why?" he prompted.

"Why I never believe anyone can love me. Not even Javi." Her voice grew muffled as she ducked her head and seemed to fold inward, shoulders rounding. "Not if he knew every awful thing about me. The truth."

His heart contracted so hard it hurt. "Javi loves you. That wouldn't change if you told him about your addiction."

"Yes, it would. No one can love the person I used to be."

He opened his mouth and the words *I do* nearly flew out. With lips clamped shut, he breathed in, then out through his nose, thinking hard.

Surely by now, her father must regret turning Sofia aside. Any parent would. Most likely he'd been caught up in the moment, blinded by his anger, stubborn, furious that he'd failed to control his daughter and watched, helpless, as she'd slipped into a world of drugs.

He thought back to his own angry words with Jesse, how he hadn't meant to deny his brother the right to come home so much as he'd wanted to teach him a lesson…and then it'd all gone horribly wrong. If he could have a second chance, a do-over to make that right, he'd take it in a heartbeat.

Perhaps Sofia's father felt the same way.

If James could locate him, invite him to the holiday party, then he and Sofia might make amends. Once her father saw how far Sofia had come, he would forgive her and Sofia would feel good about herself. Worthy. Lovable. See that she was perfect just as she was—not how others expected her to be. And maybe, just maybe, she'd decide she didn't need to go to Portland to prove herself after all.

He might not be free to love her the way he wanted to, but he could love her from afar while still having her in his life. He would be damn lucky for even that much.

"Does your father still live in Albuquerque?"

"Possibly. Why?" When she raised her face, the moonlight cascaded across her lovely features, the sight so beautiful it sucked the air right out of him.

"No reason." Then, after another pause where they listened to the trees rustle and watched the stars appear and disappear above scuttling clouds, he said, "You know, you don't have to be like everyone else to be important."

"Excuse me?"

"People want and need and value you because of who you are. Because of your story. Because of your challenges. That's what makes you unique."

She leaned closer still, lifted her face to his, and her sweet breath rushed across his chin. "James. That's beautiful."

"You're beautiful." And then, unable to help himself, he brushed her lips with a brief, tender kiss before turning Milly around and heading back home.

CHAPTER SIXTEEN

"IT'S LOVELY, SOFIA!"

At Joy's exclamation, Sofia tore her eyes from the transformed feed barn the following day and returned the woman's smile, her heart so light it could float right out of her chest.

Everywhere her eyes landed, the vast, open space captivated her attention—the foam "snow" they'd heaped along the walls and in corners, the rotating "stars" projected on the dark ceiling, the streams of silver snowflakes that fluttered from the rafters and the miniature "forest" they'd created at the entrance with four large artificial Christmas trees, creating a bower for the guests to stroll through. A Narnia movie set couldn't have been prettier or more magical.

"Not too much?"

"There's no such thing as too much when it comes to Christmas. Right, Ma?" Jared swung his mother into a hug, then twirled her around in a quick two-step to the country Christmas tune playing from Justin's DJ table. In a pine-green cable-knit sweater and a chocolate-brown rancher's hat that matched his polished boots, Jared was all smooth, Western cowboy charm.

"Just like you can't be too skinny or too rich." Joy laughed, easing back, slightly breathless. Color ran high in her cheeks and her hazel eyes sparkled behind her glasses.

Since her secret date with Boyd, she'd been full of giddy smiles and faraway looks. It'd thrilled Sofia when Boyd RSVP'd to her last-minute Evite and agreed not to spoil the surprise for Joy. She couldn't wait for the pair to go public with their new relationship at tomorrow's party. She also feared that if any of the Cades knew ahead of time they'd shut down the idea before giving it a chance— especially James. Guilt over hiding it from him rolled heavy in her stomach. He'd labored tirelessly beside her all week. Was she wrong to keep him in the dark?

Joy's smile snared her attention again and firmed up Sofia's conviction. She would not let this wonderful woman spend another holiday without a love of her own.

Sofia would bear the brunt of any anger

and keep Joy from being blamed if need be. The lesser of two evils.

Hopefully, with everyone in a happy, charitable holiday mood tomorrow night, all would be forgiven and the families could at last mend their feud. They wouldn't dare get into a fight at a party, for goodness' sake. It wasn't like they were bloodthirsty heathens. Plus, Joy and Boyd deserved this second chance with their children's support.

If only Sofia's new beginning didn't entail her leaving the people she'd grown to love. Especially James.

"And no one can ever ride too well," Jewel added, stopping to link her arm through Sofia's. A scarlet head scarf, flecked with the paint she'd used to create the "stained glass" winter scenes she'd created on the windows, concealed all but the ends of her mahogany braids. James had staked spotlights in the ground beneath the windows to make each picture glow to life.

"Or eat enough barbecue." Justin ambled over with his familiar stalking gait, teeth flashing white against his short, dark beard in a rare smile. A faint peppery scent, along with the cold, emanated from his white-dusted leather jacket. The black-and-blue encircling his left eye socket and his red, cut knuckles suggested another barn brawl last night. "Just finished setting up the pit for the pig roast."

"Thanks, Justin. Thanks, everybody." Sofia gazed at the people she now considered family. "I couldn't have done this without you."

Joy slipped an arm around Sofia and squeezed. "We only helped here and there. You and James did all the heavy lifting."

"Where is James, anyway?" Justin asked.

"Look, Mama!"

Sofia's pulse slammed at the sight of her son near the tip-top of a twenty-foot ladder. With tall, broad-shouldered James right behind him, Javi secured a white unicorn piñata that immediately showered glitter on the carefully swept and mopped barn floor. Where had James found that crazy thing? Or any of the outlandish decorations festooning the walls? When Javi suggested a Narnia theme, James had gone all out locating decorations that'd turned this old feed barn into a fairyland.

"It's beautiful!" she called, as was the rest of the room. They'd hauled over the psychedelic electronic tree, which now rotated with a mechanical hum in a far corner. Wrapped presents, which had been arriving for the past couple of days via the Secret Santa Sofia had arranged, were heaped beneath the synthetic branches. Tables bedecked in shining silver coverings and evergreen, pinecone and red-ribbon bowers awaited the dozens and dozens of cookies she and James had wearily finished baking this afternoon. White candles, encased in old-fashioned wrought-iron lanterns, appeared at regular intervals. Sofia could already imagine their ambient glow and vanilla scent when they lit them tomorrow. At the far end, James and Jewel had hauled in the sleigh and glammed it up with red and green garlands for photo ops.

"You two be careful up there!" Joy hurried to the ladder.

Sofia watched her, marveling. She never would have imagined seeing a project through to the end like this before. Yet somehow, she'd managed—hopefully—to arrange for nearly everything: music, food, activities, decorations, invitations. It struck her suddenly that maybe she was good at party planning, bringing families and communities together, the two things she'd never had growing up.

A career like this would complete her in a way she'd never imagined possible. She now understood the value of sticking with something through its ups and downs without a guarantee. While the comfortable, secure medical office job in Portland had its merits, she wondered if event planning was her true calling. If tomorrow went off without a hitch, maybe she should reconsider her future.

"Careful on the way down," she heard Joy cry as James wrapped an arm around Javi as they descended.

She recalled a ranch board meeting where they'd debated renting out this barn for weddings and other events for additional revenue. Could she start her own business here? Give Javi a home on Cade Ranch where he belonged?

Relapse was a real threat and not ever truly outrun. But she'd learned to face it in NA. Perhaps she didn't need to leave Carbondale or reinvent herself to control her worst demons. Maybe she was fine just the way she was. Faults and all.

Her eyes lifted and met James's when his feet hit the ground. The longing she spied in their depths shook her deeply. It matched her own. Did he care for her as she cared for him? Last night, his quick, tender kiss had left her speechless.

Yet now she was full of questions she didn't know if she dared to ask.

Yesterday, she'd confessed a secret so dark and deep she hadn't even admitted it to herself, that her mistakes made her unlovable. Yet James insisted the opposite, that her flaws, her weaknesses, her hardships were her strengths. He made her feel beautiful and worthy and special and she ached to tell him how much he meant to her, too.

"Are you all set?" Jared asked.

When she nodded, his strong arms engulfed her in a quick hug. Then, to her surprise, his brother and sister followed suit. "Thanks for all this," he rasped. "What you've done for Ma—"

"For all of us," Jewel interrupted. "After Jesse, we stopped being a family. You reminded us there isn't anything more important. Made us remember who we were."

"What she said," Justin said, gruff, his eyes squinty and raw. He tipped his black hat. "Much appreciated."

"Oh. No. Really. Thank you for taking me and Javi in. I'm—I'm really going to miss you."

Jewel squeezed the air out of Sofia in another hug. "Me, too. I always wanted a sister. Now we've got each other. Much better than these clowns."

Jared's lips curled. "Yeah. I always wanted a sister, too. Thanks, Sofia."

"What he said," Justin added, then instinctively jerked away from Jewel's possible left arm jab.

"That's the nicest thing anyone's ever said about me," she crowed instead, smile wide and beaming.

"Ah. Come on, Jewel. Everyone knows you're the toughest Cade sibling."

Jewel nodded, pleased as punch. With a wave, the teasing, affectionate trio clomped outside. A burst of frigid air momentarily overpowered the space heaters when they opened, then shut the oversize door.

"Sofia? What's wrong?"

She brushed the damp from her eyes as Joy approached.

"Nothing."

"Nothing?"

"I know this sounds weird, but I've never been so happy and it's making me cry."

Joy rubbed her arm. "I know what you mean, honey."

"I just wish it didn't have to end."

"Does it have to?"

Sofia felt Joy's gaze on her as she studied

James and Javi admiring decorations. "I can't stay here," she whispered.

"Because of James?"

Sofia whirled. Her lips parted, but before she could speak, Joy held up a hand.

"I don't mean to pry, but I can't help noticing the way you two look at each other. You're in love with him."

Sofia nodded, glum. "I've no right to, but... I'm sorry."

"Sorry?"

"I should be here with Jesse. Not James. This isn't the way it was supposed to happen."

"Who's to say what's supposed to happen? What's right? Jesse died—a terrible tragedy—but from that, you and Javi came to me. So maybe life does have a greater plan, an unknowable one, and perhaps it's better that way...not to know. Don't let guilt stop you from finding happiness the way it did for me and Boyd. We've both been widowed for many long lonely years, and if it hadn't been for you bringing us together, we wouldn't have found each other again."

"I hadn't thought of it that way."

"Love brought you here. Don't let it drive you away. Jesse would want you to be happy."

"Am I interrupting?" James's deep voice set her heartbeat soaring.

"Nope." Joy reached up and brushed a fleck of glitter off his cheek. "In fact, I was just offering to put Javi to bed so you two could finish up."

The music filled in the quiet after Joy and Javi disappeared. In the still moment, Sofia was acutely conscious of the rise and fall of James's chest and the faint, spicy scent of his aftershave.

"What would Jesse want you to be happy about?"

She studied him a long moment, terrified to share the feelings brimming inside her. "You."

"Me?"

She ducked her head. "Forget it." Stupid idea. This brave, honesty thing.

James slid his hand in hers, checking her forward flight. "I can't forget it." His tone had turned ferocious. Fierce. His eyes blazed. "I can't forget a single thing about you. The way your gums show just a little too much when you're smiling big and natural. That squinty left eye you get when I've really fired you up. The way you smell first thing in the morning, like warm milk heated with vanilla, and the way you make me feel every time your eyes meet mine."

She stepped closer and twined her other hand in his. Deep inside, her heart drummed. "And how do I make you feel?"

The music shuffled to a slow, dreamy tune and he swept her in his arms.

"Let me show you," he whispered, his thumb roaming over the back of her hand in a sweet, subtle stroke. "Dance with me?"

JAMES PULLED SOFIA closer and urged her backward so that they glided across the sparkling floor. A lush, instrumental tune floated in the air, in his bloodstream, fogging up his thoughts, leaving him free to simply indulge in the magical feel of her moving nimbly against him. He stroked a hand down her spine, then settled it on the sweet curve of her waist. His gaze locked with hers.

"God, you're beautiful," he said, the words hoarse and gruff with the tumbling emotions swelling inside.

When she ducked her head, he gently pressed a fingertip beneath her chin until she lifted her face and met his eyes again. "Please don't hide from me."

"I wasn't. I just feel—feel—"

Their bodies swayed as one, jigsaw pieces fitting where the edges and curves and angles snapped together into something bigger, something unbreakable.

"—so happy," she finished. A tremor shook through her and he tugged her nearer still, his protective instincts rising as they always did around her, the urge to care for her body and soul seizing him. "You make me so happy."

His heart beat a fast tap. "And that's a bad thing?"

"Because of Jesse."

He cupped the back of her head, guided it down to his shoulder and closed his eyes, savoring her warm softness as they slowly twirled. A blast of heat from one of the space heaters curled around their feet. "You want him here."

It was more a statement than a question. Of course she liked his fun-loving, easygoing brother more. Jesse had charmed everyone while James, well... He'd always been the uptight, controlling Cade whom people respected but didn't shine to too exactly.

He'd never minded that role until now, when he desperately wished this woman might return his feelings.

Her glossy black mane swung back from

her face as she tilted it to study him. "No. I feel guilty because I'm glad you're here and not—not—Jesse." Tears welled in her eyes. "That makes me a monster."

He cupped her shaking shoulders and their feet stilled. Something exploded in his chest. His heart maybe. She cared about him. She experienced the same powerful emotions that had taken him by storm from the moment he'd laid eyes on her. "Then I'm one, too, because I want you here, would have wanted you even if Jesse had brought you home, and I'm glad I don't have to compete for you."

She brushed something from his cheek, her touch achingly tender. "I'm not sure it would have been much of a competition."

"We'll never find out, just like we can't change what happened."

The sparkling light reflected in her brown eyes. "No. And maybe we shouldn't wallow in it, either."

He nodded. "Ma's right. Jesse would want us to be happy. He cared about that most of all."

Suddenly, the heaviness that'd been buckling his shoulders since Jesse's death eased. The grief, the remorse he'd been carrying all these years was his own making. Not Jesse's. He saw that now.

Jesse would want him to be happy. And nothing made him happier than Sofia.

And Javi.

"You care about others as much as Jesse did," Sofia insisted and her indignant expression, her defense of him, stirred him deeply. "You just show it differently. I used to believe you wanted to control me because you didn't think enough of me, and maybe that was true at first. Now I know it's coming from a good place. You just want to keep everyone safe."

"Protected," he murmured, touched that she alone understood him. It felt like a homecoming. "I want to be that person for you and Javi. Controlling you or anyone is wrong, but I'll always be the kind of man that looks out for others, especially my family."

"Am I part of your family?" She choked up a bit on the last word. His eyes whizzed to the ceiling and he blinked fast, thinking about her lonely, difficult life.

With every breath he took while on this earth, he'd make it all up to her.

"Yes. More than that, even."

He cupped her face, then bent to kiss her, lips grazing her mouth as gently as he could manage considering how much he ached for her. How out of control she spun him. Sure, he'd wanted this for a long time, but this was all too new, too miraculous to be rushed when he wanted to enjoy every moment.

He kissed her that way for a long time, savoring her sweet taste, exploring every nuance of her mouth. The rightness of this moment shook him like an earthquake, ripping him up inside so it felt like his heart split wide, letting the light rush in. He wanted to take her away somewhere even more private. A mountain retreat where they'd hole up for weeks with nothing but the wild and each other to explore.

But for now, this...

She was warm and sweet in his arms, her kisses tentative at first and then more aggressive as he prolonged them. He relished the feel of her fingers walking up his chest to curve around his neck, nails gently scraping through the hard facade he showed the rest of the world to the man he was beneath.

How fragile a person became, he marveled, when you entrusted your heart to another. Yet he wouldn't have it any other way, even if he could control his feelings for Sofia. She brought him to his knees with one look, yet he'd never felt stronger, more alive than when she smiled at him. It was a strange juxtaposition, this helpless potency she alone drew out of him.

He tunneled his fingers in her loose waves, drawing her in closer still, deepening the kiss. Her legs seemed to turn soft and boneless, but his arms stole around her waist to support her. She trembled slightly.

"James," she whispered as she broke the kiss, her eyes full of the moonlight spilling through the window. "I don't want this to end."

They stared at one another for a moment, the sound of their ragged breathing filling their ears.

"You and me both." He growled the words more fiercely than he'd intended, but it was impossible to imagine ever letting her go, now or in the future.

He bent to kiss her neck in the hollow of her throat and felt her pulse race beneath his lips, his whole body yearning to be closer to her scent, to her softness, her taste. He wouldn't deny himself any longer, not now or ever again.

Tomorrow, at the party, he'd convince her

to stay. *Yes*, that was what he'd do. It would be a great way to end a fantastic evening.

They'd planned everything perfectly.

What could go wrong?

CHAPTER SEVENTEEN

JAMES HURRIED THROUGH grooming Milly, one eye on his watch. The Cade family Christmas party started in just three hours.

"Uncle James, will Mama go to jail?"

James's hand stilled on the horse comb and he turned to peer down at Javi. Blowing softly, Milly sidestepped in the horse barn's main corridor.

"Why would you think that?"

"'Cause she said so." Javi's face was pale, brown eyes wide. "On the sleigh ride. I was sleeping. Then I heard her say it."

James's mind flew back to that evening. They should never have talked so openly in front of Javi, even if they had believed him to be asleep.

"I'm sorry you heard that, bud." He untethered Milly and led her back to her stall. "I promise you've got nothing to worry about."

"But I'm only little." Javi grabbed the feed

bucket and shoveled sweet-smelling corn-meal. "I can't save her from addition."

"Addition?" James snapped off the fau-cet after filling Milly's water trough. Then the word Javi meant hit him. A big word. One Sofia never wanted Javi to know. His gut twisted.

"Do you mean 'addiction'?"

Javi nodded and his dark hair swooshed to cover his blotchy face. "What's addiction?"

Oh. Lord. Here it came.

Javi deserved to know, and Sofia's delay in leveling with him had ended just as James worried it might—with a young child scared and confused.

"Will she do bad things like Daddy?" Javi's voice quavered. "Is she gonna get sick and die?"

James caught Javi tight in his arms and held the trembling boy. No child should suf-fer this way. "No. She won't die."

"But addiction is bad."

James swore under his breath. Javi was his nephew, and if Sofia couldn't bring herself to explain things as important as this, then he would. A mother's wish was important. But what if the parent was incapable of making a decision in the best interest of the child...

a decision in her own best interest, too? Perhaps, once she saw that Javi still loved her after knowing the truth, she wouldn't need to run off to Portland. With no secrets to hide from, they could begin their life as a family, right here.

Starting now.

If James hoped to one day be a father to this child, then he had an obligation to tell Javi the truth. And he wouldn't shirk that responsibility, no matter the cost, though he prayed Sofia would understand.

"Is her addiction because of me? Sometimes I'm too loud. And I don't listen."

"You're not to blame," James said firmly. Poor Javi. He was scared. Confused. "Addiction is when a person can't stop doing something, like when we eat a bowl of chips but then we wind up finishing the bag."

Javi snuffled and leaned back. His eyebrows met over his nose. "That doesn't sound bad. How come you go to jail?"

"Sometimes the things you're addicted to can be bad."

A tear slid down his cheek. "Then Mama could die like Daddy and go up."

"She's not going to die, Javi. Promise."

"But I'm too little to save her. I'm not Batman."

He brushed back his damp hair. "You don't need to be because—"

"I can save myself." Sofia's tight voice cracked through the stable and he whirled, dismayed at the pain distorting her features.

Pain and hurt that he'd put there.

But Javi deserved to know the truth.

Javi raced to Sofia and flung his arms around her waist. He buried his face in her stomach. His voice emerged, muffled.

"Just because you do bad things doesn't make you bad, Mama. I love you."

Her chest rose as she breathed deep before releasing a shuddering sigh.

"Mama?"

"I know, sweetie. I know that now and I love you, too. Come on. Supper's ready and then we've got the party to dress up for."

"Sofia," James called and she pivoted at the door, her shoulders high and jaw tight. "Can we talk?"

"Later. Too much to focus on right now."

He watched her disappear around the corner of the door, torn between forcing the conversation as he would have in the past or letting her go.

In the dimness, the horses nickered and his heart thudded in his ears as he forced himself to stay behind.

To let her be.

Would she come back?

"YES—I WILL MARRY YOU!"

A raucous cheer rose from the party crowd a few hours later, thunderous in the packed room. James clapped and hooted as his older brother, Jack, dressed as Santa, rose from bent knee, swept his girlfriend-now-fiancée, Dani, into his arms and kissed her so passionately the jubilant group whooped even louder.

"Isn't it a miracle?" his mother crowed beside him. "Never thought we'd get Jack home again and now here he is, with a wife-to-be."

"Santa's name is Nick, not Jack," he heard Javi say beside him.

James nodded absently, his eyes scanning the room for Sofia, a strange longing scraping through him. He was happy for his tormented brother who'd finally found the peace he sought after apprehending Jesse's killers and discovering the love of his life six months ago.

Would he and Sofia find that same joy?

"Is she going to be Mrs. Claus?" Javi asked,

pointing at Dani. In a green dress shirt that highlighted the red in her hair, the freckles dotting the upward tilt of her nose and her dancing, mischievous eyes, she resembled an elf. It was easy to see why Jack had lost his heart to the vivacious stable manager who'd enchanted his family from the moment they'd met her.

"You might say so." James dropped a hand atop Javi's carefully slicked back hair.

A clapping Sofia, tucked beside her NA counselor and a slouching teenager from the same support group, caught his attention. In a rose-hued chiffon dress that revealed one smooth shoulder and silver heels that high-lighted her shapely calves and delicate ankles, she knocked the breath clean out of him. She had her hair fixed different and he liked it. Piles of dark curls twisted atop her head, then fell around her long slender neck. She could have stepped right off the pages of some fairy tale. In fact, she'd put any of those princesses to shame, he'd wager.

She was just as beautiful.

And just as remote.

She might as well be hidden in some tower, for all the access he'd had to her this evening.

Since the barn incident, he'd hoped to catch

her alone, but she avoided him, bustling from table to table, guest to guest, ensuring everything went off without a hitch. Not that she need worry. She'd planned the event perfectly.

About an hour ago, the guests began arriving and there'd been nonstop action ever since. From signing the holiday-themed guest book, to posing for pictures on the sleigh, to grabbing plates of barbecue, to dancing to Justin's surprisingly appropriate holiday mix, their chattering, animated neighbors were enjoying old-school Cade hospitality.

"This must be Jesse's boy," someone pronounced in the stern, nasal voice that haunted most of James's childhood. One sidelong glance at the tall, steel-haired woman confirmed his suspicion. Lillian Grover-Woodhouse, the strict principal of their local school.

"This is my grandson, Javi." Joy used the subdued tone she'd always adopted when called down to Mrs. Grover-Woodhouse's office for one of her troublemaking offspring. "Say hello, dear."

"I don't want to call her 'dear,'" protested Javi, turning and burying his face in James's side.

James pressed his lips together to keep from laughing.

"Well!" Mrs. Grover-Woodhouse tutted a moment, nonplussed at this challenge to her undisputed authority in the small community. "I certainly hope he'll be joining us at school soon. It appears it might do him some good."

Javi tipped his head back and regarded her upside down. "My teachers don't like me because I don't bring in paper."

Mrs. Grover-Woodhouse's stern face softened. "Young man, no educator of mine would ever feel that way. We care about all of our children, and we always have enough paper."

"And crayons?"

Her straight shoulders curved as she bent ever so slightly to peer directly into Javi's eyes. "Every single color," she avowed.

"I want to go to school here!" Javi whirled between him and James's mother. "Please, Grandma. Please, Uncle James. Can I?"

"That's up to your mama, honey."

And you, he swore he heard his mother add silently, or he could read it in her eyes, at least, as she studied him with raised eyebrows. She'd been hinting around about him and Sofia and he knew without her needing to spell it out that she'd be thrilled to see them together.

As would he.

He nodded, mind made up. This "let fate take the reins" approach was wearing a hole in his patience. He and Sofia needed to settle things and not waste another moment of the wonderful party apart.

After several minutes exchanging pleasantries and shaking hands, Jack finished crossing the room. His older brother and fiancée seemed to have cornered Sofia beside the punch bowl.

"Congratulations." James gave his brother a quick, one-armed hug, then kissed Dani's cheek.

"Thanks. There's no greater feeling," Jack said without taking his eyes from a blushing Dani.

"We're trying to convince Sofia to plan our wedding here this summer." Dani tore her gaze from her fiancé and smiled at Sofia. "She's done an incredible job with the party."

"I couldn't have pulled it off without James," she murmured, eyes averted.

"He didn't boss you around too much, then?" Jack thunked James on the back hard enough to make the air whoosh out of him.

Sofia's curls swirled as she shook her head. "I wouldn't let him get away with it."

Jack squinted at her, then peered at James before his deep rasp of a laugh emerged. "She's a keeper, bro. Don't let this one get away."

"That's what I'm telling her." He angled his head, hoping to catch her eye.

Look at me.

"And that's not bossy at all," Dani drawled. She ladled punch into a red Solo cup and handed it to Jack.

He swallowed back a laugh. "Of course."

Sofia, he noticed, hadn't even cracked a smile. He shifted closer to her. "Dance with me?" he murmured.

Before she could answer, a loud, chattering group bottlenecked beneath the Christmas tree bower and the room fell silent.

"What are *they* doing here?" Jack slammed down his cup and a wave of punch splashed onto the table.

James's mouth dropped open. The Lovelands. Here. On Cade land. Strolling in like they owned the place, acting as though they had any right to be here.

"I invited them," Sofia said, as calmly as if making a weather observation.

James gaped at her. "Without telling me?"

He'd thought they'd moved past secret-keeping and on to a place of trust.

"I didn't think you'd approve."

"Darn straight."

A dark suspicion grew. Did this have something to do with Boyd's interest in his mother? He and his siblings had worried when mysterious presents began arriving. Since nothing seemed to come of it, however, they'd dropped their fears. Apparently they had been lulled into a false sense of security, never noticing the devil standing on their doorstep. And Sofia had invited him right in.

"Who are the Lovelands?" Dani asked in the tense silence.

"What you call creatures lower than snakes," James hissed.

"Welcome!" His mother's voice rang into the quiet and the crowd parted, making way for her as she advanced on the family. Boyd stepped forward and his giant-sized sons, Daryl, Cole, Travis, Maverick and Heath, moved to flank him, wearing identical scowls, arms crossed over puffed chests. His fair-haired daughter, Sierra, a wildlife veterinarian, peeked over her father's shoulder.

Boyd wore a dark blazer atop a crisp white shirt, gray dress slacks over alligator boots and a bolo tie with a large turquoise stone. His thick white hair was mostly hidden beneath a wide rancher's hat.

He handed Joy a bouquet of red roses and a murmur ran through the electrified crowd. His mother buried her nose in the flowers and her face suddenly transformed, her features smoothing, her expression opening. For an instant, he didn't recognize her. It was like looking at a stranger…or someone he'd forgotten, he hadn't seen her in so long.

It reminded him of how she used to look at his father.

Did she care for Boyd? Love him?

A knot formed in the pit of his stomach. No opportunistic Loveland, seeking to fix his financial woes, would court his vulnerable mother. James wouldn't stand for it.

Sofia dropped a hand on his tensing bicep. "Don't do anything stupid."

"The stupid thing was inviting them in the first place." He clapped a hand to his forehead. "I didn't mean that."

"Yes, you did." Hurt weighed down her quiet voice.

Boyd bowed, then extended a hand to Joy. Just as the pair reached the dance floor, the music zipped off. Justin's teeth appeared in a grizzly-bear snarl.

"Play the music!" hollered one of the Loveland brothers. Daryl, James supposed, the only mouthy one in the taciturn bunch.

The Lovelands were known in the community as stubborn, grudge-holding, silent types, men of action, not words. Whenever anyone needed a hand, the Lovelands showed up. They didn't have much to donate beyond their time, but they gave it generously; he'd admit that much.

"Just like a Loveland," Justin taunted, stalking from behind the DJ table. His eyes glittered. "Coming here and acting like you own the place when you can't even afford yours."

"You take that back, you son of a—" Daryl strode forward and then a scuffle broke out, a flurry of shoves followed by swinging fists. It happened so fast, James barely had time to reach the melee, Jack hot on his heels.

Before he arrived, Daryl took an uppercut to the jaw from Justin, stumbled, then crashed into a decorated tree. The tinkling sound of breaking ornaments could just be heard over the shouting and cussing.

Jared ducked to avoid Maverick's massive fist, then pummeled the Goliath in the stomach. Unaffected, steel-man Maverick put Jared in a headlock and the two twirled around like enraged bulls, knocking over the cookie table. Its contents slid to the floor in a shower of crumbling bits.

Jewel leaped on Maverick's back. "Let him go!" she shouted, boxing his ears until Maverick crashed to his knees and released her dazed brother. Jewel raised a heavy boot, her face hard-boiled and bright red. Before she could stomp Maverick, Heath Loveland grabbed her from behind and carried her, howling and thrashing, from the violent tussle.

Travis, a county sheriff, brought his phone to his ear as James and Jack waded into the melee.

"Knock it off," growled Jack, bodily separating Justin and Daryl.

Jewel managed to free herself from Heath, then headbutted her captor hard enough to make him career into the punch bowl. Glass and red sprayed onto the shocked guests.

"And stay down!" she yelled, bloodthirsty, fist cocked, at a wide-eyed Heath.

James helped a staggering Jared to his feet and was rewarded with a solid hit to the nose from Maverick. Well. At least he spared Jared's pretty face.

"Jewel! Boys!" His mother waded into the ruckus. "Stop! This is unacceptable."

"And I'm taking everyone down to the county jail," Travis shouted as he pocketed his cell phone. A siren sounded in the distance, followed by another, shocking them all into silence.

"I'll help," Jack added, grim. As a Denver deputy sheriff and the older brother of a wild bunch of siblings, he didn't look the least bit ruffled, despite the white beard now dangling from one ear.

Within minutes, officers processed the scene and led most of the Lovelands and Cades out to squad cars. The horrified guests hurried away, thanking a red-faced Joy for an "entertaining" evening. James surveyed the party ruins. A tornado couldn't have done more damage. Cookie pieces and sticky punch coated the floor. A crystal bowl that'd been in his family for generations lay in glittering shards. Haphazardly leaning or fallen Christmas trees partially blocked the exit.

Everything. Everything he'd worked, striven, sacrificed for—all his efforts to protect his family—had fallen apart at Sofia's hands tonight. They were humiliated in front of their neighbors and friends. He shouldn't have trusted Sofia so completely. Had been a fool to believe he could cede control to someone else, especially an outsider.

"I'm sorry, Joy," he heard Boyd say as he led her outdoors. Javi scampered after them.

A soft hand fell on his arm. "Let them be, James."

He shook loose. "You had no call to do this."

"James…" she pleaded but he pivoted and stalked away, fuming.

"We'll talk when I get back from the station," he bit out over his shoulder, then exited, nearly bumping into the teenager he'd spied with Sofia earlier.

"Cool party," the youth observed with an anarchist's grin.

James didn't break stride or dignify the cheeky comment. Brushing by Joy and Boyd, he hopped in his truck and gunned it down the long drive.

He needed as far from here—and Sofia—as he could get.

CHAPTER EIGHTEEN

AN HOUR LATER, Sofia dumped yet another full dustpan into the garbage and blew the hair up off her damp forehead. Her back ached and her head throbbed. At least her feet no longer hurt since replacing her heels with sneakers after tucking Javi into bed. Days and days of careful planning—reduced to rubble in just minutes.

Worse, all the progress she and James had made, the closeness that'd grown between them, had disintegrated along with the punch bowl.

It stung that he'd told Javi the truth about her addiction. Shame filled her every time she'd glimpsed his trusting face tonight. His nature was to rescue others and now he viewed her the same way, the one person he should count on, not worry about.

He deserved a better mother than a former addict, and while she was proud of the work she'd done in NA, she hadn't wanted him knowing about any of it. Admitting, accepting and facing her past was one thing, but having her son struggle to understand it was another level entirely. Telling him was her choice to make, not James's, yet once again, he'd seized control and done as he pleased, even if it meant letting Javi think the worst of her.

James doesn't think you're a horrible person, though, whispered a voice inside.

Yes, that'd been true, but she could imagine what he thought of her now after the party debacle.

She still believed she was right to invite the Lovelands, though she'd wished for different results. Sadly, Joy had broken things off with Boyd to keep the family peace, despite Sofia's objections. She vehemently disagreed that Joy's happiness should take a back burner to her children's stubborn grudges. If Sofia stayed in Carbondale, she'd do everything she could to reconcile the families.

If she stuck around…

The barn door creaked and a stooped, gray-haired man shuffled inside.

With a hand shading her eyes, she squinted at the figure. "I'm sorry. The party ended a while ago."

"Looks like I missed quite a shindig," drawled the stranger.

It was a voice she had heard before, deep and raspy. It made her bones crack and splinter, made her feel the hard, cold rejection of a childhood long since past but never forgotten.

"Dad?"

He picked his way through the debris and stopped a couple of feet in front of her. Jowls now hung from his jaw. Pouches bagged beneath his sunken eyes. Deep lines carved the skin between the corners of his mouth and chin. His critical gaze, raised eyebrows and a skeptical eye-squint, hadn't changed, though.

Her heart threw itself backward and clung to the bars of her rib cage.

"Your fella there, James, invited me. Said you were putting together a soiree. Told him I'd have to see it to believe it. My Sofia. Never could finish tying her shoes, let alone something big like this."

He whistled as he rubbernecked, his square head pivoting. "Some things never change."

Her hands balled at her sides, his stinging judgment finding its mark as it always had. She pursed her lips to keep from lashing out. She wouldn't give him the satisfaction of seeing her lose control. Besides, why waste her breath? He'd made up his mind about her long ago and wasn't about to change now.

"Why are you here?"

"Heard I have a grandson. James, at least, thought I should know about him."

She felt herself flush hot. How dare James accuse her of inviting unwanted outsiders when he'd done the same thing...even worse—he'd phoned her estranged parent. James's actions proved that once again, he thought he knew best and didn't trust or respect her enough to make her own decisions.

"Yes. He's five and his name's Javi."

Her father scratched his head. "Strange name."

"I like it."

He swatted the air, as if batting her words away like buzzing gnats, annoyances of little consequence. Just like her. "Would like to see him."

Over her father's shoulder, she noticed Riker, the teenage boy she sat next to in support group, slip inside. Since he wore only a T-shirt and jeans, she presumed he'd come back for his coat. She recalled how he'd finally opened up at a recent meeting about his varsity letter jacket. He'd recounted how nothing he did ever pleased his old man, especially when his drug usage got him kicked off the football team—his father nearly booted him from home.

"Javi's asleep." She turned and grabbed up her broom.

"That's it? That's all you got for your old man? You always were ungrateful—"

She squared her shoulders and whirled to face her father full on, aware of Riker's watchful gaze. Maybe she would fail to make an impression on her closed-minded parent, but she could set an example for the troubled teenager.

"Ungrateful?" The broom clattered to the ground. She crossed her arms. "What did I ever have to be thankful for? Huh? Those piano lessons you bought so you could yell every time I hit a wrong note? The homework help you never had time to give? You always made room in your schedule for lectures when I got bad grades, though, didn't you?"

"You needed discipline," he sputtered, his skin growing mottled. "Structure."

"I needed love, Dad. Love."

His mouth opened, then closed, and a muscle jumped in his jaw. They stared at each other for a tense minute and even Riker froze in place.

"I was a single parent," he protested, his strident voice faltering, dipping.

"So am I," she pronounced, infusing each syllable with strength and conviction. Righteousness. "And I've done the best I can, despite not having a high school degree, resources, family. I haven't been able to give Javi much, but I've always given him love."

And perhaps that was the greatest thing of all. Much more important than the material things she'd beaten herself up over for not providing. She saw that now. She was a good mother. And an addict. And a high school dropout. And only ever a temporary worker so far, but she had a heart and that just might be the most precious commodity anyone could possess and give to others.

"If I'd known about Javi…"

"What? You wouldn't have kicked me out? Abandoned me? You decided long ago that I wasn't good enough, but you know what? You don't get to decide anymore. I do." She tapped her chest. "Me. And I think I'm pretty awesome."

Riker shot her two finger guns and a wink behind her father's back, grabbed his jacket and eased outside.

"Well, you haven't gotten a job yet," her father protested. "A place to live. I told James I could help you with that. Got some business connections in…Portland…was it?"

"You think I need your help *now*?" A hysterical laugh bubbled up inside her and she strained to hold it back. "I needed it when I was a teenager, let out of juvie with no place to go. Where were you that day, Dad?"

He hung his head. "Teaching you a lesson."

"Lesson learned." Her faltering voice dropped for a moment and she drew in a deep breath before continuing. "I can take care of myself just fine—so you can leave and feel good about that."

"I feel good about nothing." He shoved his hand in a pocket, yanked out a white handkerchief and dabbed his glistening face. "You think I don't have regrets?"

She blinked at him. "Do you?"

"Doctor said it's the baby or your wife," he mumbled to himself. Suddenly his knees buckled, and he grasped the table edge.

Alarmed, she fetched a chair and held it steady as he sank down.

"What did the doctor say?"

He leaned his elbows on his knees and his back hunched. "Your mother had a complicated pregnancy. Was a miracle she conceived you at all, considering her lupus. In fact, she was advised against it, told to terminate the pregnancy, but she wanted a child more than anything." He swiped the handkerchief over red-rimmed eyes. "Said she wouldn't stop one of the Lord's miracles. Made me promise that if anything ever happened, that I choose you."

Goose bumps broke out over Sofia's entire body and her head spun. She'd always thought of herself as her mother's killer, her father's widow-maker. Never had she considered that they might have wanted it that way.

That *she* might have been wanted.

"Your mother was bleeding heavy and unconscious. Her blood pressure was skyrocketing. Then we lost your heartbeat," her father continued, his voice broken and raw. "The doctor said it was her or you." He cleared his throat and his mouth worked silently. Then, "And I chose you, just like she wanted."

"Why didn't you ever tell me?" Her poor father. Her poor mother. What a horrifying sacrifice they'd made for their child. For her. An unparalleled act of love. Her heart thundered in her chest as she grieved for this incredible mother she'd never known and the deep, shattering pain her father had endured.

"Didn't want you blaming yourself. Still.

I blamed myself. Every time I looked at you, I saw myself letting her go. She has a place here inside of me." He laid a hand over his heart. "Where I carried her, same as she carried you. When she left, that place became nothing but a big, empty wound."

"She wanted you to make that choice, Dad."

He swiped his fingers along his eye bags, head falling back, and loosed a long breath. "What she wanted was for you to grow up perfect and I failed her in that. Failed you. I'm sorry, Sofia. That's why I really came, I guess. To tell you that. You deserved two parents and I couldn't even give you one. Not a decent one, anyways, though I thought I was doing my best. No matter how hard I pushed, you pulled away. Did things your own way."

Her mind reeled at an apology she'd never imagined receiving. "I never was any good at being controlled."

He laughed briefly, but there was a stretched sound to it, like it was straining against the solid weight of pain dragging downward. "Didn't figure that out until after you disappeared and it was too late. Always knew I'd be no good as a parent. Wish it'd been me that'd died that day. Not Cora."

His head dipped and his shoulders shook. Tears dripped unchecked down Sofia's face.

"Oh. Dad. No." And in an instant, she knelt on the floor before him, her arms thrown around his neck. "Someone once told me that despite terrible tragedies, life has a greater plan, an unknowable one. But everything happens for a reason and it's up to us to determine what that reason is."

"I wish I'd told you I loved you."

"You just did."

She dropped her head on his shoulder and she felt his arms come around her and his mouth press against the crown of her head.

"I'm glad you came."

And she was. Despite the pain and suffering he'd put her through, it was Christmas, a time to let go of grudges and forgive. Besides, hadn't she just witnessed what happened when people refused to make peace? She couldn't accuse the Cades and Lovelands of hanging on to hate if she did the same. NA had taught her that forgiveness was the only way to let go of her pain and find peace.

"Thanks for that, darlin'," he said softly, but not weakly.

She stood, extended a hand and helped him to his feet. "How long are you staying?"

"Actually, I'm in the middle of a business trip. My flight leaves tomorrow morning. If I can, I'd appreciate the chance to meet Javi before I go."

Her smile wobbled. Forgiving him was one thing. She could do that and move on. However, letting him back into her life, having a relationship, even a small one, filled her with trepidation.

What if he hadn't really changed? He'd been critical of the party and her life just moments ago. She didn't want that around Javi.

"I'm not sure—"

"Please, Sofia. Give me a chance to prove I can be different, a good grandfather to Javi and maybe a father to you again, if you'll let me."

Her nostrils flared as she drew in a deep breath, considering. Maybe she could call a temporary truce for Javi's sake to see if her father had really changed. Maybe they could heal the hurt between them.

"Okay."

"Thank you, Sofia."

She ducked her head, overwhelmed and a bit off balance at the rushing countercurrents of emotions swirling inside her.

"You look good, honey."

Her hand flew to her lopsided hair, then felt the sticky mascara streaks on her cheeks. It was the first compliment he'd ever given her. "Thanks, Dad. See you tomorrow, then. Javi will be happy to meet you."

After donning his hat, he tipped the brim and sauntered outside, leaving her to continue picking up the pieces of the party, and her life.

It must have been close to midnight when the sound of wheels on snow roused Sofia from her seat by the kitchen window. Her heart thumped as she glimpsed James hop from his truck and slam the door shut.

She snatched the door open and frigid air clawed at her face. "Where are the rest?" she called.

He raised weary eyes, then clomped up the porch stairs, stomping snow off his boots. He entered the house without a word.

"Are they getting a ride with someone else?"

Pulling open the fridge, he bent slightly and peered inside. "Nope. Travis decided to teach them all a lesson and keep them overnight."

"Oh." She slumped against the counter. "In the same cell?"

James turned with a soda in hand. "Travis and Jack agreed that if everyone could make it until morning without killing each other, they might let them go."

"Sounds like Travis and Jack are getting along."

He popped the tab and raised the can for a long swig. After a moment, he lowered it and studied her with dark, serious eyes, a bitter wrench to one side of his mouth. "They're tolerating each other because they're forced to."

"Kind of like the way you forced me and my father together?"

He released a short breath that vibrated his lips. "Forgot about that."

"When were you planning to tell me?"

James's head jerked away from her accusing tone. "At the party."

"When it'd be too late to stop it."

His jaw tightened. "I thought it'd help. You said you never felt worthy because of him, and I hoped if he saw you again, things would change."

Technically, he'd been right, but that didn't excuse his high-handed actions.

"You went behind my back and took charge of my life, first telling Javi about my addiction and then bringing in my father."

"You were never going to do it on your own."

"That doesn't give you permission to take over. I spent too much of my life being controlled, first by my dad, then by drugs, then my fears. I won't live like that anymore. How can I trust you?"

"Trust?" He stared at her, eyes bulging, incredulous. "I can't trust you, either. You invited the Lovelands without ever saying a word, when you knew I wouldn't approve."

"It's your mother's life. Not yours. Stop interfering. Stop trying to control her."

"You invited in an outsider who'll only break her heart." Anger compressed his words into hard chips, slamming down on the counter between them. "She's suffered enough and come too far for me to see her go backward again. You don't know Boyd Loveland."

"But I know Joy Cade. I trust her to make her own choices. So should you."

He shook his head and shot her a bullish stare. "I should have taken control of the party from the start. We would have avoided this mess altogether."

"You'd control everything if you could,

even if it means ruining other people's lives, like your mother's?"

His chin jerked up and down.

"She deserves happiness," Sofia fumed. "Only now she's upstairs crying, miserable because she broke things off with Boyd because of you."

"It's for the best," James said heavily, then lifted the can for another long swallow. "Trust me."

"That's it, isn't it? You don't trust anyone's judgment but your own."

"Tonight didn't disprove that notion."

"That's hypocritical. You're all over me for inviting the Lovelands, but not the least bit sorry for calling my father."

His flinty expression gave nothing away.

"Are you still contesting Javi's trusteeship?" she asked suddenly, the need to know right now, this instant, pounding urgently inside her.

When he dropped the can on the counter, it wobbled, tipped, then fell with a metallic ting. "Yes."

The air rushed right out of her. After everything, she still wasn't good enough, couldn't prove herself to James. Well, she was done chasing after anyone's good opinion. The only one that really counted was her own.

"Then it's goodbye."

He straightened his slouch and his face looked slapped blank. "Wait. What?"

"I can start the job at any time. Javi and I will leave in the morning."

He'd lifted his hands and seemed to forget them in midair, trying to get his head together perhaps. "Tomorrow? Two weeks before Christmas?"

"It's better not to drag this out, and Joy's splint comes off tomorrow anyway. You don't need me."

"Don't leave because of this," he insisted, sounding winded, like he'd been sucker punched.

"I won't be around someone who doesn't believe in me, who'd rather control than trust me. That's not possible for you, is it? Trust?"

They stared at each other for a charged moment. James opened his mouth to say something, but he couldn't make it work. A few heartbeats later, his broad shoulders sagged. "No."

Though she tried to stop them, tears of hurt welled. "Then please leave."

The desire to say more was hot in her throat

but she forced herself to remain quiet. Calm. Strong. Her self-control balanced on a fragile edge—dancing along a cliff. She could throw herself over it once he left.

She tilted her thumb at the door and his lips squeezed together so tightly they turned white. With a last, anguished look, he jerked himself around and marched stiffly outside.

A dead, empty space opened inside her and she was left gasping and paralyzed, watching the one thing she'd always wanted from the world—a family, a home, a love of her own— dissolve to dust and blow away.

She moved to the window and stared at the dark, wishing James back, yet knowing she couldn't go forward if he did return. It cleaved her heart to let him go, but she'd learned too much, come too far, to be with a man who didn't trust her completely.

She was worth more than that.

And ironically, it was James who'd taught her so.

CHAPTER NINETEEN

A MINIATURE TRAIN trundled on tracks inside the dim living room. James watched it wind through the cluster of ceramic village homes Sofia and he had arranged weeks ago. It chugged around the ice skating pond and rattled past the Christmas tree farm.

Tendrils of warmth curled from the dying hearth fire and Clint stretched out on his back before it, front paws flung straight overhead, legs splayed and tail puffed to absorb every glimmer of heat. The flicker of light cast by the glowing hickory logs illuminated the figurine trio standing before one of the pines. A father, mother and child.

His throat tightened. Once he'd hoped that would be him, Sofia and Javi, but that dream died when she'd packed up and left two weeks ago without a goodbye.

How had everything gone so wrong?

It was Christmas Eve. He and Sofia should be tucking Javi's presents under the tree, cuddling on the couch, whispering about their future. Just weeks ago, she'd kissed him tenderly on that sofa and the ground had opened, swallowed him, buried him in that unforgettable moment. Now she slept thousands of miles away in Portland, and he brooded here with nothing but his pride for company.

His heart moved sluggishly in his chest. Leaning forward, he picked up the trio, wishing it was Sofia he held. Touched.

Her accusations roared in his ears.

"You don't believe in me," she'd insisted.

But he did. Or he'd hoped to, until she'd let him down.

"You want to control me, not trust me."

His fingers tightened around the ceramic family. She'd been right about that. After the party debacle, when he'd discovered she'd misled him and kept secrets, Jesse's old hurts and betrayals rushed back, cutting him fresh and deep.

Now, with some time and perspective, he'd begun wondering if his urge to manage everyone stemmed from fear, not love. Bending others to his will, lashing out when they made different choices, mistrusting without proof weren't the actions of a caring man.

He'd treated Jesse that way and lost him.

Now the same had happened with Sofia and Javi. As for his mother, she'd taken to spending most of her time in her room again. His siblings barely spoke to him, though their accusing gazes said plenty.

They blamed him for Sofia's departure.

And he did, too. It seemed like he was the common denominator in an equation he couldn't solve, no matter how many ways he puzzled over it.

"You miss them."

He jerked at the soft voice and whirled. "You're up late."

His mother tightened her pink robe's belt. "I couldn't sleep."

A sigh escaped him. "Me, neither."

"Want some warm milk?"

"Sure." He padded after her into the kitchen.

Grabbing a stool, he sat at the counter and watched her pull a carton from the refrigerator. "Want cinnamon in it?"

"Sounds good." He toyed with a glass jar's metallic fastener and studied the peanut butter blossom cookies piled inside. He recalled the salty sweet dough Sofia coaxed him into licking straight from the beaters and how they'd laughed like naughty children.

"What's making you smile?" His mother shot him a sidelong glance before pouring the white liquid into a small saucepan and flicking on the heat.

"Nothing."

Just Sofia's gummy smile. The beauty mark on her left cheek. The crazy snort she made when she laughed hard.

Nothing at all…

"You miss her."

"And Javi." He flipped open the cookie jar and grabbed a couple of treats. "Want one?"

"No, thanks." She plucked a wooden spoon from a holder and stirred the heating liquid.

"How's the wrist?"

The spoon stilled, and she studied the faint pink scar. "Better. The physical therapist is happy."

"What about you?"

She grabbed cinnamon from a cabinet and sprinkled some over the milk. The sweet, pungent scent pulled a sneeze out of her.

"I've been better."

"Tomorrow's Christmas and you haven't put much out for presents besides the ones Sofia wrapped for you."

His mother used to go to extravagant lengths to fill their stockings with unexpected items.

Now they hung from the chimney like dead balloon animals.

She grabbed two mugs, set them on the counter and poured the milk. "Guess I'm not as much in the mood to celebrate as I thought."

"Me, neither." He gulped a mouthful of the rich, warm treat.

"It's not the same without them."

"I'm sorry, Ma."

She lowered her cup. "For what?"

"Driving Sofia away. Causing a scene at the Christmas party. Hurting you again. We should have been respectful to Boyd at least."

She brought her mug to her lips and the large cup obscured her expression as she sipped. Then, "Maybe that just wasn't meant to be."

"What do you mean?"

"Boyd and I dated in high school and things ended over a mix-up. Maybe that was a sign way back then that we weren't right for each other after all."

He pictured her beaming, beautiful smile at the party. She'd been lit from the inside with joy, and he'd pulled the plug. Regret sawed his gut.

"You two looked pretty happy."

A wistful gleam entered her eyes and she let out a breath. "Honey, you're the one I feel bad about."

His fingers drummed on the side of his mug. "I don't want you worrying about me."

"You're in love with Sofia."

His mouth refused to deny the accusation, so he shook his head instead. No need to get his mother worked up over the depth of his feelings...and his loss.

"So why are you holding on to that ceramic family like it's a lifeline?"

His fingers unfurled to reveal the trio in his hand, their outline a red mark on his palm.

A long breath escaped him. "I messed up, Ma. I've been too controlling."

"Can't disagree with you, honey. You've been this way since Jesse, and I need to accept some of the blame for that because I let you take over things while I was busy grieving."

"You couldn't help it, Ma."

"But I should have." Her tone turned fierce. "We can't always control the things that happen to us, but we can control how we feel about them, how we react. I'm your ma and it was up to me to take control of the family." She brushed at her eyes. "Now. I'm telling you straight. Sofia and Javi are the best thing that's ever happened to you. And don't give me any of that guilt about Jesse."

"I wasn't going to."

"Good." His mother shoved up her robe's sleeves like a prizefighter stepping into a boxing ring. "How are you going to make it right?"

He bit a cookie in half and chewed, the buttery crumbles barely registering. "Nothing I can do. She doesn't want anything to do with me."

"Can you blame her?"

The rest of the cookie dropped from his fingertips. "No. She thinks I don't trust her. Says I only want to control her."

"What do you think?"

"I don't know."

A napkin appeared and his mother briskly swept the crumbs up. "The giving of love is an education itself."

"Huh?"

Her robe's matching pink slippers scuffed across the wood slatted floor as she crossed to the garbage can and tossed the paper. "Eleanor Roosevelt said that. It means that love requires change, especially in ourselves. We have to be willing to grow, to become better people, to be worthy of it."

"I've always tried to do right."

She smoothed a warm hand over his cheek. "I know, honey. You were always my responsible one, managing every moment, preventing each catastrophe, but you can't stop all bad things from happening no more than you can plug a leaking dam with your thumb. Life can't be controlled or scripted. Neither can love."

He leaned his cheek into her palm and closed his eyes. "It'd be easier if it could."

"But would it be better? Think about all of the wonderful things that happen to us when we least expect them."

"Sofia and Javi," he murmured, then straightened. His mother was right. The natural order of things was not order. Life was a beautiful mess, and if he could get out of his own way, maybe he might enjoy it.

Grow, even.

"Sofia said loving someone and believing in them isn't the same thing."

"I agree. To truly love someone," his mother continued, "you need to open yourself up to the negative as well as the positive—to grief, sorrow and disappointment, as well as to joy, fulfillment and a faith, a trust in others that's maybe never been possible for you before, honey. But you're a man of courage. Conviction. A loving heart has no room for fear."

"Love's an act of heroism," he said, speaking his thoughts as he considered his mother's words.

She nodded, eyes sparkling. "So's trust."

"I've been a coward for losing faith in Sofia."

"But you can change that."

He nodded. Yes, he could. Right now. This moment. If he caught the next flight to Portland, he could reach her by morning.

She might not accept his love. In fact, he had no expectations other than a door shut in his face. But love was about giving, not getting. Hopefully she would accept his overdue apology, and one other, very important thing that he'd planned on mailing her but would now deliver in person.

He owed her that much and more.

He leaned over and bussed his mother on the cheek. "Merry Christmas, Ma."

Her eyebrows rose. "It's not midnight yet."

He swung around the counter, stuffed a sealed envelope from the mail pile into his pocket, grabbed his keys, coat and hat, and turned at the door.

"I won't be around to say it then. I'm catching a flight."

"To…?"

"Sofia and Javi."

Sofia fitted a plug into a socket, and a small Christmas tree, set before a bay window, glowed to life. Rubbing the early-morning sleep from her eyes, she stepped back and admired the colorful sight. Small white lights, set deep inside synthetic boughs, illuminated the red, gold and green bulbs she and Javi purchased last night with the first paycheck from her medical receptionist post. Having enough money to modestly furnish the one-bedroom loft she'd rented and decorated for the holidays thrilled her to her toes.

At last, she'd realized the fresh start of her dreams.

A stable job. A new city. Secure housing.

Everything she'd thought she wanted.

Yet nothing she did, no amount of cookie baking, present wrapping or Christmas movie viewing, erased the longing that left her sleepless and wistful since leaving Carbondale.

She could make a wonderful life here, yet this wasn't the career, the city or the home she wanted. Nothing against Portland. In fact, she was beginning to appreciate this quirky, welcoming city.

Its only crime was not being Carbondale, the residence of the boisterous, passionate, colorful Cade family she'd grown to love as her own. She missed Jewel, Justin, Jared and Joy. As for James, she couldn't begin to untangle the knot of emotions that twisted inside her every time she thought of him…an almost nonstop occurrence.

The heart did not recognize physical distance, she'd discovered. Nor did it listen to reason. She missed him. Loved him, still.

The clank of hot water rumbling inside an old-fashioned wrought-iron radiator wrenched her from her thoughts. Despite the steamy warmth spiraling through the room, she pulled a bright red wool sweater over her yoga pants and shivered as she plugged in a sugar cookie–scented candle, then an animated Christmas carousel. She surveyed the small, high-ceilinged room.

A plush beige couch and matching armchair faced a small flat screen mounted on hangers attached to a brick wall. Sprigs of holly mixed with white mums and pine boughs burst from a ceramic bowl atop a glass coffee table. A green-and-light-blue woven rug covered much of the polished oak floor. Beside a toddler-sized nutcracker soldier, a wireless speaker connected to her iPhone crooned "Believe" from Javi's new favorite Christmas movie, *The Polar Express*.

The Cades' presents created a festive pile

beneath the tree. Javi would be so excited to see the thoughtful gifts that had arrived earlier this week. She'd hidden them at a neighbor's apartment and retrieved them last night after he'd fallen asleep. Should she wake him now or let him sleep a bit longer?

He'd been up late talking to Joy via Skype. Another hour or so more wouldn't hurt, anxious as she was to unwrap everything and reconnect to the family she missed with all her heart. Were they awake yet? Colorado operated in Mountain Time, so it'd be 8:00 a.m.

Jewel was most likely stealing an extra piece of bacon from one of her brothers' plates while Justin huddled over a cup of black coffee. With one eye on the local paper's sports section, Jared would be texting a new girlfriend. Joy, no doubt, bustled around the table, supplying eggs, toast and juice. As for James—her heart rate stuttered—he would be leaning in the doorway, a bowl of cereal in hand, overseeing the scene, ensuring everyone else's comfort and happiness the way he always did.

Yes, that was a form of control, but it was also an act of love. She could accuse him of plenty, but never of selfishness. He demanded much, but he gave even more.

How she wished she were beside him, leaning her head on his strong shoulder, an arm slung around his waist...

She forced away her longing and glanced outside. Fat snowflakes spiraled lazily from gray cloud cover. A thick blanket of white covered pristine roads. Snow piled atop brick buildings and frosted leafless branches. The mute, peaceful world resembled a page from a fairy tale.

One without a prince.

Not that this princess needed rescuing, she firmly reminded herself. So far, she'd achieved her goals and accomplished new ones, like attending her first Portland NA meeting earlier this week. Lots to be grateful for and feel blessed about. She was free to live her life as she wished and had put her problems behind her at last.

Only...what to do about her broken heart? Every time she pictured James's disappointed frown, heard the distrust in his voice, a bit of her withered inside.

Not that she needed his approval. Making mistakes made her human, not less than others. From the moment Joy gave Sofia a shot to prove herself, and showed her she truly cared and believed in her, Sofia had begun seizing control of her self-esteem. And once Sofia saw what she could accomplish, had earned James's hard-won faith in her, she'd begun believing in herself, too.

Once she'd been sensitive, worried that others, especially James, could negatively influence her, but the person she needed to rely on, she'd discovered, was herself. Only then could she be a strong, equal partner. It was up to her, not outside forces, to keep her anchored and able to embrace life—and love—without risking addiction.

So why had she run the moment he'd voiced his displeasure? Perhaps she should have stayed and worked through adversity as she'd learned to do in NA.

Life, and relationships, was all about compromise. Planning the Christmas party with James proved she did have the stick-with-it mind-set necessary to pull off a big event and be part of a loving relationship and family. Being a good partner/mother/daughter didn't mean being perfect. It meant doing the best you could every day that you could.

A Christmas card, taped to the window frame, caught her eye. A glossy Christmas tree graced the cover. Inside, her father's writing covered the blank paper. He'd wished her a merry Christmas and signed it "love."

Her eyes stung. She'd been furious with

James for meddling in her relationship with her father. Yet he'd been right. She needed to reconcile her past to have a better future. Deep down James had meant well.

Regret washed through her.

She'd always wished to give Javi a real Christmas. While she now had the material things she'd wanted, she saw they didn't define the Christmas spirit—people did. Without those she loved—and she loved James—Christmas was just another day.

If not for her hasty retreat, she'd be celebrating Christmas at Cade Ranch and she and James might have forged a future together.

Now it was too late.

She jumped at a soft knock at the door. Peering out the window, she spied a taxi pulling away from her curb and a glimpse of what looked like a man wearing a familiar jean jacket standing on her stoop. Her pulse slammed in her veins.

Her sock-covered feet skidded as she bolted for the door. She flung it open and the tall, handsome cowboy standing on her doorstep, hat in hand, squeezed the breath out of her.

James.

Snowflakes clung to his long lashes and his deep brown eyes turned her insides warm and gooey. "What are you doing here?" she gasped.

"Howdy, Sofia." A sheepish note entered his deep baritone. "Merry Christmas."

"Merry Christmas. But why—what—"

"I came out to apologize and give you this." He thrust an envelope in her hand. She didn't spare it a glance. Her thirsty eyes couldn't drink their fill of him. With cold staining his cheeks red, his lean jaw covered in a dark, gorgeous bristle, his hair grown out a bit, he'd never looked more fiercely attractive. It took every ounce of control not to fling herself in his arms this very moment.

Restraint, she urged herself. *Hear him out.*

"Won't you come in?"

"I won't impose on your holiday. Just wanted to tell you in person how sorry I am for blaming you about the party. That was my and my siblings' fault, not yours."

She slid on boots, donned a coat and hat, and joined him outside, shutting the door behind her. "I should have included you in the decision to invite Boyd and his kids."

He nodded. "True. But I would have only shut you down instead of listening to reason. You were right about that and a whole bunch else."

Her mouth lifted in the corners and pleasure curled, warm and bright inside.

"I was also wrong to invite your father without your say-so."

"I wouldn't have listened, either, and it turns out you were right. Dad and I did need another chance. Thanks for that."

A slow smile twisted up one side of his mouth. "Glad to hear. Despite how it looks, I've only ever wanted the best for you and Javi."

"I know."

His eyelashes dropped to his cheeks. "What you don't know is that I do believe in you. Trust you, too." He shook his head, staring at his feet, his words emerging faster. "Guess I didn't realize it, either. Not until…well…" He pointed at the envelope in her hand. "You'll understand when you read that." He half turned toward the road. "I'd better head out and catch another taxi if I'm going to make the noon flight to Carbondale. Thanks for hearing me out. I hope someday you might see your way to forgiving me."

"I already do. We all make mistakes."

His eyes delved into hers and his leather-gloved hand rose to cup her cheek. "You are beautiful, Sofia," he rasped, voice hoarse. "Merry Christmas. Give Javi my love."

Then he tramped down the steps, leaving deep impressions in the gathering snow.

The crinkling sound of paper, crushed in her balled hand, captured her attention. A hurried glance revealed a law firm's return address.

What?

She ripped it open and yanked out the sheet that granted her sole stewardship of Javi's trust in Cade Ranch.

James said he trusted her and here was tangible proof. He'd dropped the lawsuit.

Panic swept through her.

And now he was walking out of her life.

No! She couldn't let him leave.

"Stop!" she hollered and slipped and slid in the gathering snow after him. He paused beneath a lamppost. White fell around them in a thick shower.

"James Cade. You are done controlling every minute of our relationship."

A grin formed on his handsome mouth and humor glinted in his eyes. "Pardon?"

"You don't get to just show up when you want, then leave when you're done."

"Thought I was giving you space."

She stepped close enough that the tips of her boots touched his and she draped her wrists on either side of her dark-haired Adonis's neck. "I decide when I need space."

He tipped her chin up so their gazes met.

"I'm guessing this isn't one of those times?" The rich rumble of his voice sent a bolt of joy through her, so warm, so sweet, she wanted to melt right into him.

"Definitely not." She raked her fingers through his thick brush of hair. "I've been running all my life, from my dad, my addiction, jobs, then you…but you…you were always right behind me…even now. Here you are. And I'm thinking, why am I still running?"

He squinted at her quizzically. "Been wondering that myself till I realized it was me. I drove you away and I never want to be apart again. You're the one, Sofia. No. You're not just the one. You're the only one."

She blinked back tears, wanting to be sure she understood before she lost her heart to this man forever. With what little voice she could scavenge in the midst of a huge well of emotion, she asked, "So you're saying…?"

"I love you." His hands bracketed her waist, his fingers straying onto her hips as he tugged her gently against him, sealing their bodies together.

She rose on tiptoe and whispered, "I love you, too," against his lips.

With a groan, his mouth captured hers in a long, sweet caress. Snowflakes settled on their fused lips and mingling tongues, melting, fresh and pure and cold. After a moment, he pulled back and their speeding breaths frosted the air white.

James studied her, his brown eyes turning dark as onyx despite the strengthening morning light. "Before you, I thought I knew what a home was. Livestock. Timber. Land. Traditions. Responsibility. A place to oversee and control. But you showed me that home is about the people you love and I can't wait to build one with you. I want to chase after fairy tales together. I want Javi and the rest of our kids to see a love like we have, and I want them to know what an amazing woman you are."

"Kids?"

He rained kisses on her damp cheeks. "One. Two." His lips whispered across her ear, sending a delicious shiver all the way to her toes. "Three…maybe six. I like big families."

"You don't have the final say," she reminded him, mock stern but serious, too.

He dropped his head, then rolled his eyes up with such a hangdog expression it made her giggle. "I'm never going to be cured of this control thing, am I?"

"No. But it will be fun challenging it."

"You might be the only one who can," he

groaned. "Guess that's why I'm head over heels for you, darlin'. You're the best thing that's ever happened to me." Suddenly he bent on one knee in the snow and lifted her hand. "Will you marry me?"

Tears sprang to her eyes and her throat clamped so tight she could only nod, surprise and bliss rendering her mute.

"Is that a yes?" The hopeful, fearful light in his eyes loosened her tongue.

"Yes," she gasped and he bolted to his feet and caught her close, his heart beating so fast and hard she could feel it through the layers separating them.

"I love you," he murmured, reverent.

Her lips wobbled into a smile. "I love you, too." She cleared her throat. "Now. About those kids..."

One eyebrow rose. "What do you have in mind?"

"Since we already have a head start, how about coming inside and spending the holiday with the one you have?"

A vulnerable expression replaced his amusement. "Will Javi accept me as his father?"

"Yes!" piped up a small voice. Sofia staggered as her son, dressed haphazardly in an unbuttoned coat over Batman pj's, launched himself at the two of them.

"Santa got my letter!" Javi pumped his fist skyward.

James swung him up into an embrace with one arm and reached his other hand to clasp Sofia's. "What letter?" he asked as they swished through the snow back to the loft.

"At the lights thing."

The Festival of Lights, she thought. "You asked for a family."

Javi beamed and his head swiveled between the two of them. "With Uncle James."

"Me, too." Sofia ruffled her son's hair.

James smiled at her over Javi's head as she opened the door and let them inside. "Then he gave us all our wishes this year."

"Merry Christmas!" Javi shouted and scampered off to tear into his presents. "Can I open this one first?"

He pointed to a large box and, after a quick kiss, James joined Javi on the floor. Sofia perched on the couch and watched the animated pair, marveling, recalling her darkest times, Christmases when she'd nearly given up but had pushed on for Javi's sake. Now she saw that she deserved happiness, too, and had found it at last.

Thank you, Jesse, she thought. *And merry Christmas*.

The spirit of Christmas was about giving without a thought of getting, yet she'd received more than she could have ever imagined.

James was her miracle. Her dream-come-true happiness.

Her love.

* * * * *

*Be sure to check out
the next book in Karen Rock's*
ROCKY MOUNTAIN COWBOYS
miniseries coming out in February 2018!

FALLING FOR A COWBOY

Also, don't miss these other great reads!

*A COWBOY TO KEEP
UNDER AN ADIRONDACK SKY
HIS KIND OF COWGIRL*

*All available now from
Harlequin Heartwarming.*

Get 2 Free Books,
Plus 2 Free Gifts—
just for trying the Reader Service!

Love Inspired®

YES! Please send me 2 FREE Love Inspired® Romance novels and my 2 FREE mystery gifts (gifts are worth about $10 retail). After receiving them, if I don't wish to receive any more books, I can return the shipping statement marked "cancel." If I don't cancel, I will receive 6 brand-new novels every month and be billed just $5.24 for the regular-print edition or $5.74 each for the larger-print edition in the U.S., or $5.74 each for the regular-print edition or $6.24 each for the larger-print edition in Canada. That's a saving of at least 13% off the cover price. It's quite a bargain! Shipping and handling is just 50¢ per book in the U.S. and 75¢ per book in Canada.* I understand that accepting the 2 free books and gifts places me under no obligation to buy anything. I can always return a shipment and cancel at any time. The free books and gifts are mine to keep no matter what I decide.

Please check one:
☐ Love Inspired Romance Regular-Print
(105/305 IDN GLWW)

☐ Love Inspired Romance Larger-Print
(122/322 IDN GLWW)

Name _____ (PLEASE PRINT)

Address _____ Apt. #

City _____ State/Province _____ Zip/Postal Code

Signature (if under 18, a parent or guardian must sign)

Mail to the **Reader Service:**
IN U.S.A.: P.O. Box 1341, Buffalo, NY 14240-8531
IN CANADA: P.O. Box 603, Fort Erie, Ontario L2A 5X3

Want to try two free books from another line?
Call 1-800-873-8635 today or visit www.ReaderService.com.

*Terms and prices subject to change without notice. Prices do not include applicable taxes. Sales tax applicable in N.Y. Canadian residents will be charged applicable taxes. Offer not valid in Quebec. This offer is limited to one order per household. Books received may not be as shown. Not valid for current subscribers to Love Inspired Romance books. All orders subject to approval. Credit or debit balances in a customer's account(s) may be offset by any other outstanding balance owed by or to the customer. Please allow 4 to 6 weeks for delivery. Offer available while quantities last.

Your Privacy—The Reader Service is committed to protecting your privacy. Our Privacy Policy is available online at www.ReaderService.com or upon request from the Reader Service.

We make a portion of our mailing list available to reputable third parties that offer products we believe may interest you. If you prefer that we not exchange your name with third parties, or if you wish to clarify or modify your communication preferences, please visit us at www.ReaderService.com/consumerschoice or write to us at Reader Service Preference Service, P.O. Box 9062, Buffalo, NY 14240-9062. Include your complete name and address.

LI17R2

Get 2 Free Books,
Plus 2 Free Gifts—
just for trying the Reader Service!

LIS17R2

HOMETOWN HEARTS ♥

YES! Please send me **The Hometown Hearts Collection** in Larger Print. This collection begins with 3 FREE books and 2 FREE gifts in the first shipment. Along with my 3 free books, I'll also get the next 4 books from the Hometown Hearts Collection, in LARGER PRINT, which I may either return and owe nothing, or keep for the low price of $4.99 U.S./ $5.89 CDN each plus $2.99 for shipping and handling per shipment*. If I decide to continue, about once a month for 8 months I will get 6 or 7 more books, but will only need to pay for 4. That means 2 or 3 books in every shipment will be FREE! If I decide to keep the entire collection, I'll have paid for only 32 books because 19 books are FREE! I understand that accepting the 3 free books and gifts places me under no obligation to buy anything. I can always return a shipment and cancel at any time. My free books and gifts are mine to keep no matter what I decide.

262 HCN 3432 462 HCN 3432

Name	(PLEASE PRINT)	
Address		Apt. #
City	State/Prov.	Zip/Postal Code

Signature (if under 18, a parent or guardian must sign)

Mail to the **Reader Service:**
IN U.S.A.: P.O. Box 1867, Buffalo, NY. 14240-1867
IN CANADA: P.O. Box 609, Fort Erie, Ontario L2A 5X3

* Terms and prices subject to change without notice. Prices do not include applicable taxes. Sales tax applicable in NY. Canadian residents will be charged applicable taxes. This offer is limited to one order per household. All orders subject to approval. Credit or debit balances in a customer's account(s) may be offset by any other outstanding balance owed by or to the customer. Please allow 4 to 6 weeks for delivery. Offer available while quantities last. Offer not available to Quebec residents.

Get 2 Free Books,
Plus 2 Free Gifts—
just for trying the
Reader Service!

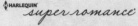

Get 2 Free Books,
Plus 2 Free Gifts—
just for trying the Reader Service!

READERSERVICE.COM

Manage your account online!

- Review your order history
- Manage your payments
- Update your address

> ### *We've designed the Reader Service website just for you.*

Enjoy all the features!

- Discover new series available to you, and read excerpts from any series.
- Respond to mailings and special monthly offers.
- Browse the Bonus Bucks catalog and online-only exculsives.
- Share your feedback.

Visit us at:

ReaderService.com